PATHWAYS INTO

PATHWAYS INTO EVIL

COPYRIGHT 2023 © Alan D Baker

Cover design by Alan D Baker

This novel is the work of fiction, with the exception of historical events involving names, countries and organisations. Present day businesses, organisations, places, events and products described in the text, either originate from the author's imagination, or exist and are used fictitiously. Any resemblance to actual persons, living or dead and events is entirely coincidental.

See 'Researching the novel' for additional information on knowledge sources. See 'Pronunciations' for adapting text in this novel for optical text readers. You will find these topics along with 'Acknowledgements' after the end of the novel.

PATHWAYS INTO EVIL

CHAPTER 1 - **Night drive**

February 26th 9:30 p.m.

A white Mercedes sped down the South Wales section of the M4. Motorists whose powers of concentration were now deteriorating with the maturing night, were angered as the Mercedes effortlessly slipped past them.

The somewhat tiresome driving conditions on the Welsh M4 were usually no different from other parts of the country. But during February the motorway had become prone to mists in the evenings, with the inevitable result of scarcity of traffic. However, the translucent substance that had nearly obscured the previous night's sky was absent.

Directly above in the zenith was the constellation of Ursa Major (the Great Bear).

In the northwesterly sky, the Andromeda constellation (Mythical Princess) was upside down, head first and slowly sinking towards the horizon. To the right of her belt and positioned upright north to south was Andromeda, the nearest galaxy, but only appearing as a haze.

In the western sky many constellations were slowly climbing out of the haze to make their presence known for the evening.

In the southeastern sky, the moon was rising and full, puffy clouds were sweeping over it and causing alternating flickering light and dark inky coloured shadows. Behind the moon was the great constellation of Leo (the Lion).

In the southern sky between the Canis Major (the Greater Dog), and the Canis Minor (the Lesser Dog) was the upright Monoceros (better known as the Unicorn). To the right of Monoceros was the constellation of Orion (the Hunter). Orion consisted of an immense rectangular constellation of four stars, and three centered parallel stars known as the Orion's Belt. The stars of the belt pointed north to a star cluster, known as the Pleiades, and sometimes referred to as the Seven Sisters.

PATHWAYS INTO EVIL

On the opposite side of Orion's Belt in the western sky, the stars pointed to Sirius, which in reality was a binary star, a main star Sirius A, and a tiny blue dwarf star Sirius B, which was the size of the Earth.

Sirius was in the constellation of Canis Major, and is one of the nearest stars. In reality it was a white star, but from its low horizon, gases in the nearby night sky, emanating from a nearby steelworks, mingled with its colour, intermittently flashing its light from glistening white to blood red.

#

The Mercedes slowed down and left the motorway at Junction 40, the Taibach interchange section, then headed for Port Talbot.

Port Talbot is one of Europe's largest steel manufacturing towns. In the nineties the council decided to take advantage of its assets, and built a modern town centre. The new centre consisted largely of multi-story buildings, and it occupied approximately a quarter of the space of the old town.

The Mercedes swiftly past through the town centre and headed south for Aberavon Beach. The beach was one and a half miles away and part of Port Talbot.

#

PATHWAYS INTO EVIL

Somewhere in the three miles of promenade, Policeman Alan Williams peacefully strolled on his night patrol. Four days earlier he had been on special duty in Cardiff.

A protest movement against laboratory animal experimentation was centred on the Welsh Assembly building, 'The Senedd', when it was suddenly hijacked by a militant neo-fascist group calling themselves the 'New World Order'.

Dozens of youths were encouraged to go on a rampage. Sixty people had been arrested before the police were able to take control of the chaos. Hundreds of thousands of pounds of damage had been done. The sad fact was, that claims of secret societies controlling the wealth of nations needed to be investigated by the authorities, and it troubled many people in power.

However, he thought, the Cardiff protest was four days ago, and tonight would be different. He was thirty miles from the Welsh capital, and the atmosphere was serene, and seemed almost like compensation for his previous anguish from dragging away protestors that were blocking access to the Senedd, and then having to arrest some youths that were fighting back at him.

The night air being blown from the sea was chilly, but also refreshing and would keep his mind alert.

Alan was walking eastwards. About halfway along the promenade and within sight of the Aberavon Beach Hotel, he cast his eyes back on a white Mercedes. It was parked in a parking bay, about 300 feet away, and next to the side of a dual carriageway (named after the late Princess Margaret). He had blindly walked past the car a few minutes earlier. Then he had been looking out across the bay towards Swansea City. The city street lighting was lit up like strings of pearls, but as the clouds moved across the sky and then past the moon, looking around, the white car now stood out like a sore thumb in the night.

The driver's window was rolled down, but from looking directly into the car, only a shadowy figure could be seen. Curiosity pulled him to the car like a magnet. Thirty feet from the car, he heard the driver talking over a handheld transceiver. Intrigued, Alan walked towards the vehicle, but the driver easily spotted him. The car's headlights flashed onto full beam, deliberately blinding him. The engine sprang into life and the car screeched forward. He felt a severe pain from the impact of the car's wheel arch against his leg, and then let out a loud groan as he dived for safety towards a grass verge.

Couples who were out for an evening walk, froze momentarily as they witnessed the scene, and then rushed forwards to help the constable. Lights lit up in the hotel and some people peered out from opened windows.

The Mercedes sped down the dual carriageway, its disc brakes squealed as it turned sharply into the concreted beach slope leading to the beach. The lock sealing the metal gates at the entrance to the slope had been intentionally forced open earlier. Both gates swung violently apart as the car's bumper made contact with them. The chassis bumped violently as it hit the sandy beach at the bottom of the slope. The Mercedes then dimmed its headlight and headed east along the beach until it was swallowed up in the evening darkness.

Emergency 9 9 9 calls were made from the hotel. Within ten minutes, two police cars pulled up at the scene. The policemen made their way to the constable, but were soon surrounded by concerned bystanders, all trying to explain what had happened. Some twenty minutes later, two senior officers, Inspector David Jensen and Inspector Geoffrey Hughes, arrived separately by car from the Swansea Central Police Station. They left their cars and approached the injured constable.

Alan was now able to stand up and walk, but with a pronounced limp. Jensen looked hard at the man; then recognised him. He could see that life was returning to his face, "How'd you feel now AL?"

"Don't worry about me Sir, I was winded when the car hit me, I've pulled a leg muscle and sprained my ankle too. Just get that bastard!"

"I thought the Mercedes was nicked. The driver was talking over a handheld transceiver. On approaching the Merc, the headlights turned onto full beam, then it took off at me like a rocket!"

"AL, where did he go?"

"Down the beach slope, Sir."

Jensen looked back at the beach slope, then looked up and around. He spotted Ray Phillips a local police sergeant talking to a couple that had witnessed the incident. Jensen raised his voice, "Ray, when you're free? Look after AL, and call an ambulance for a check-up, he might have a fracture."

Ray excused himself from the couple, then walked over to Jensen.

"I've spoken with Alan ten minutes ago. There's an ambulance on the way!"

"Thanks Ray, can you also call up another three men? I'd like them armed too, just in case!"

Jensen turned to Geoff, "Geoff, I'm going down to the beach, but I'll need a backup!"

The two men walked back to their cars, and equipped themselves with Glock 17 pistols and standard issue torches. They then descended down the beach slope and followed the tyre tracks.

After walking for about 15 minutes, they saw a faint luminescent glow, which on approach grew brighter to the unmistakable profile of a two-door Mercedes-Benz E Class AMG. On reaching the car they could see it was abandoned, and all lighting turned off. The car was relatively new, about three years old. The driver's door and boot were left wide open. Jensen's torch beam revealed an electronic ignition key in a compartment under the dashboard.

Jensen quickly examined the rest of the car.

"Take the car up Geoff, before the sea makes fast work of it!"

"I'll have a look around here to see if I can find the driver, but I doubt I'll find anyone. Whoever dumped the car is probably gone. It would be silly to hang around near here!"

Geoff was stunned at the comment, and raised his voice, "What sort of nutcase would leave a £30,000 AMG Merc, in the wet sand?"

Jensen did not answer.

As Geoff was about to start the engine, a distant humming noise coming from out in the bay became more audible. The hairs on the back of their necks began to rise and prick.

The strange humming noise grew much louder; swirling blades shot sand into the night sky, then a large craft made itself visible by activating an onboard search light. It found what it was looking for, then slowly descended from the sky and hovered three feet above a six-foot square grey canvas platform. Jensen walked quickly towards the craft.

Under the belly of the craft two metal arms activated, extended, then grasped the handle protruding from a metal box container. Then the onboard search beam instantly deactivated. In front of Jensen and appearing silhouetted against the night sky was a large military sized drone. It was impossible to spot any identification marks. Within seconds, thrust was applied to the Rota blades and sand was blown in all directions. The drone ascended through the air; picked up power, and shot away disappearing into the night sky.

Astounded, Geoff started the car, and switched the Mercedes headlights onto full beam. He then manoeuvred the car so that its headlights pointed at the platform. Geoff then got out of the car and walked alongside Jensen towards the platform. They realised the canvas platform came from the boot of the car. They examined the material and found it was lined with thick rubber.

"What the hell! What do you make of all this?" said Geoff.

"I don't know? Whatever is going on, I think this is the beginning of some nasty puzzle that we might get the answer to, tomorrow."

Jensen looked across at Swansea Bay, viewing the street lighting leading to the picturesque village of Mumbles, about two miles west of Swansea. His ears strained as he recognised the swirling blades of the drone returning. The drone was on them in 20 seconds, creating swirling sand and hovering about 30ft away, some 10ft above the beach. This time he saw two protrusions sticking out from the font belly of the craft. Alarmed, this was a different drone!

Jensen recalled a similar incident several years earlier in Thailand. He yelled, "Geoff, let's get the hell out of here!"

Rushing away Jensen turned and fired several shots at the drone. Seconds later a screeching projectile was launched. Jensen and Geoff dived for the sand. The missile tore into the Mercedes and blew it apart. Fragments of the car exploded into the night sky. It turned the beach for a few seconds into daylight. Pieces of contorted metal fell back to earth as fireballs. The larger fireballs did not want to die, and on impact with the beach, speckled the sand with hundreds of tiny fireballs.

One bullet managed to damage the drone. The drone spluttered, tried to gain height by revving its motors, but failed to generate enough power, so activated a software routine and blew itself to bits.

After the noise had died, Jensen and Geoff slowly got up and found their footing, but were covered in wet sand. They walked back towards the promenade stumbling at times, as the explosion had left their ears ringing and had affected their balances.

They both had injuries but not serious. In place of the expensive car, was now a huge sand crater, lit-up by burning tangled metal, oil and leather.

On approaching the promenade, Jensen turned around and scanned the beach. He knew that the sea would soon claim the remains of the Mercedes and drone. The jagged metal was a hazard and would soon have to be removed before swimmers and surfers could use the beach again.

As Jensen looked east towards the steelworks, he saw a small momentary glint of red light coming from large boulders lining the pier. He couldn't see any defined shape, but then on reflection, he froze momentally for a few seconds, sensing possible trouble and wondered whether his past was catching up with him.

#

A sniper peering out through an infrared optical gun sight, attached to an Accuracy International Sniper Rifle followed Jensen and his colleague as they made their way back to the promenade.

Except for the rifle's barrel and nozzle, the sniper's position was almost hidden by giant concrete jackstone boulders. Thousands of these chest high boulders interlinked to form a sea breaker wall, which run for the full length of the 900-foot pier.

The sniper's finger was on the trigger, but there was no reason to squeeze it. If anything had gone wrong, he was the backup to put a few rounds into the fuel tank of the Mercedes, destroying any evidence.

He did not want to give away his position, so released his grip on the trigger. He placed the rifle up against a jackstone. Then he picked up an LCD panel that was receiving Bluetooth transmissions from a cluster of instruments that he had earlier placed nearby. He switched-off the LCD panel and returned it to its leather holder. The LCD panel had displayed wind direction and speed, temperature, atmospheric pressure and humidity.

He detached the 5-round magazine containing .338 Lapua Magnum rounds and put it to one side, then detached the infrared optical sights from the rifle. The rifle and detached components were then put away into a large fishing rod bag.

He collected the cluster of instruments, and placed them into a family sized plastic lunchbox, along with the LCD panel. Taking all his deadly items, he navigated his way past the concrete jackstones, slowly climbing to the concreted platform at the top of the pier.

He then walked to a small carpark at the front of the pier, where his Lexus was waiting. The rifle and its components would not be leaving the country. Instead, they would be stored in a lockup storeroom until one day he might find some use for them again.

The Mercedes driver made his way for a rendezvous outside the Naval Social Club, which for himself was not far away, but to the sniper was much further away, and on the opposite side of the beach front. The Mercedes driver had his handheld transceiver to contact his colleague should he fail to recognise him, or the Lexus.

Avoiding any police contact, the sniper planned a detour, by driving his Lexus through the housing estate behind the beach front. Soon, he and his colleague would be leaving the steel town, their contracts completed, and both looking forward to spending their easy earnings in a warmer climate.

#

Jensen and Geoff met up with Ray and Alan on the promenade. Ray was relieved to find both men were not seriously injured. Both men had suffered small cuts from which trickling blood had congealed. Their uniforms were torn in several places, and had damp patches which were sprinkled with wet sand, and now gave out the odour of the salty sea.

Jensen spoke, "Lads, I'm going to nip across to the Aberavon Hotel to see if I can get some dry towels. Ray, when I get back, I want those officers I asked you to call up, and yourself to join me. We'll be checking the pier wall, but I suspect that if anyone was there for mischief, they will have moved on by now!"

CHAPTER 2 - **Whitehall calling**

February 27th 8:45 a.m.

From a large window on the 3rd floor in Whitehall, the Secretary of State for Defense, the Right Honourable Peter Mathews MP, was looking downwards onto the pavement below. People were walking quickly as if anticipating a rain shower.

He pushed back the heavy red velvet curtains and walked over to his large teak desk. On the top of his desk were several morning newspaper editions, some of which included the incident at Aberavon Beach. He had heard the early morning news on Radio 4, and had watched a short television news broadcast of the incident. Fortunately, there was no news on what destroyed the Mercedes.

Peter wore a dark blue suit, was in his mid-forties and had an athletic build. He was ex-military from serving seven years in the Royal Navy. He ended his naval career serving as a lieutenant commander.

He was slightly troubled; for he knew David Jensen from the axed International Business Innovations Department, whose functions were now absorbed into M I 5 and M I 6. They had both worked from the same office in Whitehall for over three years. At times, they had not got on well with each other, and he would have preferred Jensen to have disappeared from his life!

Wing commander Raymond French, attached to Whitehall, knocked on Peter's office door and walked into the room.

"Hi Raymond, any further updates?"

Raymond was slim and immaculately dressed in his uniform. He took off his hat revealing dark brown hair. He wore a trimmed moustache consisting of a slightly lighter brown colour. He focused his dark piercing green eyes on the Defence Secretary.

"Yes, Sir!"

Raymond then put a blue file on the teak desk and flipped it open and scattered a dozen photographs. They were motorway snapshots of a white Mercedes travelling down the M4 from London. The car drew automatic attention because its speed rarely fell beneath 67 mph. The cameras traced the car and took snapshots every 20 minutes, until the car could be seen leaving the motorway at Junction 15 for Swindon.

Peter looked-up from the scattered photographs, "So, what happened in Swindon last night?"

"Theft on top of this suspicious incident!"

Raymond revealed two further photographs hidden underneath the pile. The photographs were taken from a Gene Solar Systems Ltd. security camera. They showed the white Mercedes parked along a connecting road to the company's main entrance.

"Just within this hour, Gene Solar reported that twelve bio-chips were missing, and emailed us these photographs of the Mercedes. One of their lead researchers Dr. Cheryl Brenton has also gone missing too!"

"Gene Solar use scanning security cameras to cover the outside roads. From the time encoded in the photographs, the Mercedes was parked 100 yards away, and stayed parked approximately from 5:30 p.m. to 6:15 p.m. It must have been a remarkable job as no alarms were activated."

"Bio-chips, the next great leap. Raymond, I thought that security in that place was very highly rated, and impossible to break into!"

"Yes, that place has hundreds of alarms. But clearly not good enough!"

Peter was troubled, "Well that leaves an inside job using this researcher or some rogue group with access to security plans. Just how much could these chips be worth on the open market?"

"I asked Accounts the same question a few minutes ago, Sir. If these chips are kept energised with a special liquid nutrient, they could be worth billions, specifically as replacements for temporary memory storage systems. These prototypes have a short life of only a couple of years. But assuming someone might have the knowledge to link them up to a missile guidance system, then we might have a serious problem?"

"Good God! That's why we gave Gene Solar the research grant for!"

Peter raised his tone, "Another bloody mess! So, some power could shortly have the ability to copy all the research we've paid for over the last five years!"

The phone rang, Peter flinched as a red L E D illuminated on its front. He picked it up, knowing it was the Prime Minister Richard Harris on the line.

Richard was Scottish, worldly wise and generally spoke with a touch of jovial sarcasm.

"Hello Peter, I have the M I 5 Chief Rosemary Yates with me, I also have a file in front of me on Inspector David Jensen. I see you are old acquaintances!"

"Yes, you're correct Prime Minister. I worked with David Jensen for three years, but I haven't been in contact with him, let me see now, for about four years."

Richard made a deliberate pause, then spoke, "Get him some transport Peter, he has a link with the missing woman. I want both of you in a meeting, along with Rosemary, later this afternoon."

"Yes Sir." The Defense Secretary then looked up at the Wing Commander.

The Prime Minister continued, "I don't want any press asking awkward questions." There was another pause, "Peter, when Jensen arrives, can we use your office?"

"Yes Sir, that will be fine!"

"Good, thanks Peter!"

A humming tone indicated the Prime Minister had finished the call.

"Raymond, the Prime Minister wants to meet Inspector Jensen this afternoon. I'll shortly contact him. I want you to organise a helicopter trip. Make it available from RAF Saint Athan in South Wales. I'll want him to be picked up in Swansea from a suitable safe location, then fly him near here. If it's not being used, they can land in Horse Guards Parade!"

CHAPTER 3 - **Investigation meeting**

February 27th 3:45 p.m.

Peter was sitting behind his large teak desk. Sat in front of him was the Prime Minster, the M I 5 Chief Rosemary Yates, Raymond and Inspector Jensen.

The Prime Minister was the first to speak, he turned to Jensen and smiled. "There has been quite a lot of turmoil in your life during the last 15 hours Inspector, possibly reminiscent of your days working here for the International Business Innovations Department. I expect you want to know the main reason for bringing you to this meeting."

The Prime Minister turned to Peter, "Peter, would you update Inspector Jensen please!"

"Yes Sir. Gene Solar Ltd., based in Swindon have reported 12 bio-chips stolen from one of their laboratories yesterday evening. Inspector, we are aware that your responsibilities are within the Western Division of the South Wales Police, but the information collected by several Whitehall departments believe that the drone and missile incident you witnessed last night are linked to Gene Solar Ltd., and possibly to a past acquaintance of yours."

Jensen looked startled! "Who?"

Peter continued, "You did a Law Degree at Swansea University. According to several lecturers that we interviewed for your Whitehall IBID Security Pass, you were well acquainted with Cheryl Brenton and was thought to be in a relationship with her."

"As you are already aware Inspector, Cheryl did a Joint Honours Degree in Chemistry and Biology, at Swansea University. After graduation she went on to do a PhD. in Biochemistry, at the University of Hong Kong."

"She still has a brother living in Honk Kong. She returned to this country five years ago, and worked for several research companies, before finding a position at Gene Solar Ltd. in Swindon. That was 18 months ago. She was promoted nine months ago to a senior researcher within a laboratory there. As of yesterday, she's gone missing."

Jensen was bemused!

"I'm sorry to have wasted your time, I took Cheryl to several plays at the Swansea Grand Theatre. I also spent some time with her, along with other friends at Aberavon Beach during the summer holidays. But there was too much studying to do for my LLB Law, to have any serious relationship with her. I've not seen Cheryl since we graduated. We had a falling out shortly after graduation!"

"Nevertheless, Cheryl's a possible national security risk now," said Rosemary. "We'd like you to find her, and it's vitally importance to get these bio-chips back or destroy them."

Jensen was puzzled, "What's so important about these bio-chips?"

Peter interjected, "Gene Solar Ltd. is under contract to produce these devices to work with a future National Defence Shield. These bio-chips are prototypes and have a limited life, but we expect the development will lead to a more stable product with a long-life expectancy. That information by-the-way, was Top Secret until yesterday, when a batch was stolen!"

"Help us," said Rosemary, "I think there was no coincidence to what happened to you last night!"

Jensen was not convinced, "Although my colleague Geoffrey Hughes and I were nearly killed yesterday! From what I remember about Cheryl, I do not think that any lingering emotions of a possible vendetta entered the equation!"

Jensen thought for a good minute, "OK, but I want a word with my Police Chief first!"

"I'd like to see around that Gene Solar lab this evening, and also, I want to see Cheryl's home in the morning. I'm assuming it's in the Swindon area?"

Peter interjected, "Yes, she lived locally! I'll get a representative from the Cranfield University Defence Academy, at the Shrivenham Campus to meet you at Gene Solar Ltd. After all, they arranged the contract with them. We'll also provide you with a master key set, so you should be able to get access to her home. If that fails you can use the services of a local locksmith. There's two in the area that have worked with us in the past. We'll notify the Swindon Gablecross Division Police HQ of your visit to prevent any unnecessarily embarrassments."

Jensen turned to Peter, "Peter, is there any further information on the drone?"

"No, it's remains are still being analysed by the 157th Welsh Regiment. It's an Army Logistics Regiment. You might be aware that they have one of their bases in Swansea."

"Yes, I've been there a few times. Was there anything else in the sea at Swansea Bay last night?"

Rosemary interjected, "The Mumbles Coastguard have reported two tankers delivering iron ore and coal supplies from Brazil and Venezuela. The supplies were for the Tata Steelworks. One tanker was leaving the harbour for more iron ore supplies in Peru. There were also two fishing boats, and one yacht."

"What is known about the yacht?" asked Jensen.

Raymond answered, "It's one of those super-yachts, on its way to Cyprus. The captain's name, is Stefan Balaskas. He claimed they were returning from Cork and were just sightseeing off the Welsh coast before returning to Limassol."

Raymond continued, "The yacht was later anchored off Falmouth for the night waiting for refueling this morning. The Falmouth Coastguard took the opportunity to search the vessel. Cheryl was not onboard. We're still tracking the yacht, as we're not happy with the captain's report."

"OK," said Jensen. "Cheryl could try to slip onboard at dozens of other locations. Which makes me wonder, why the drama last night at Aberavon Beach? Can someone get me any further information on all those ships?"

Rosemary interjected, "Leave it to my department! We'll check them all out for you!"

"Thanks Ma-am!"

Before Jensen left Peter's office, Rosemary informed him that Gene Solar Ltd. resembled a university campus. Throughout the campus, security cameras were placed at strategic points on all outside and inside buildings. There were six medium sized three-floored buildings, but all these were dominated by a central building of five-floors. The central building contained the Main Reception Room, and Main Security Guard Office, along with other offices and laboratories. The remaining six buildings consisted of security sections, offices and laboratories.

From Whitehall, Jensen booked a hotel room in Swindon and hired an Audi A4, for three days.

Before returning to RAF St. Athan, the crew of the helicopter dropped Jensen off in Swindon at the Shaw Ridge Linear Park. From there and a ten-minute walk, Jensen found his way to the Village Hotel where his room was waiting and his Audi A4 was parked.

Thirty minutes later he drove to the local ASDA centre and bought clothes, including pajamas, a toothbrush, and an inexpensive electric shaver.

CHAPTER 4 - **Gene Solar Ltd**

February 27th 8:15 p.m.

At Gene Solar Ltd. Jensen found the visitor parking bay located outside the campus. It was fenced-off from the company. He locked his car and walked towards the Information Office. The office was situated next to the main gates entrance, which Jensen observed was manned outside by two security staff. From what he observed, before any vehicle could pass through the gates, it would entail ID security badge checks, and further security codes to be entered into a button panel.

On entering the office, cameras scanned Jensen's face and tried to match his image against the company's database. As he was not on their database, he was stopped by a security guard. He thought that even with this degree of security, 12 bio-chips were missing.

Jensen was escorted to the Main Reception Desk. He gave his name, and was told to take a seat while processing was done. Twenty minutes later he was interviewed, photographed and then led into the main campus.

Jensen was escorted by another security guard to the central building and then left to enter it. He pushed the large revolving door, walked through it, and then walked towards a second reception desk. A security guard approached him but this time the guard was stopped by a woman who came over to meet him. She was in RAF uniform.

"Hello, you must be Inspector Jensen!"

"I'm Angela Carter from the Cranfield Defence Academy."

Jensen shook her hand. "Glad to meet you."

She was a trim 5ft 6 inch blue eyed blonde. Her hair was cut short, making her appearance somewhat stern. She wore the full RAF officers' uniform, with dress and tunic jacket. Two stripes on her sleeves indicated the rank of flight lieutenant.

"Where do you want to start?" said the security guard.

"Cheryl Brenton's desk please!" said Jensen.

The security guard led them to her desk in an open office. The office was lit by secondary fluorescent lighting, so Angela decided to switch on the main lighting, in case they missed anything important. They examined her desk for several minutes, but found nothing to help them, as the desk draws only contained several company brochures and information leaflets on upcoming events at the town's Wyvern Theatre and Arts Centre.

"You would expect to see a photograph of a loved one, or parent," said Jensen looking at the security guard.

"Sir, as a defence contractor, after work, we have a clean desk policy here. Cheryl has a personal safe, inside we found a large purse containing several photographs, including one of yourself that we think, was at a university event."

Jensen was startled!

The guard added, "Sir, M I 5 want the purse and its contents, but we have photocopies of all the contents. I'll provide you both with copies before you leave tonight."

"Thank you," said Jensen. "Can we now see the lab where Cheryl worked?"

"This way Sir, Madam, you'll both have to wear special outer garments before entering the laboratory."

The laboratory consisted of an air purified room containing four workstations with electronic microscopes and chairs. Jensen walked over to Cheryl's workstation; her microscope was fitted with several lenses. Angela informed Jensen that the microscope had been loaded earlier with a bio-chip on request from her commanding officer. She then briefly instructed Jensen in the use of the equipment.

Jensen then peered into the eye pieces, rotated two knobs and focused on what appeared to be a silicon chip with several small channels leading away from it to another device. Intrigued, he adjusted the lens to focus on the mysterious object. He initially laughed at what he saw. Then, after a few seconds recoiled in horror.

Angela felt his pain. Jensen composed himself, walked back to the microscope, and refocused the knobs. The device was a semitransparent object resembling a wrinkled grub. It was joined end to end in the shape of a polo mint, and pitted throughout with miniature holes. It was half submerged in a pink liquid, and fed by miniature channels from a tiny transparent container. It moved slightly up and down, like the motion of breathing.

Jensen raised his tone, "Angela, what the hell is that?" He then walked away from the microscope.

Angela had seen it all before and was no longer revolted by the sight. She walked over to the microscope and peered through the eye pieces.

"It's a small brain, grown from the cells of a cephalopod squid. In its natural state the esophagus passes through the main brain, that's why there's a hole in the middle. Cephalopods are highly intelligent animals, they have three hearts, and a smaller brain in each arm. Normally, the brain that you were viewing would be covered in a harness that contains thousands of miniature electrodes. They've removed the harness to give you a better understanding. The harness connects to the miniature interface above it, which looks a bit like a silicon chip."

"Dozens of these tiny brains provide immense storage capacity for silicon chip technology. The life expectancy of this brain is two to three years; the same life expectancy of a mature squid. However, the long-term goal is to learn from this research, and then to build a synthetic intelligence that's required for the defence shield. This research is a subfield of AI that deals with systems that can reason, learn and act independently."

"Angela, ignoring the future development, you are informing me today that you are experimenting with living storage intelligence!"

"Yes, at this stage of the development."

"Does the RSPCA know what's going on here?"

"No!" She then said sternly, "It's Top Secret!"

Jensen took his eyes away from the microscope and then searched around the workstation. It was all clean! "OK Angela, I've seen enough horror for today. Let's pick-up those photographs. I'll need to see around Cheryl's home in the morning."

CHAPTER 5 - **Pinewood Drive**

February 28th 10:00 a.m.

Angela parked her BMW Z4 in front of a garage attached to 21 Pinewood Drive. Jensen agreed to be picked up from the Village Hotel, as it was pointless taking two cars and causing congestion issues.

No. 21 was a bungalow attached to the end of a row, that consisted of two further full-sized houses. Pinewood Drive, was in the Shaw area of Swindon. From there several roads led to Whitehill Way, which led to the Great Western Way dual carriageway, which in turn connected to the M4 motorway at Junction 16.

Although one of several bungalows in the Shaw area, the grounds were quite large. A six-foot red brick wall ran from the building adjacent to the road. Pinewood Drive was a horseshoe shaped road which contained over 100 houses, and several closed roads connected to it. Those roads led to more houses, flats and garages.

The front lawn was shared by two other houses, and subdivided by two paths which connected to a small driveway off the main road. The door leading into No. 21 was not visible from the road, but in full view from a budding eight-foot Weeping Cherry Blossom tree growing in the bungalow's front lawn. Jensen took out the master key set provided by Whitehall. After several attempts using different keys, he entered the building.

Jensen walked through a small green painted parlour, into the living room. He found the light switch, and switched it on. Angela followed and then opened out two red blackout living room curtains.

The living room walls were decorated in an expensive golden and green wallpaper. A two-seater green leather sofa stretched across the far wall, and a complementary green leather chair was located against the near wall next to a bookcase. The bookcase was crammed with books on many topics. A 37-inch Panasonic L E D TV was positioned in the far corner next to the window. Two small glass top tables, were positioned in front of the sofa, their purpose looked to rest drinks on, and to eat small meals from.

Angela did not waste much time in finding the bathroom, bedroom, kitchen and conservatory. She then searched through all the drawers in the bedroom, while Jensen put the kettle on in the kitchen.

Jensen walked through the kitchen into the conservatory and past a circular wooden dining table with three red leather chairs surrounding it. He looked out onto her garden. He viewed a central lawn surrounded by four flower beds.

Across the far side of the garden was a large Maple tree just beginning to bud. Behind the tree was a six-foot light brown, almost golden, closed-board fence which stretched the length of the garden. To the right of the fence were two large darker brown wooden panelled gates, and the six-foot high brick wall he had eyed earlier. Jensen could see several bird baths of different sizes, portraying a very pretty laid out area.

Jensen thought, Cheryl's home was ideal, he wondered what led to her disappearance, and her betrayal of the country? Had she been blackmailed, or could she be really innocent all along?

Angela began to look frustrated, "There's nothing here of any relevance!"

The kettle water boiled. Jensen found two tea spoons in a tubular copper container, and teabags in a kitchen cabinet. He added the teabags to the two cups and poured hot water over them. He then added milk from Cheryl's fridge, removed the teabags and passed one cup to Angela.

Jensen spoke, "Cheryl wasn't the type of girl to take her work home with her then!"

Jensen looked into Angela's eyes, "So, if you were part of a team to steal bio-chips, where would you go after the job's done?"

"She's unlikely to visit her parents in Dorset," said Angela. "It's too close to the action; maybe she's gone to Hong Kong to see her brother Richard."

"Possibly," said Jensen. "But when I knew her, Cheryl did not give me the impression of wanting to bring any trouble to her brother. But Cheryl did have quite a few friends in Swansea. Maybe that's where we start?"

"You mean get M I 5 and M I 6 to investigate her old university chums?"

"Yes, why not? Come to think about it, one of her close friends was Lian from Singapore. After graduating, she went off to France to teach English. Another of her close friends was Mary from Horsham in West Sussex."

"OK" said Angela, "Let's put all the photographs we find here, with the ones from Gene Solar and see if you can recognise anyone, besides yourself."

Jensen raised a smile, "You know, you're very funny at times!"

12:00 p.m.

They viewed several photographs of her brother with background scenes that were taken in Hong Kong. There was another photograph of her parents with a Dorset address written on the back of it, and another with a London Thames scene with her friends Mary and Lian.

One of the photographs that the security guard identified was of himself after graduation. After staring at his picture for about 10 seconds, a distant memory rekindled in his brain. Jensen walked to the living room bookcase and started removing books from the top shelf. He then opened each book in turn and flicked it over so that the pages hung downwards, and then gave each book a good shaking.

Angela was amused, "What's got into you now?"

On shaking the third book, a couple of photographs fell out.

Angela giggled, "So, she used to hide away photographs that were special to her."

Jensen nodded, "Yes, I almost forgot. Cheryl used to put photographs in her textbooks, to brighten up her revisions when approaching exams."

Jensen and Angela went through the remaining bookcase, book by book. Eventually they found a further 10 photographs. Most of the photographs were centered on city scenes.

There were picture scenes from London, Paris, Rome, Madrid, Singapore, Fujian, Shanghai, and Beijing. In many of the photographs she was with people that he did not recognise, but then he hadn't seen her for years. One photograph that had fallen out of a travel book, titled 'AMAZING PLACES 200 Extraordinary Destinations', drew his immediate attention. In the foreground was a yacht heading out for sea on a bright sunny day from a marina. He recognised the marina. Jensen knew the area; he had visited it several years earlier on a sailing course. It was unmistakable Limassol in Cyprus.

Jensen looked up at Angela, "We can pass several of these photographs on to M I 5 and M I 6 to see if they have any face matches on their records. This one's very interesting though, it's a yacht leaving Limassol. You can just make out the name on the stern, it's called the Bluebell."

"It's the same yacht that was in Swansea Bay on the 26th. At this moment it's making its way back to Cyprus. Now, at normal cruising speed, it will take the yacht a couple of weeks to get there. I'II need to get to Limassol before it arrives, but after reconsidering your earlier suggestion, I still think I have enough time to visit her brother in Hong Kong first!"

CHAPTER 6 - **Hong Kong**

March 3rd 2:30 p.m.

Jensen was tired after a 13-hour British Airways flight from Heathrow to Hong Kong. Whitehall was paying his expenses, so he had taken Premium Economy class. Another hour passed while he went through passport control, and a taxi journey which took him to the Ocean Park Marriott Hotel.

It was a damp day and many skyscrapers were covered in low clouds and mist. The streets were always over-crowded with business, but it was no longer a British colony, and it showed. The new National Security Law was now in place. The Chinese Communist Party (CCP) were now in full control.

While on official business for Whitehall and for leisure, he had visited the city several times in the past. Hong Kong had many attractions then, the Big Buddha in Lantau Island, Ocean Park, Disneyland, Happy Valley Racecourse, the Observation Wheel, in Victoria Harbour, Victoria Peak, and Cable Car rides, came to his mind. However, what always made him uneasy, was looking up at the skyline and seeing grey housing block accommodation going on forever. Fortunately, on that day the mist took the madness of that sight away.

Jensen knew Hong Kong had always big problems. All land belonged to the Hong Kong government and leased for a period of 99 years. Taxes were low or non-existent, because the government acquired its wealth by leasing land to multi-corporates at vast fees.

Only 25% of Hong Kong was leased for building on. The remaining 75% was green, and could be built on in parts, but the Hong Kong government refused to lease this land out. This meant prices were sky-high in the concrete jungle. This led to the term caged accommodation, where some people could only afford accommodation in housing blocks which were about the same size, or, even smaller than an American car parking area.

Jensen compared Hong Kong with Singapore. Although, recent events revealing housing problems and an overworked population had changed some of his thinking, but, what a contrast! Although an autocratic state, and dominated by the People's Action Party, Singapore had a better solution to the housing problem, by applying thinking which was years ahead. In 1960 Singapore set up a housing and development statutory board to build affordable homes. All land again was owned by the government and on a lease for 99 years. But there, all flats were built below cost, and financed by the government. Profiteering from the housing market had been dispensed with. Tower blocks were built in different sizes and painted in different colours to prevent the impression of blandness of living, and each block assigned shopping areas and schools.

In Singapore people were forced by law to save 20% of their monthly wages so that in later life, they could afford to buy accommodation and have a pension. Most people only needed to wait three years before they were eligible to purchase government accommodation, if available!

A quick thought flashed through Jensen's mind, back home, Swansea Bay in South Wales had none of the economic madness he saw around him in Hong Kong, and he was grateful for that!

Cheryl's parents were now retired and were living in South West England, in Dorset. They had been interviewed by the local police, along with an undercover M I 5 agent, but they knew nothing of their daughter's whereabouts. The police suggested to them, that they should contact their son Richard to see if he knew anything about her disappearance. Richard was based in the city and worked for a communications company called Zerif. Jensen was aware that while in Hong Kong under the CCP clampdown, he could be followed, and any communication by phone or mobile would be traced.

Zerif was part-American and part-Chinese owned. The station transmitted news, TV programs, films and music which it streamed through satellites. Records showed the station was highly profitable. President Trump had prevented the selling of satellites to Chinese companies which were allied to the Chinese Communist Party. However, bandwidths were still available to be leased. The Chinese ownership part of Zerif enabled them to make use of these satellites. These frequency bands were used on times for CCP propaganda.

After a meal at the Marriot restaurant, Jensen left the hotel to find a bus to Repulse Bay where Richard lived. He soon found a bus heading to the bay. Repulse Bay was just a 20-minute ride from the hotel.

Earlier, he had looked up the area and its history on his smartphone. The bay was named after a British warship H.M.S Repulse, which was Commissioned in August 1916, but was sunk by Japanese bombers in December 1941.

The bay had been developed from 1910 to attract tourists. The development started with the beach and was followed by the Repulse Bay Hotel in 1920. To attract swimmers to the bay, a bus route was created which ran from the centre of Hong Kong. Today it's one of the oldest routes on the island.

The beach was eventually extended to 960 feet, which was one of the longest on the island. Until the 1960s, residential blocks were restricted to only three blocks with each having six storey apartments. These were luxury apartments with servant quarters. Later the Repulse Bay Hotel was demolished in two stages during the 1970s and the 1980s.

A shopping mall was built on part of the old hotel and designed to imitate colonial architecture. Today the bay is one of the most expensive housing areas on the island with some buildings reaching thirty floors.

Jensen easily located Richard's apartment block, and his flat at 'The Lily, 229A Repulse Bay Road'. The apartment block was a spectacular design, and curved inwards towards its middle floors and then outwards again towards its upper floors, resembling a lily. It was divided into four 28 story block towers, with every apartment overlooking the bay.

Before his planned surprise visit that evening, he decided to make a good look around the area. The area was indeed one of the most scenic places he had ever seen. It had spacious areas with clean looking tower blocks, a golf course and plenty of green parks. From the sandy beach Jensen looked out to several smaller islands in the bay. He understood why famous people such as Ernest Hemingway, William Holden and Jennifer Jones had stayed at the original hotel.

7:30 p.m.

Jensen pushed the doorbell button on Richard Brenton's flat door. Richard came to the door, checked through the optical spyhole and then unlocked it. He looked a little surprised as if he rarely had visitors. He was medium height, about 5ft eight, and slim. Like his sister, he was half English from his father and half Chinese from his mother.

Jensen showed Richard his Police ID. "I'm sorry to disturb you, I'd like to ask you a few questions about your sister Cheryl."

"What's happened to Cheryl?"

"She's gone missing from her job at Gene Solar Ltd. in Swindon. She might also be implicated in the disappearance of microchips."

"What!"

"Come in, come in. Please sit down on the sofa. Would you like a refreshment?"

"Yes, a cup of coffee if you have one, please?"

Jensen closed the flat door behind him. "As your phone line might not be safe under the clampdown, I thought I'd call on you directly."

"I've no secrets to hide from the CCP Inspector." Richard gave a concerned look. "I don't know of Cheryl's current whereabouts; I've not heard from her for some time."

"You look familiar Inspector, have we met before?"

"Yes, Cheryl introduced us 15 years ago at Swansea University, when you and your father and mother, paid her a visit."

Jensen then turned the conversation back on track, "How long has it been since you've seen your sister?"

"About nine months ago. Cheryl was here last July."

"Did she ask you for anything out of the ordinary?"

"She stayed for several weeks and wanted me to take her around the Zcrif broadcasting station. She was very interested on how we communicate through our satellites."

"Did you not think that was a little suspicious?"

"Not really, she was happy for my career progression and always very inquisitive!"

"Cheryl said she was researching for a possible promotion in a research company in Swindon. So, I gave her all the help I could."

"Mr. Brenton, we can no longer trace her through her mobile. Do you have any other contact information?"

"Let me see now, I have her home telephone number, but you should already have that, and of course our parents contacts."

"What about any friendships?"

"Yes, you are correct, Cheryl had several good friends. I'll try to remember their names and put them down on a list for you."

"Do sit down Inspector, while I make you a cup of coffee."

7:55 p.m.

Jensen finished his coffee, got up from the sofa and walked over to the large living room windows overlooking Repulse Bay.

Richard could see that Jensen was engrossed in the spectacular view. He handed Jensen a list of three names and places where they worked. "I hope these names help you. Yes, it's a great view of the bay from here, fortunately, the flat and sea view comes with my job."

"Is there anything else I can do for you Inspector?"

Jensen took a card out of his wallet and passed it to Richard, "Should Cheryl get in touch with you, she can contact me through any of these numbers."

Richard put the card down on a table, then led Jensen back to the flat entrance door and opened it. Jensen then walked through to the corridor outside.

Richard said cheerfully, "If she calls, I'll get her to contact you. Goodbye Inspector." He then closed the door.

Richard realised that Cheryl could not be contacted at this time, so walked over to his drink's cabinet and poured himself a glass from a Maotai bottle. The liqueur was popular in China; he enjoyed its crisp and complex flavour. He then walked over to the large windows and looked out into Repulse Bay.

As Jensen walked away, he felt Richard knew far more than he was letting on. There was no mention of

Cheryl's parents. He assumed they would have been concerned and had contacted him.

9:50 p.m.

Jensen walked slowly past the Observation Wheel on the Victoria Harbour Promenade. The views across the harbour of the multicoloured neon lights of the skyscrapers, which lit up the city, was just spectacular!

His flight back to the UK was the following afternoon. Jensen realised the whole trip had been strange? Since the handover on the 1st of July 1997, he'd been to Hong Kong on several occasions and he often experienced difficulties with the authorities. This time and under the CCP clampdown, he was allowed to go and do almost what he wanted!

CHAPTER 7 - **Limassol**

March 14th 10:00 a.m.

Jensen looked-up the recent United Kingdom involvement in the history of Cyprus.

Cyprus was placed under the administration of the UK from 1878, but decided to annex the island in 1914. This unilaterally annexed military occupation remained until 1925 when it became a Crown colony. The island mostly consisted of Greek and Turkish Cypriots. Greek Cypriots made up the largest percentage of the population. This led to power struggles, and demands from the Greeks and the Turks that the whole island be incorporated back to their home countries.

Following national violence, the UK granted independence to Cyprus in 1960, on the 16th of August. However, on the 15th of July 1974, the Greek Cypriot Nationalist Guard and the Greek military junta staged a seizure of power, (coup d'état) overthrowing President Makarios III. This led to a Turkish invasion on the 20th of July, taking control of the north and dividing Cyprus along what became known as the Green Line. In turn, this led to the present-day capture of territory in Northern Cyprus, cutting off a third of the country. Since that time 165,000 Greeks have been displaced to the south and west territories of the island, and 45,000 Turks have been displaced to the northern territory.

Today, Cyprus is controlled by two sectors. The Greek sector is under control of the Republic, and consists of 60% of the landmass, and is located in the south and west. The Turkish sector, is under control of the Turkish government of Northern Cyprus, and consists of 36% of the northern landmass. A further 4% of the area is made up of a United Nations buffer zone, which separates both sectors.

#

Jensen slowly walked away from the Four Seasons Hotel in Limassol towards the marina. It was a warm day, in the mid-sixties Fahrenheit, and fortunately the air was moist from the ocean. The vast hotel was a delight, and as a bonus his room faced the sea. Colourful potted shrubs had been placed on every balcony.

On the surface, the trip to Hong Kong had appeared to be a waste of time. Richard had produced a list of three names. He knew about Lian, the teacher of English who worked in France. There was a male director of a small firm in Fawley near Southampton, and also a male friend now living at Agudela in Portugal. M I 5 and M I 6 had contacted them, but all came up blank, as did the checks on the ore tankers and fishing boats in Swansea Bay on the evening of the 26th of February.

The intelligence services were keeping an eye on the Bluebell since it was searched by the Falmouth Coastguard. They were also secretly logging phone calls made by Cheryl's parents. They informed Jensen that Cheryl's mother, Hui-ying, had telephoned Richard on the 2nd of March. When he paid Richard a visit on the 3rd of March, for one reason or another, he had kept quiet about his mother's phone call.

Jensen was informed that the Bluebell was hours away from docking at its port bay, so he wanted to view the docking berth area. The area presented many scenic views. Hundreds of white yachts were lit up by blue waters. The marina was very clean too, most of the buildings gave the appearance of being no more than 20 years old. They were painted white or cream, and most had flat roofs, whilst a few buildings had conventional sloping roofs in bright red or orange ceramic tiling.

Money talked here; hundreds of boats were docked within the marina; it could cater for 650 berths and some yachts up to 360ft. There were plenty of viewing stations, shopping areas and numerous cafés.

There were recently-built modern villas too. Some of the exclusive accommodation's had swimming pools and docking ports at the rear of the gardens and were fronted with roads and sometimes sea views too.

Jensen found he could peer through the large front windows of the villas into open plan dining and kitchen areas. Expensive cars, Bentleys, Mercedes, and BMWs were parked on the forecourts, presenting an envious lifestyle.

The marina had white curved boulder breakwater sections. Cream-coloured arched bridges linked up the sections which enabled you to quickly cross its length.

Jensen thought as if he had been transported to a different world. On retirement, if he ever had the money, it would be a nice place to settle down.

Jensen located the docking port for the Bluebell. It was adjacent to a Spanish looking villa with a ceramic red tiled roof. He spotted a man and woman who were not moving far from the villa and assumed they were making a bad job of surveillance.

After a quick phone call, he saw the woman answer a mobile phone call and slowly walked away with the man to be replaced shortly by another couple who were less conspicuous.

Jensen then went for a walk along the concreted promenade. He compared it to the promenade where he grew up at Aberavon Beach. The top concreted promenade at Aberavon Beach ran for about two-miles and rose some seven feet in a curve from another concreted platform below it. This was followed by many breaker boulders which now covered the original concrete steps, and led down to the sandy beach. The furthest part of the promenade nearest to River Neath, still displayed the original steps. The Aberavon Beach promenade was lined with cafés and fast-food outlets. Recently, it also contained several giant steel sculptures in recognition of the steelworkers whom had brought prosperity to the area. The air there would be quite cold at this time of year.

The palm tree lined concreted promenade at Limassol ran for about three quarters of a mile. It did not have a sandy beach, but adjacent to it were thousands of cream and grey-coloured boulders acting as a breakwater. The boulders gently sloped downwards some six feet from the promenade to meet up with the sea.

Both sides of the walkway were lined with palm trees. There were smaller paths leading from the main pathway to cafés and fast-food outlets. In Limassol it was warm all the year, around 50 degrees Fahrenheit in January and 81 degrees in June. What both areas had in common were large merchant tanker ships moving throughout their bays. Jensen walked the length of the walkway, then returned to the marina.

2:30 p.m.

A surveillance operator alerted Jensen by mobile that the Bluebell was approaching the marina. Jensen walked quickly towards the villa.

As the Bluebell approached the marina, ten heavy duty air bags, known as fenders, were inflated and five were secured to each side of the yacht's outer upper hull. This prevented any side damage to the yacht on contact with any other yacht.

The Bluebell then swung around so that the stern was facing the mooring in front of the villa. The yacht had three upper decks painted in a light aurora blue. Jensen had read from the intelligence report that the design model was a Angeletti Sapphire, 200ft in length, and was built in Italy.

The Bluebell's diesel engines were reversed and powered-down so that the stern could be moved slowly to the docking port. An inflatable dinghy with two men onboard powered to the docking port, and then one of the men collected several rope lines to be passed to the yacht.

Jensen kept his distance but focused on the crew. Five ship hands were on the stern to handle the lines that were passed from the inflatable dinghy. When the yacht's stern was about 30ft from the docking bay, the anchors were dropped. A boarding bridge usually referred to as a Passerelle was then pre-extended.

A deck officer then appeared at the stern and started talking through a handheld transceiver to Captain Stefan Balaskas on the side-bridge. A stevedore (dockworker), waited for the mooring lines to be passed from the deckhands on the yacht.

Jensen could see that a large 10ft sofa, positioned about 15ft from the bow, had plenty of cushions, this indicated that guests were onboard. The crew were all in uniform, which indicated that the owner was on board too!

A deckhand then prepared a heaving line with two shackles attached. The shackles were very strong U-shaped pieces of metal with removable bolts across their openings. They were used to secure the yacht to the quayside. The deckhand then threw the heaving line to the stevedore and the shackles were pulled in.

The deckhand then threw another heaving line attached to a mooring line, and it was collected by the stevedore. The stevedore hauled in the line and pulled in the mooring line. The quayside had heavy metal round docking bars that looped out from it. The stevedore then moved back the bolt in the shackle, and fed the shackle around the docking bar, then fed the loop at the end of the mooring line into the shackle, and finally secured the bolt between the U-shaped pieced metal. The stevedore walked to the starboard side of the yacht and a second heaving line attached to a mooring line was thrown to him. With the remaining shackle, the procedure was repeated to secure the yacht to the starboard quayside.

The deckhands on the Bluebell then took up the slack by slowly winching in the mooring lines by use of small electric controlled revolving capstans operated by foot pedals. Two further mooring lines were secured to the yacht through the same procedures.

A small overlap was left for the Passerelle to be fully extended and lowered to the quayside.

The deck officer then carried two further shackles and cross-spring line ropes across the passerelle and passed them to the stevedore to be secured to the quay. As before, the cross-spring-line on the port side was secured to the starboard yacht quayside, and the starboard cross-spring-line rope was secured to the yacht port quayside using the shackles. This was a method of enabling the yacht to be square against the quayside preventing any damage to the yacht or any other yacht nearby.

A box was then placed under the Passarella on the quayside forming a step-down to the quay. Finally, a fresh water hose and electrical lines were connected to the yacht.

3:30 p.m.

Jensen waited for the crew to disembark. Two Mercedes taxies pulled up at the front of the villa. Several deckhands departed from the yacht, they were carrying suitcases, and their leather shoes. They swapped their crew shoes for the leather ones and placed their crew shoes in the larger box under the Passerelle. They then walked around the villa and piled into the taxies to take them home.

Shortly after Captain Stefan Balaskas and his First Officer Eamon Thanos left the yacht. They were also carrying suitcases and leather shoes. They repeated the shoebox procedure, and then walked around the building to the front of the villa. They waited several minutes until another taxi pulled up. They then got into the taxi and drove off. Several more taxies pulled up as more of the crew departed.

4:10 p.m.

Some forty minutes later, and after most of the crew had left, a woman walked across the Passarella. She was carrying a small suitcase and her red shoes, followed by two men, both carrying suitcases and brown leather shoes. They repeated the shoebox procedure, by placing their boarding shoes in the box and putting on their outdoor shoes.

The woman wore a large white hat and wore a body length white dress to match. She was slim. Asian in appearance, and had long flowing black hair.

Jensen felt sad, it looked like it was Cheryl! But it had been years since he had last seen her.

The other two men were casually dressed for the Cypriot climate. One was burly, looked in his fifties, and projected an air of confidence. He was broad shouldered, about 6ft in height, and wearing sunglasses. He had short cut dark hair, and was wearing a blue shirt, and dark blue shorts. Jensen identified him from photographs as the owner of the Bluebell, Alekos Alisavou, a Cypriot. The other man looked younger, possibly in his thirties. He had brownish skin, slightly shorter and was thin in appearance. He was wearing green checked shirt and long white trousers.

The woman spoke to the thin man as they left the jetty and walked towards the villa. The owner took out a set of keys for the rear door and all three entered.

As a precaution, the intelligence network had assumed that the villa would be checked for bugging devices, so did nothing to the inside of the building. However, from a nearby villa, secretly hired out to the British Intelligence Services, invisible laser beams were focused to point at several of the villa windows, where hopefully minute vibrations inside were turned back into sound and speech.

7:30 p.m.

Jensen was back in his room at the Four Seasons Hotel. As the villa was secretly under continual surveillance, he relaxed. Jensen viewed the harbour, poured himself a glass of brandy and then sank back into a large green sofa. Ten minutes later a knock at the door broke his relaxation. On answering the call, he was surprised and pleased to see it was Angela Carter.

"Hi Angela, come-in." He closed the door behind her.

"David, I've been here for a week. Peter thought it a good idea for me to come too, but to stay in the background. I've got some blown up photographs of the Bluebell crew, and one is of interest to you!"

"Cheryl?"

"Yes," said Angela. She then put down several photographs on a nearby table.

He voiced in anger, "Hell, how could she get involved with these bunch of idiots?"

He thought, 'What has Cheryl got caught up in now, and realised that unless a miracle occurred, his ex-girlfriend was heading for a long-term prison stay!'

Angela felt his anguish.

"My poor dear, let's take a break, I've found this marvellous restaurant. It's out of the way and about five miles from here. Are you coming?"

Jensen thought for 20 seconds, then whispered to himself, 'What the hell!' He got up from the sofa, walked over to his bed and picked up his jacket. They then left the apartment and took a lift to the basement carpark where her hired BMW Z4 sportscar was parked.

CHAPTER 8 - **The Bluebell**

March 16th 3:00 p.m.

Fully manned, the Bluebell gently slipped its moorings and headed out into the Mediterranean.

Jensen was notified shortly after of the yacht's departure, but there was nothing further he could do at this stage. Because the investigation was connected to the UK Defence Shield, nobody would contact the local Greek government in the south of the island, nor the Turkish government in the north. Both governments might also have spies in their ranks, which risked a diplomatic crisis if information was not handled professionally.

Jensen decided to explore the Old Town of Limassol and wait for the reports to come in.

#

Clear of the marina Captain Balaskas powered-up the Bluebell's engines until it was travelling at 11 knots and heading in the direction of Alexandria. Alekos wanted to take the yacht there as a recently acquired report suggested the area had become a hub for intelligence gathering. Alexandria was 259 nautical miles away, and it would take some 24 hours to get there. Once anchored, there would first be additional and personal business with a schooner captain.

Inside the Bluebell Cheryl attended to her bio-chips. The UK government awarded the bio-chip technology to Gene Solar Ltd. because it had grave concerns over conventional data handling for the UK Defence Shield. Analysis showed that magnetic and optical data-storage systems had a short shelf-life for several of the planned ocean and mountain destinations. Also, running conventional data centres consumed vast amounts of energy.

Her bio-chips were contained in glass baths. Each bath needed to be sustained by a mixture of nutrients containing plant starches and fruit juices.

These ingredients combined to form a type of glucose, plus a very small portion of drugs to prevent electrode rejection. Sodium and potassium ions made at her Swindon home, were then added to the glucose as they were essential to pass through the membranes to enable electrical activity of the neurons. Cheryl topped-up the glass baths with the glucose, and was careful not to pull on any of the connecting gold input and output interfaces, which led from the bio-chips.

She had played an important role in the procedure of bio-chip engineering. She reflected over her research. Originally, her bio-chips were grown in the lab from cells taken from the hippocampus of a cephalopod squid. These cells as in humans, were the primary cells for making long term memory. They were then placed into seed trays, and bathed with a mixture of nutrients and growth hormones. Following bathing, they were placed in a bioreactor to encourage them to grow. A cell soon doubled, and then doubled again. In time there were trillions of them.

When the brain grew to the size of a kidney bean, it was nearly complete. It then contained a prefrontal cortex, that was used for short term memory, and a temporal lobe containing a hippocampus, that was used in the processing of long-term memory, and finally a cerebellum for skill memory. The cerebellum was not used in this early stage of development.

A harness was then placed over the brain. On the underside of the harness were thousands of miniature electrodes which were designed to transmit and receive data. Each electrode was point-25mm in length, with a diameter of 9 µm. Each electrode had a unique ID from which a computer could identify it. Within days, the brain grew into the electrodes. After this period, miniature wires leading from the harness were connected to larger interfaces on the exterior of the brain. Supplemental chemicals were then added to the nutrients to inhibit any further tissue growth.

The larger interfaces were then connected to a computer. Finally, a computer program was run to generate specific neurons in the brain.

ASCII data was converted by the computer into binary. Because each data string generated, originally contained nothing but zeros, the computer simply wrote over the 0's with a 1, when a 1 was due by the ASCII conversion. The computer was able to identify every electrode, so simply wrote the string to the brain by applying a micro-voltage to a specified 1. As 0's carried no voltage, they were not required.

The process generated neurons and formed short term memory in the prefrontal cortex. Unless the generated neurons were fixed, the brain would either reconfigure them, or delete them in a short period of time.

To make the memory permanent, a timed pulsed frequency signal was sent from two dedicated transmitters attached to the underside of the harness. They lasted for a period of five milli-seconds, and were repeated twenty times. The pulses and frequencies used with the 1's, made the neurons permanent, and stored them as long-term memory in the hippocampus.

A specified pulsed frequency signal was programmed to be associated with a string of data, that was 8-bits in length. Other specified pulsed frequency signals could represent the same combinations of 8-bit lengths.

So, an ASCII code consisting of eight values, converted into Binary would equal 8 blocks of 8-bits, totalling 64-bits. For example, using the code ApXU0023:

    A, would be '01000001'
    p, would be '01110000'
    ...   .
    2, would be '00110010'

3, would be '00110011'

To recall data, a specified pulsed signal frequency was sent from the two dedicated transmitters for the same period of five milli-seconds. Any fixed neuron that recognised that pulsed frequency signal was stimulated and automatically fired. The micro-voltages that were detected, were then transmitted through the same electrodes that originally created the neurons.

The micro-voltages were then fed back into the computer along with the frequency and placement value of each active electrode. The data would then be converted back into blocks of 8-bits, and then generally back into ASCII. Any other temporary neurons created in the process would generate only low levels of micro-voltages, and would be safely ignored by the computer.

Her bio-chips were alive and stored information at the molecular level. They could not be used for calculations at this early stage of development, other chips did that work. Those chips passed processed data through the electronic channels to her bio-chips.

In the early days she encountered a severe problem. All living things have to sleep; so, further bio-engineering was needed to keep the bio-chip awake for prolonged endurance periods.

After months of research, she discovered that certain species, as the Albatross, Alpine Swift, Great frigatebird, Fregata minor, Dolphin and Killer Whale, can endure very long periods of staying awake. One theory is that these animals have unique brains that allow them to switch off half, and to take it in turn to swap between them. Enabling the birds to half-sleep on the wing.

The solution was to use DNA splicing, by altering the squid's DNA sequence through adding part of its sequence from the DNA from an Alpine Swift. When she grew the cells into a bio-chip brain, she now wrote data to both halves. But also, she would use several of these bio-chip brains in tandem for any failure. After the DNA splicing, the effects of long-term sleep deprivation on the bio-chips did not really worry her, as the aim of the research, was to create a synthetic brain that could be programmed through electronics and software, in about two years' time.

However, her bio-chips opened up the possibility of future development leading to 16-bit, 32-bit or 64-bit operation, and integrated with quantum memory states, 0, 0 or 1, 1, 1 or 0, through creating different sets of the original 8-bits. This would be useful to any defence shield when driven by quantum computers, which were currently under development by other UK defence contractors.

Being able to store vast amounts of data, they did away with the need for large memory banks. They also did not require much cooling. Consequently, the cost of upkeep was a fraction of a typical databank.

The end product would eventually be a non-living synthetic brain which would function for at least fifty years. However, for the moment, her newly acquired bank balance from her latest employers meant that future research would be left to other scientists back at Gene Sola Ltd.

The vast amount of data collected could be searched for patterns, and when combined with Cheryl's research algorithms, had proved at the Gene Solar laboratory, were ideal for satellite intelligence codebreaking.

Alekos was in the business of extracting sensitive data from military satellites. He had informed Cheryl that there were three satellite types he was interested in:

> Low Earth Orbit (LEO) – small field of view.
> Between 99-1242 Miles (160-2000 km)
> Earth orbit between 90-120 minutes

Travelling speed at 17,000 mph, 28,000 km/h
11.25 orbits per day.

Medium Earth Orbit (MEO) med. field of view.
Between 1243-22236 Miles (2000-35786 km)
Earth orbit between 2-6 hours.
Travelling speed at 14,000 mph 22,000 km/h
Two orbits a day.

Geostationary Orbit (GO) easy capture
At 2236 Miles (35,786 km)
Travelling speed at 7,000 mph 11,000 km/h
Earth orbit in 24 hours.

Geostationary satellites can, and do, linkup to other geostationary satellites covering the globe. Some LEO and MEO satellites were on circular orbits travelling west to east, while others were on elliptical orbits covering the Northern and Southern Hemispheres. However, some specialised satellites, travelled pole to pole, spying for military developments and troop movement analysis.

#

Onboard the yacht, Senior Electrical Engineer Nicolás Remis, checked a handheld transceiver that Alekos would be using a day later to contact a business colleague. It was adapted for the 399.9 - 403 MHz band.

This band included navigation, positioning, time and frequency standard, mobile communication, and meteorological satellite.

He then checked the frequency chart for VSAT (Very Small Aperture Terminal) antennas. There were three large domes positioned at the top of the yacht's masts. Within the domes, were the satellite dishes, which would normally be fixed to a specific band, for example, Band C which had a frequency range of 4 to 8 GHz.

When this antenna was linked to a router, it would enable anyone of the crew to receive internet on their laptops. The satellite dishes on the Bluebell were very special, in that they had been modified to scan all the satellite bands and connect to a powerful transceiver. The transceiver was located in a hidden room on the yacht.

In the onboard hidden room, Nicolás linked-up a cable from the router to the transceiver and then linked-up another cable from the transceiver to his laptop. He then switched on the power and run a maintenance program to check that he could receive all the satellite bands: L, S, C, X, Ku, K, and Ka.

CHAPTER 9 - **Alexandria**

March 17th 7:34 p.m.

The Bluebell dropped anchor 15 miles off the port of Alexandria. It was a warm evening; the waters were calm. The night sky was clear of cloud and full of constellations.

In the southwestern sky, the Orion constellation had risen to its highest elevation along with Canis Major (the Greater Dog), Monoceros (the Unicorn), and Taurus (the Bull). They were now were starting to set towards the horizon.

The eastern sky towards Alexandria displayed the constellations of Leo (the Lion), Ursa Major and Minor (the Great and Minor Bear), and Hydra with its five heads rising from the horizon. Out to sea in the western sky the reverse was happening, with the constellation of Andromeda slowly setting.

#

Off the North African Coast, Adisa Akerele was sailing onboard his schooner. Adisa was born in Liberia, and had grown up there. He was fifty-one, stood about 5ft 10 inches in height and was of medium build. He had long flowing black and greyish hair that at times obscured his brown eyes and thin black beard.

In the late 1980's and during his teens, he became involved in diamond smuggling within Liberia and the neighbouring country of Sierra Leone.

During the 1980's, Liberia was under the dictatorship of a Liberian Army officer, Samuel Doe. He had overthrown the democratic government of William R. Tolbert in 1980. Tolbert was killed and all high-ranking officials in his government executed. Doe headed a military junta until 1985, when he ordered an election that was marked by fraud to become the 21st President of Liberia. His regime lasted until September 1990 when he was overthrown, and executed by a splinter group of Prince Johnson's rebel army, during the First Liberian Civil War (1989-1996).

For a further six years, rebel army groups fought for control of Liberia. In 1996 West African peace keeping forces disarmed the rebels and brought peace to the war-torn country.

Charles Taylor, was formerly removed from the Doe government in 1983, on alleged accusations of one-million-dollar embezzlement charges. After being trained as a guerrilla fighter in Libya, he returned to Liberia in 1989 and became the leader of the strongest rebel group, the National Patriotic Front of Liberia. He was elected the 22nd President of Liberia, from the 2nd of August 1997. Prince Johnson initially worked with Taylor, but due to internal power struggles in the government, left to create his own party called the Independent National Patriotic Front of Liberia. However, rebel forces supporting Taylor forced Prince Johnson to flee to Nigeria.

The civil war in Sierra Leone, lasted from 1991-2002. At this time, guerilla armies ruled Sierra Leone, many of its people were enslaved and forced to work in the diamond mines. These mines were basically mud banks with mud drenched rivers flowing through them, where the enslaved had to sift the water for the precious stone. Disobedience frequently resulted in hacked off limbs by machete blade. The diamonds were later traded to buy arms to finance the conflicts between the guerilla armies.

Due to its atrocities, the Revolutionary United Front (RUF), then the dominant guerilla army, attracted world attention, which led to a United Nations (UN) ban on diamonds from Sierra Leone. So, the RUF then started dispatching uncut diamonds through Liberia with Taylor's support in exchange for arms.

In June 1998, Adisa nearly lost his life at the age of 25, from fast and frighteningly close slashing motions from a machete blade being targeted at him. The machete was being wielded by a RUF mercenary. But when he shot dead his attacker, and shortly after extracted a large uncut diamond from his inside jacket pocket, it would change his life!

Two years later, Adisa traded the diamond for £70,000 in London. From that moment on, money outweighed ethics and morality.

When the UN discovered Liberia's involvement in the illicit diamond trade, an embargo was placed on all trade of guns for diamonds. Taylor lost control of power on the 11th of August 2003 in the Second Liberian Civil War (1999-2003), and fled to Nigeria.

Prince Johnson, not involved in Liberia's second civil war returned to Liberia in March 2004, leaving again briefly due to death threats. However, in the 2005 elections won a Senate seat in Nimba County. He served as the chair to the Senates Defence Committee. In 2009 the Liberian Truth and Reconciliation Commission recommended that Johnson should be included in a list of 50 people that should be barred from public office for being associated with warring factions. However, this was overruled by the Supreme Court in 2011 for being unconstitutional.

Taylor's past caught up with him on the 26th of March 2006, when facing arrest and deportation back to Liberia, he decided to flee the country. But he was caught on the 29th of March by border guards, when trying to cross the border into Cameroon in a Range Rover, that was carrying Nigerian Diplomatic plates. He was also in possession of a large sum of money in US dollars.

A Special Court for Sierra Leone, that was setup by Sierra Leone and the United Nations, agreed to the judgement, that, he be tried in Leidschendam, a province of South Holland. On the 26th of April 2012, the court found Taylor guilty of 11 charges of 'aiding and abetting' war crimes, and crimes against humanity, and sentenced him to 50 years. He was transferred to British custody and began his sentence at HMS Prison Frankland in County Durham, on the 15th October 2013, where he remains until today.

In May 2021, Prince Johnson was promoted by the Liberian government to head the West African Nation's Senate Committee on National Security, Defense, Intelligence and Veteran Affairs. However, due to the condemnation of the man and pressure exerted by several United States Embassies, he was forced to step down from the post in July of the same year. Today, he remains a Senior Senator for Nimba County in the Liberian government.

#

By the end of the civil war in Sierra Leone in 2002, Adisa had made a fortune. He then decided to cut back on activities and enjoy his wealth.

Today, Adisa now owned a luxury 31-metre, 103-foot, two mast schooner, which he named the Eclipse, and employed three crew. His business was spread over the Mediterranean. His schooner was usually hired by the wealthy for sightseeing trips at €22,000 per week, but if there were no bookings then there was always plenty of cargo to transport to various ports.

Adisa had contacts with dealers that traded in heroin and cocaine. This enabled him to sometimes participate in smuggling cocaine from the Congo, heroin from South Africa, and conflict diamonds smuggled into Liberia, and from his old patch in Sierra Leone. This business was still far more lucrative than his sightseeing tours.

Shortly after anchoring the Bluebell, the owner and Operations Manager, Alekos Alisavou picked up his handheld transceiver and contacted Adisa.

"When can we meet my friend?" said Alekos. "I'm now at our agreed destination."

"My Eclipse will be with you within an hour!" came the slightly crackling reply.

8:30 p.m.

Fenders were secured to the upper outer hulls of both yachts. The Bluebell's stern lower deck boarding platform was opened, and minutes later the Eclipse carefully came along side. Ropes were thrown from the Bluebell's crew to secure the boats.

"How's my friend?" said Adisa.

Adisa's men passed 15 four-inch cans to Alekos's team. Although the cans were labelled as mixed fruit, they were filled to the brim with powdered heroin. When they had finished, Aleko's men had exchanged 23 1-kilogram bars of gold worth 'One Million 311,000 Euros'. Alekos and Adisa knew the final street price would be considerably greater, but cartels in the pipeline would need paying.

Alekos then received a small packet of 10 uncut diamonds from Adisa, estimated at €29,750. This was a private deal; Alekos checked the diamonds until he was satisfied. He then handed Adisa an additional 500-gram gold bar.

He knew they were probably mixed with conflict diamonds from Liberia, Sierra Leone, or the Republic of Congo, also known as 'Blood Diamonds'. Alekos had two daughters in private colleges and an expensive wife. The money to keep them all happy had to be found from somewhere; in this case from unscrupulous diamond dealers in Antwerp!

"A pleasure doing business with you Alekos. We meet up again on the 6th of April."

Adisa looked straight into Alekos's eyes, "Alekos, we've done this exchange now over 20 times, my men want fancy trinkets to impress their women. Next time, for 15 cans of heroin, we want an extra two kilograms of gold. Because of our friendship, the diamonds remain the same price!"

Alekos was taken aback; he knew that most of the gold would end up in Adisa's pocket.

"My friend "said Alekos, "You know that I can do trade in Lebanon, with the merchants in the Beqaa valley."

Adisa's poker face initially slipped and projected a little fear as he thought through the opposition quickly, then he recovered and grinned.

"Indeed, but the Syrian Army now guard the poppy and cannabis fields. You will have trouble dealing with them! Hezbollah occupy the area too!"

"Alekos, you will make enemies of them!"

Alekos knew that showing any fear while negotiating would not do his image any good.

"OK, I will talk to my colleagues and get back to you."

"Talk?" said Adisa. "Why do you need to talk to your friends? Are you not the 'Big Man?'"

Alekos responded, "I need to talk to my carriers and their contact's, you do not expect me to pay the full burden, do you? They might not be happy with the new price!" He was bluffing, he was part of a syndicate and knew that a 10% increase in price would not please his bosses, the 'Financiers'.

Adisa's face showed concern, then he smiled, and he put out his hand to be shaken by Alekos.

Alekos shook hands Adisa, "OK, I'll be in touch, within a week …OK."

Adisa smiled again, he turned and boarded his schooner.

Adisa then turned to look Alekos in the eyes again, "If everyone is happy with the new price, next time we can party a little, yes?"

"Next time I'll bring bottles of spiced rum, we can celebrate on your yacht!"

Alekos smiled back, however, the thought of Adisa's bunch of vultures celebrating on his yacht did not please him.

The ropes securing the boats were then released and the Eclipse drifted away. Five minutes later Adisa turned on his diesel engines and powered out of sight.

#

10:30 p.m.

Alekos sat with Nicolás and Cheryl on swivel chairs, in the hidden control room within the Bluebell. In front of them was a large LCD screen connected to a high-powered laptop. The laptop was linked by a router to a transceiver which connected in turn to the satellite dishes. Nicolás took control of the laptop and through a software interface, unlocked the V-SAT antennas from the C Band at 6.25342156 GHz. This band normally linked the Bluebell to the internet. Then with a touch of a software switch, electronics took control, and the Bluebell's antennas began to scan on different frequencies across the night sky.

After several minutes a green L E D lit up and then turned blue, indicating that a satellite was detected in Ku Band at 14.376549876 GHz. If it was a spy satellite, it needed an activation code to prime it, and if successful would download the information that it had acquired earlier.

Nicolás flipped a switch which linked the laptop to a set of bio-chips. Within seconds, hundreds of thousands of possible activation codes and small self-activation programs were sent into the laptop's memory and then transmitted through an antenna-transmitter to the satellite. But the excitement was quelled when nothing was transmitted back. Disappointed, Nicolás cut off the switch to the bio-chips.

Nicolás tried again, and the antennas searched through the night sky. After what seemed to be an eternity, the green L E D lit up again and turned to blue. This time Cheryl leaned forward first to flick the switch that linked the laptop to her bio-chips. Hundreds of thousands of possible activation codes and self-activation programs were then sent to the satellite.

After 25 seconds, a second green L E D lit up and turned blue, indicating an activation code had been successful, and a downlink of data from the satellite would commence shortly. Nicolás took control of the laptop and flipped a switch linking the laptop to another set of bio-chips.

Alekos eyes were fixed on the large screen which now lit up displaying downloaded data. It took a good 10 minutes for the download to complete. The data was always encrypted, however, they had help from another set of bio-chips, and a software program loaded into the laptop which was designed to crack the encryptions. However, it might take several days of processing to be successful.

Alekos was pleased and sat with Nicolás and Cheryl for a further two and a half hours, while they repeated the process. When they finished for the night, they had collected downloads from four satellites. Nicolás then linked his software to a further set of bio-chips containing millions of deciphering codes and dozens of deciphering routines. He then left the computer to decode the data. The original V-SAT channel was then restored. The secret room was then vacated and sealed from sight.

Alekos invited Nicolás and Cheryl into the large Main Deck Saloon.

"We can celebrate now," he said. He opened a bottle of Champagne, handed out wine glasses and poured the golden liquid into them.

"Tomorrow, we can take a break while the software is decoding the information. We'll take the Bluebell into the harbour and pay Alexandria a visit for a few days. Everyone, enjoy the wine and have a restful night's sleep."

CHAPTER 10 - **On reflection**

March 21st 8:00 a.m.

The Bluebell powered away from the port of Alexandria and headed for Limassol. Cheryl was standing at the stern on the Fly-bridge Deck. She was above the Main Deck and looking back at the city. Although Alexandria was the third-largest city in Egypt, with a population of over five and a half million, and full of historical sites, she was happy to be returning to Limassol.

Alexandria's city centre was encased in grim high tower blocks that reminded her of her once home in Hong Kong, and she felt someone should have warned her of the constant traffic noise. Within the centre it was almost impossible to walk in any direction without hearing the constant honking of horns. One enraged motorist completely lost control, and got out of his car to assault another driver, which led to a punch-up. Alekos informed her that the locals loved drama.

There were plenty of hotels, restaurants and bars for the tourists, such as the 'Mirage Hotel', the 'San Giovanni Stanly Hotel', the 'Cap D' Or', 'Bleu', and the 'Spitfire Selsela Café' on the water front. The 'Club 35' was an exclusive nightspot where celebrity's hang out to dine and dance the night away. But Cheryl did not want any of that. She wanted somewhere peaceful.

To find peace, she had visited several mosques away from the centre. The mosques were beautiful, especially the Abu al-Abbas al-Mursi Mosque, which had intricate details and resembled being carved out of cream coloured ivory.

She had hired a guide to see the archaeological remains of the city that Alexander had built, and later the Romans. Alexander had built the first university in the city dating from his conquest in April 331 BC. She was shown his classrooms. Most of the remaining walls were now only about four-feet high, some passageways had steps leading down to lower floors, where stone slabs placed in the rooms had served as seats for students to sit on. She was shown twenty-two classrooms, and then led to the Roman remains of a bathhouse.

As they walked down stone steps to basements, the guide told her to take care as there were no handrails to protect her. The basements would have contained Roman slaves. These slaves would have spent most of their grim lives feeding stone furnaces with wood fuel to heat up the water. The small walkways over the bathhouse were also dangerous with drops of over 12 feet to one side.

Cheryl noticed that parts of the site were overgrown with weeds and garbage had been thrown over it. Only a small number of people were visiting the site. This forced her to ask the guide: "Why do people not care about this site?"

The reply from the guide was startling. "Today, we are Egyptians, Alexander's army, and the Romans, have long gone!"

#

Breaking herself away from her memories, Cheryl brought herself back to the present day, and breathed in some gusty and slightly salty sea air, making her cough. As she viewed a small sailing yacht heading for the port of Alexandria, she caught a second view through the corner of her eye. It was Alekos coming to greet her.

Alekos looked happy, "Cheryl, I've just left Nicolás, your bio-chips have worked. We have decoded data from three satellites. I've called a meeting in the saloon for 11 O'clock."

Cheryl raised her hand and gave a smile, "I'll be there!"

#

8:30 a.m.

Jensen woke from his bed in the Four Seasons Hotel. He walked to the balcony, took a good look over the harbour, then walked back into the bathroom and took a shower. After the shower he then dressed and went to the hotel restaurant. He was not very hungry so settled on cereal mixed with fruit, and a cup of black coffee. He then bought a local newspaper and returned to his room.

Little information had reached him. He had originally assumed that Alekos was only engaged in low-level smuggling, and the bio-chips would be just another trinket to be sold on to a third party. But he now speculated whether Alekos and his operation, were far more dangerous than he had originally thought?

While waiting to be contacted he looked up the history of Limassol on his smartphone. This kept his mind occupied but also changed his thinking on the island's past.

The city of Limassol is situated between the ancient cities of Amathus and Kourion (also known as Curium). In 1191 AD, Richard the Lionheart's fiancé Berengaria and his sister Loanna (Queen of Sicily) had been travelling in different ships to Richard, and because of a bad storm arrived in Limassol.

The Byzantine governor of Cyprus, Isaac Komnenos (also known as Commenus), was a hard man and fell into an argument with Berengaria. This resulted in him denying any supplies to the queens and not allowing them to leave their ship.

Only when Richard arrived, on the 1st of June, were the queens allowed access to the island. Richard then went after Isaac with his army and overpowered him. Richard then released imprisoned crews from three earlier shipwrecks. The ships had belonged to his fleet, but had sunk in sight of the port of Limassol. Richard promised not to put Isaac in irons, but instead kept Isaac a prisoner in chains of silver. Richard took Isaac's daughter as ransom and then took over the island and gave himself the title of 'Lord of Cyprus'. He married Berengaria of Navarre on the 12th of May 1192, at the Chapel of St. George in the fort, which was near the harbour in Limassol (Navarre still exists today as a province of Spain).

Richard had been an arrogant man for most of his life. When his father Henry II, wanted to give Aquitaine, a part of France to his youngest son John. Richard opposed him, as he had grown up there. When Henry invaded Aquitaine, Richard joined his two elder brothers and joined forces with the King of France Phillip II, and attacked his father. They chased Henry from Le Mans to Saumur, surrounding him, and forcing him into defeat. Later his father had to acknowledge Richard as the King of England. This led to his father's early death in July, in the same year of 1189. Richard was crowned on the 3rd of September in the same year.

Although Richard was born in England, and spent most of his childhood there, most of his adult life was spent in the Duchy of Aquitaine in France. After being crowned, his life was spent on the 'Third Crusade', lasting from 1189 to 1192, or, being held in captivity, or on defending his territories in France.

Richard survived the 'Third Crusade' and set about returning to England. But through his arrogance, he had made enemies with most of his allies during the crusade against Saladin. On sailing home, bad weather forced him ashore near Venice. So, he had to travel in disguise through the territory of the Duke of Austria, Leopold V.

Leopold was another enemy Richard had made in the Holy Land. But Richard was caught, and passed to the Holy Roman Emperor Henry VI of Hohenstaufen. He was imprisoned in Trifels Castle in southwestern Germany until a ransom of 150,000 marks, the equivalent of 100,000 pounds of silver, was paid to the emperor. He was released in February 1194. The ransom also included the release of Isaac and his daughter into the care of Leopold. Richard returned to England to be crowned for a second time. A month later he left for Normandy to put down rebel forces and intermittent warfare against Phillip II, where he remained for five years.

On the 25th of March 1199, Richard was in Limousin France suppressing a revolt by Aimar V of Limoges, at Châlus-Charbol Castle. On that day in the early evening while walking around the castle perimeter without his chainmail, Richard was wounded in the shoulder by a crossbow arrow shot from the ramparts by a marksman. Unable to remove the arrow, a surgeon was called, but on removing the arrow, the wound suffered further injury. The shoulder wound turned gangrenous and shortly after he died in his mother's arms, on the 6th of April.

Before Richard died, Pierre Basile (but known by several names), the young boy marksman and knight, who fired the shot was captured. He was forgiven by Richard and given 100 shillings for compensation for the loss of his father and two brothers from fighting against his army. Soon after Richard had died, an infamous mercenary Captain Mercadier, who was in the service of Richard, stormed the castle and hanged all the defenders. One account, states Pierre was recaptured, flayed alive and hung. Another account states Pierre was just left alone to go free.

#

10:50 a.m.

Jensen was reading a newspaper in his hotel room when his mobile phone rung. It was the Defence Secretary Peter Mathews calling from London.

"Hi Peter."

"Good morning, David, I have an update. The Bluebell is cruising away from Alexandria, and most likely heading back to Limassol."

"I'm sorry to drag you away from the sun, but I want you back in London by tomorrow morning. Normally, there are only two flights a week out of RAF Akrotiri to Brize Norton, but nothing today, so I've hired you a private jet at Paphos airport to take you to London City airport. There will be someone to meet you from the British Embassy at Gate 5 from 3 o'clock. They will know your face, but check their IDs before leaving with them!"

Peter continued, "I've arranged a meeting tomorrow afternoon with you and several other people, some you know, and some are from overseas."

"Keep your room in Limassol booked for the next couple of weeks, and see me as soon as you arrive." Peter then ended the call.

Peter had kept the message short, no doubt worried about the line being bugged.

Jensen walked over to a large wardrobe, took out his travelling case, opened-it up, gave a slight groan and started packing.

#

11:00 a.m.

The Main Deck Saloon of the Bluebell was quite impressive. A thick cream carpet run the length of the room. Four sofas surrounded a mahogany table. The ceiling was highly polished in a slightly darker cream colour, and reflected the room beneath on its surface. Two mahogany pillars reached to the ceiling, and by looking through them, there was access to a large dinner table that could seat 12 people. Behind the table was a large 100inch TV screen which hung from a matching mahogany wall. Next to the TV hung two wall lights on each side.

Sat in the centre of the sofa, nearest to the 100inch TV screen, was Alckos. He was wearing a light blue short-sleeve shirt, and white shorts. He was looking relaxed, happy and holding a blue file.

On another sofa to the left side of the mahogany table, and wearing white uniforms, sat Captain Balaskas, and his First Officer Eamon Thanos. Balaskas was in his mid-fifties, he had dark-brown eyes and short greyish hair which matched his trimmed beard. Thanos looked ten years younger, and was clean shaven, but his hair was starting to grey around his neck.

On another sofa to the right side of the mahogany table sat Nicolás. He was wearing a blue short sleeved shirt and a white trousers. He looked relaxed as if a tourist on holiday.

Cheryl entered the room. She walked past the Main Deck Saloon glass doors and sat on a sofa facing Alekos. She was in a relaxed holiday mood too, and wore a sleeveless red and white striped top, and dark navy slacks.

On seeing Cheryl, Alekos said, "Excellent, we can now begin. I've asked Captain Balaskas to take it easy returning to Limassol, so we'll now arrive in two days. The computer is still working on decoding the remaining satellite data. We'll keep the computer running until we approach Limassol."

"We have decoded a series of photographs of military sites. The satellite data is quite remarkable!" He smiled. "They show buildings that are located inside mountains, and submarines deep underwater."

Alekos, then opened the folder and passed the decrypted photographs around the table. All the photographs showed longitude and latitude locations in the left-hand or right-hand corners.

Alekos smiled, then added, "You can all see these photographs are worth a great deal of money to the right customer."

Alekos, looked up, then looked around the table. "Even better, once we have extracted all of the information, Nicolás is looking at a way to wipe the satellite's memory clean, so giving us an advantage in time when presenting the information to our customers. But for now, we do not want to make ourselves visible to any outside organisation. So, that procedure will be held back for special cases."

Alekos then looked again around the table. "For now, we tell no one!"

"Does anyone have any questions?"

Captain Balaskas spoke. "Do we continue to do business with Adisa, Sir?"

"It's still good business," said Alekos. Like Adisa, he had no morals or ethics; the only driver for his business was how to make huge amounts of money quickly.

"This time, we traded 23 1-kilogram bars of gold worth about 'One Million 311,000 Euros' for 6 kilograms of heroin. The heroin will be sold for about 'Two Million 500,000 Euros' to the dealers. We are not greedy, when it passes on the streets in Europe and North America it will be worth about 'Three Million 700,000 Euros'. We will still make a good living, but Trondheim will not be happy with Adisa's extra 114,000 Euros demand. We'll wait and see what Trondheim will do, and how they want us to respond."

Cheryl looked startled; Trondheim was in Norway. "Alekos, what's in Trondheim?"

Alekos looked back at Cheryl, "My Financiers!"

CHAPTER 11 - **The big reveal**

March 22nd 9:30 p.m.

Peter informed Jensen that infrared satellite images showed that a second boat had docked with the Bluebell super-yacht off the coast of Alexandria on the 17th, from 8:30 p.m. until 9:15 p.m. Also, that evening, unauthorised satellite activity was recorded from French, Italian and American satellite stations, during the hours from 10:40 p.m. until 1:00 a.m.

2:30 p.m.

Jensen was sitting in a Whitehall lecture room next to Peter and Raymond. M I 5 Chief Rosemary Yates and M I 6 Chief Jon Barton were sat in seats in front of them. There were also several other officials. There was an American from the CIA. Jensen recognised a man and a woman from M I 6 who he had worked with in the past. There were two other foreign Intelligence Officers, a French woman, and an Italian man. There were also several other people of different nationalities wearing Interpol badges.

The two people from M I 6 that Jensen had recognised stood up in the lecture room and broke up the chatter.

"OK, let's start, my name is Roger Phillips. My colleague is Lucy Mathews, and we work for M I 6. We have been working in the satellite surveillance unit for the last four years."

"To this meeting we have invited Brad Jackson from the Central Intelligence Agency, Sophie Gruyere, from the French Foreign Intelligence Agency, and Luciano Bellini, from the Italian External Intelligence and Security Agency. This is because satellites belonging to their countries were interfered with, in orbits above Alexandria on the 17th and 18th of March."

"Those satellites were instructed to download surveillance data by an unauthorised organisation. We had previously assumed that decryption of highly sensitive data by another country would be impossible to break. However, after a recent event which led to bio-chips being stolen from Gene Solar Ltd. in Swindon; we are no longer confident that sensitive information transmitted from satellites can remain secure?"

Roger turned to look at the American. "Brad, can you add now please!"

Brad rose then spoke, "Good afternoon, everyone! If anyone here does not know me, I've worked for the CIA for the past fifteen years. For the past five years I've been employed with the satellite surveillance team. I'm now going to show you a series of slides. Can someone dim the lights please?"

Roger and Lucy sat down in their seats. Seconds later the room went dark and then Brad pressed a button on a hand-held device to project the first slide against a large screen.

Brad continued, "You can see our latest imaging is a jump in generation on what we could do just a few months ago. We now fly surveillance stealth aircraft equipped with powerful radars and powerful camera lenses. We can combine this information with onboard infrasound emitters (below 20Hz to 0.1Hz)."

"Today, on special missions, our stealth aircraft are able to link-up with overhead satellites for prolonged periods of time. This way, even in cloudy scenarios, we can still get good results!" Brad then pressed the button slowly several times, showing a succession of several slides. "As you can see from these slides, we can now identify bases within mountains and submarines that are several hundred metres under water, and of course stamp date and time, and geographical co-ordinates into the photographs."

"We also look out through space to spy on neighbouring satellites and by chance came across this image."

After pressing the button; the slide brought the room to silence!

The projected image from the slide just managed to show an outline of a jet-black spacecraft with a bulbous front and very long body. What looked like a large antenna-transmitter, hung beneath its body. It was also equipped with thrusters enabling it to change orbit.

Brad continued, "I know it's difficult to make it out against the blackness of space. We estimate it to be 30 metres in length, that's about 100-feet, and 2 to 3 metres in width, or about 8 to 10-feet. The beam width, the widest area, is at the front of the craft, this is bulbous in shape and about 4 or 5 metres. That's about 13 to 15-feet in beam. There are no markings to indicate nationality, and we do not know where it came from. How that spacecraft got there without us noticing it, is embarrassing, considering all the electronic and optical systems that we have looking into space today!"

"After detecting this craft, we searched for anything similar, but found nothing else like it. Of course, this does not mean it's the only craft of this type in space. It's coated in a stealth paint and it's invisible to radar! Fortunately, it can be optically detected by our latest satellites, but that's assuming we know where to find it! Unfortunately, for the present, this craft has moved out of our satellite range, and we can no longer detect it."

"Why Alexandria?" asked Jensen.

Peter cut-in, "Alexandria has always had a strategic location. Being on the shores of the Mediterranean Sea, meant the city used to be repeatedly captured and ruled by many overseas invaders like the Greeks, the Arabs, the Eastern Roman Empire (Byzantines), the Ottomans, and the French."

"But recently It's becoming another Vienna for spy activity. In Africa it's second only to Algiers for espionage. M I 6 have reported seeing security agents from Russia, China, and South Africa, and have identified faces there from Middle Eastern terrorist groups."

Jensen continued his questioning, "Brad, you said, that the spacecraft has now disappeared. So, what countries are these spy satellites passing over before reaching Alexandria?"

"I thought of that, it's my next slide."

A map of the world containing major cities filled the screen.

"As you can all see," said Brad. "The coordinates for Alexandria are Latitude 31.205753, and Longitude 29.924526. If we use the 30-degree latitude and longitude lines, as base lines, travelling west, we pass through Libya, Algeria, Morocco, across the North Atlantic Ocean to Florida, but within reach of Cuba, then Texas, and Mexico."

"If we travel east, we pass through Jordan, Saudi Arabia, Kuwait, Iran, Afghanistan, Pakistan, India,

Nepal, China, and then the line passes to the Pacific Ocean between Taiwan and Japan."

"If we travel north, we pass through Turkey, the Black Sea, Ukraine, Belarus, Russia, within range of Moscow, then Finland, Norway, Svalbard Islands in the Barents Sea, which belong to Norway, and then finally the Arctic."

"If we travel south, we pass through Sudan, South Sudan, Zimbabwe, South Africa, and then onto the Antarctic."

"Does that help?" said Brad. "If I cover elliptical orbits over Alexandria, we might be here for some time."

There was some small laughter in the room.

"Well, yes, I see your point Brad," said Jensen. "In those orbits that you've already covered, there are a few hotspots, Ukraine, Belarus, Russia, Afghanistan, Pakistan, India, China, Taiwan and Cuba."

"Yes, indeed!" said Brad.

Luciano from the Italian Security Agency, cut-in, "Brad, I'm a little troubled, we've seen your impressive slides showing military installations within mountains, and submarines at great depths. Stationary orbit is acceptable, but how is it possible to link up to individual satellites in low or medium orbits for prolonged periods of time? Satellites in low orbit can travel at 17,000 miles per hour, even in medium orbit they can travel at 14,000 mile per hour. Are you now confirming you have stealth aircraft that can travel at speeds of Mach 5 or Mack 6, that leave little or no vapour trails, that would normally identify them to an enemy?"

"No," said Brad, he then thought carefully! "We just have many satellites and several stealth aircraft that follow the lead!"

A thought was shared throughout the lecture theatre, 'AURORA SR-91, or, TR3b Black Manta?'

Silence followed, Brad said nothing, but looked downwards towards the floor.

3:20 p.m.

Peter broke the silence, "Turn the lights back on please." Peter then stood up.

"Thanks' for that Brad, I can assume your team are still searching for possible launch sites for the spacecraft?"

Brad nodded and replied "Yes Sir." He then sat down.

Peter closed the meeting, and then asked Jensen and Roger to his office.

In his office, Peter was the first to speak, "I can only assume that Alekos will at some point discover the same information that we've seen here today. Because there's no actual evidence to date of spying activity originating from his yacht, I want you both to get onboard the Bluebell and look for the evidence. Do nothing else, the Navy will do the rest. Do you both understand?"

Peter looked at both men in turn.

"Yes Sir."

"Yes Sir."

CHAPTER 12 - **Trondheim**

March 22th 4:30 p.m.

A heavy dark cloud hung above the city of Trondheim in Norway. At this time of year, the city had best 12 hours of sunlight, which began from about 6 a.m. and ended around 6 p.m. But most of it was dimmed light, with only about 3 hours of actual full sunlight. In July, the sun barely set. But on this day, the temperature was in the mid-30 degrees Fahrenheit. Most people wore thick coats, insulating themselves against the cold penetrating winds.

Trondheim is just over 300 miles Northwest of Oslo, and located on the south shore of a large fjord at the mouth of the river Nidelva. Its population was normally around 200,000. However, at this time of year, it was full of students studying at the University of Science and Technology (NTNU).

In September the Student's Union had a unique way of making the First-Year's become better acquainted with each other. Small groups of five or six students were literally linked-together in a chain using long and thinnish ropes, giving each student about three feet of space from the next.

The group were then told to go on a pub-crawl around the city. So, a group of rope linked students would enter a public house, order drinks, stay for a while, then drink-up for another pub, and while leaving possibly being passed by another group of rope linked students entering the building. Although it looked very silly, everyone would be enjoying themselves and encouraged to chat with each other in the rope chain.

While the city centre was composed mostly of one-story, or two-story grey stone buildings, most houses in the city were alternatively painted in a multitude of colours from green, yellow, red, blue or white, which countered any monotony.

The picturesque houses were all built from high quality wood, which combated the winter weather.

Multicoloured warehouses on the wharfs lined each side of the river bank. They rested on large heavy wooden or concrete pillars. Many had four or five floors.

The days of sailing ships loading cargo from the wharfs were long gone. Some enterprising Norwegians converted the warehouses into modern companies, while others converted them into luxury flats, giving spectacular views of the Nidelva river.

Smallish to medium sized luxury yachts now sailed passed the wooden buildings. In the summer months they frequently carried bikini clad young beauties sunbathing on mattresses near the bow, whilst their rich owners were happily piloting the crafts.

Trondheim had the magnificent medieval Nidaros Cathedral, built over a 230-year period, from 1070 to 1300, and in both 'Romantic' and 'Gothic' style. It was sited next to the Archbishops Palace, a castle and a palace built from the 13th century. Trondheim also had the great Kristiansten Fortress.

The fort's history was a little grim, but filled with military honour. The fort was built after the great city fire in 1681, and stands guard over the city. It was built from 1682 to 1684 and further strengthened in 1691. It saved the city from several conquest attempts by Sweden in 1718. Many soldiers had given-up their lives in the battles.

Some of these men had frozen to death manning the top of the fortified walls. The enemy suffered a hellish time too, many dying of gunshot wounds or slowly freezing to death outside the fort. The fortress was decommissioned in 1816 by King Charles XIV John. In 1997, it was turned into a museum. Inside is a memorial place to Norwegian Resistance fighters that were shot against the inside wall by the Nazis.

Today Trondheim is a magnificent technology hub, mostly credited to its University, the NTNU (Norwegian University of Science and Technology).

There are plenty of museums too, such as the 'Forsvarsmuseet Rustkammeret war museum', 'The Crown Regalia' where the crown jewels and robes are kept, and the 'Rockheim' museum, which is dedicated to the history of rock music.

There are dozens of public houses, coffee bars, and nightclubs for the tourists, students and locals. Notably the most popular the 'Three Lions Bar', which hosts live music, and there is 'Heidi's Bier Bar', where staff are dress in authentic Bavarian folk costumes. For all kinds of cultural events the main venue was the 'Byscenen concert hall', now mostly used for rock concerts.

#

In a villa overlooking the Trondheim Fjord, three people were sitting within an Art Deco styled room. The room panels were extravagant and been purchased 50 years earlier from a 1930s liner that was being scrapped. The panels had been kept in storage for years, and were now restored to perfection, and rebuilt into an outhouse next to a mansion. The room was circular, about 60 feet in diameter. The walls had teak panelling, containing engravings of Venice and Milan buildings, and a scene from Santorini. The views were accompanied by engravings of military troops holding spears and swords from earlier times.

From the centre of the room, a luxurious circular thick carpet stretched outwards to 30 feet. It was coloured in sections of light and dark purple, and white, with white and dark swirls running through it.

Standing on top of the carpet were two medium sized tables containing bottles of various alcohol spirits and clean drinking glasses. Behind the tables were two large circular designed sofas, and four single chairs. They were all coloured in off-white. The room was lit-up by several pillar-styled lamps placed around the room, and secondary by three circular bands of smaller lights placed in a magnificent dark red plaster ceiling.

The three people sitting on the sofas kept many dark secrets. They considered themselves not as Norwegians but descendants from the German military elite.

#

Vidkun Quisling (18th July 1887 – 24th October 1945), a Norwegian military officer, politician, fascist and Nazi collaborator, paved the way for the German invasion of Norway. In turn, remnants from his activities, many decades later evolved into a criminal organisation which now in the present day, was led by a group of three people known as the Financiers.

Quisling had formed his own political fascist party in 1933, the Nasjonal Samling (National Party) which was based on Hitler's National Socialist German Workers Party, but it failed to win seats. During the German invasion of Norway, he tried to take power, but he was not trusted by the Germans and was unsuccessful.

However, from 1942 to 1945 the Germans found a place for him, he could act as Prime Minister of Norway; on condition he shared the administration of the state with a German civilian administrator, Josef Terboven. This pro-Nazi puppet government was known as the Quisling regime.

The German elite learned the Norwegian language and perfected the accent and mannerisms. They then mixed with the population to spy on them during the German occupation from April 1940 until May 1945. Many of the people they spied upon were unmasked as resistance fighters, and shortly after shot against the inside wall of the great fortress.

After World War two ended, Quisling was put on trial during a legal purge in Norway. He was found guilty of embezzlement, murder and high treason against the Norwegian state. His sentence was death by firing squad, which took place at the Akershus Fortress in Oslo. Consequently, the word Quisling became a byword for "collaborator" or "traitor" in several languages.

#

The German elite had married locally to camouflage their part in the ultimate game of world domination. However, by the end of WWII, the goal had changed. Now generations on, the three people sitting in the Art Deco styled room had no remaining descendant ties to Germany. The new goal was far more subtle, control of populations without people being made aware of it.

Those in the outer-periphery who might had known anything about their descendants had died fighting in WWII, or were shot inside the fortress, or were sent to the death camps, or had been hung after the Nuremberg trials, or since that time, had been quietly disposed of. They were sitting on huge wealth from tax havens from around the world, the very same bounty that had originated from Nazi plunder.

Harald Haugen sat on the large circular sofa on the left side of the table. He looked across the table at his two colleagues. Svein Thorsen and Anne Westrum, were sitting opposite him.

Harald was a big man, clean shaven, silver haired and had blueish eyes. His cheeks were slightly reddish. He was in his late-fifties, 6ft 1inch tall, and accustomed to life's luxuries. He wore a thick blue and white chequered pullover, brown slacks and brown suede shoes. He poured three glasses of Courvoisier XO Imperial Cognac Brandy, and then passed two glasses to his colleagues.

"We have good and bad news from Alekos," said Harald. "The satellite imagery has been successful; some photographs are still being processed. But our narcotics business has hit a little problem, as Adisa wants an extra 2 kilograms of gold for the next delivery."

Anne was a slim woman in her early-fifties, 5ft 8 inches in height. She had dark brown eyes matching her hair. She wore a green flowing midi dress with matching green suede low block heel shoes. Her eyes radiated cold-blooded intelligence. Her colleague Svein was also in his early-fifties and an inch taller than Anne. He wore a dark grey zip neck jumper, navy trousers and black leather shoes. He had short fairish hair, a thin face with penetrating green eyes.

Anne looked at Svein. "Do we have alternative carriers?"

Svein shrugged, "Two years ago, I tried doing business in the Beqaa valley in Lebanon. But the dealers were assassinating each other to get at the cannabis and heroin. That persuaded me to avoid these people at all costs."

Anne cut-in, "Svein, what about the South Africans or the Congolese?"

"Yes, most African countries are engaged in narcotics. I've read in research papers that Africa produces over 10,500 metric tons of cannabis each year, a fourth of all the marijuana in the world. The Congolese produce more cannabis than almost any other African nation, with the exception of the South African's. Estimates of between 20-40 metric tons of heroin enters Africa each year, but it could be much higher."

"When the Americans pulled out of Afghanistan; the Taliban came out of the shadows and opened-up old heroin trade routes. They smuggled the heroine to South Pakistan, but once it left the coast, it became the responsibility of the drug cartels."

"Using human mules to avoid detection, they fly the heroin to Mozambique. From there it's across land to Johannesburg. The heroine is then sent on its way up the African West Coast, or sent on to India through Doha in Qatar. From India it reaches the America's, Europe and Australia. However, two of these human mules have recently been caught at Hyderabad in India, as red flags were showing up on their passports. They had travelled from Johannesburg to India through Doha. However, in some Taliban controlled areas, since the start of this year, the poppy cultivation is down by 80%. The farmers are being forced to grow wheat instead, at a fraction of the poppy price yield, due to the Taliban rethinking their values."

"Then that settles it," said Harald. "Search for another supplier from a cartel in South Africa. They can deliver to us using an alternative route through West Africa and then off the Northern African Coast in the Mediterranean."

Anne cut-in, "Harald, what do we do with Adisa?"

Harald thought for a few seconds then looked back at Anne and Svein, "Adisa is getting greedy, but narcotics is only 20 percent of our business. We will continue to work with him until we find alternative suppliers. When we find them, his services will be discontinued! There will be no need for any violence on our part. But if he causes us any further inconvenience, then he and his boat will disappear under the waves along with his crew. Nothing should connect back to us, as the task will fall to Alekos."

"Do you both agree?"

"Yes!" said Svein.

Harald looked sternly across the table at Anne.

"Yes, agreed, too!"

CHAPTER 13 - **Bounty**

March 23rd 9:30 a.m.

The Bluebell was within 50 nautical miles of Limassol. Nicolás located Alekos sitting on a sofa near the bow, and informed him of the latest satellite imagery. Nicolás handed Alekos a large white envelope containing a photograph. Alekos got up from the sofa, then walked into the spacious Main Deck Saloon. He sat down on a sofa, took out the photograph and stared at it for several minutes. Nicolás began to get impatient.

"Is that all Sir? I have several tasks to complete before we reach the marina."

"Sit down Nick. What do you make of this photograph?"

"It's quite remarkable Sir! It's like something from a Star Wars set. It's impossible to identify any markings on the craft. There's possibly none!"

Alekos looked at the coordinates and time recorded in the bottom left of the picture. It was the same photograph that led Jensen to be recalled to Whitehall.

Alekos looked up from the photograph at Nicolás. "When we go back to Alexandria, then at some point, target this craft to see if it's still in orbit! Nick, do you have anything else to report?"

Nicolás, got up from the sofa. "Yes sir, we have deciphered nearly all the remaining photographs. They are what we assumed, and show military installations around Asia, particularly Taiwan and troop movements at boarders, mostly India, Pakistan and China, but there's also more Russian build-up in the Ukraine."

"Excellent," said Alekos. "Harald will be pleased."

11:00 a.m.

Alekos was in the Main Deck Saloon sat on a sofa. He was engrossed in a video call to Harald on a 37-inch LCD TV. The TV was previously hidden inside its glossy teak cabinet.

Earlier, Alekos had sent more deciphered photographs to Harald, including the one of the strange spacecraft.

Cheryl was looking comfortably sat on a sofa, opposite him.

Alekos could see that Harald was pleased, both realising that the millions of Norwegian Kroner invested in the Gene Solar bio-chip operation had brought a potential huge bounty.

Alekos, then broke his conversation with Harald and turned to Cheryl. "Cheryl, I'd like to introduce you to Harald. Without his team's finance and planning, it would have taken us many years to get to where we are today!"

"Good day Sir," said Cheryl.

Harald replied, "Welcome to the firm Cheryl."

From the screen, Harald turned to look at Alekos, "Alekos, pass Cheryl the photograph."

On receiving the photograph, Cheryl looked bewildered and alarmed. "What's that?"

"That's what we want you to explore," said Alekos. "This photograph was taken from an American Spy Satellite. From the time and co-ordinates recorded on the photograph, this spacecraft was in the area over Alexandria, when we were there scanning for satellites. We must have sent your codes to this spacecraft, but none of them were able to trigger any response."

Cheryl thought for a few seconds, "It might be impossible, there might be other mechanisms involved, but I can give it a try! I'll add more codes to the bio-chips from my library, and I'll create more algorithms to generate thousands of additional codes! So, the next time we go back there, and provided the spacecraft is unmanned, we might have more success!"

"Excellent," said Alekos. "Cheryl, when we get back to Limassol, the yacht will undergo quarterly maintenance in its bay. We'll need to recheck the villa again for any listening devices. You're welcome to stay on at the villa, or I can find you accommodation in a five-star hotel. We'll leave again for Alexandria on the

5th of April. Will you have enough time to create your new algorithms by then?"

"More than enough! I'll stay on at the villa as I need access to the bio-chips."

Harald added, "Alekos, I'll top up funds in the Cypriot Bank, so you can buy the gold to cater for Adisa. I'll end the meeting now, so, until the next communication - bye!"

The TV screen turned to static, then twenty seconds later it automatically turned itself off and descended back into its glossy teak cabinet, and out of sight.

Alekos turned to Cheryl, "Would you like a cup of coffee?"

"Sure!"

#

2:00 p.m.

Jensen and Roger were flying in an executive jet from Biggin Hill, heading to Paphos airport in Cyprus. Because there was no international airport at Limassol, they would also have to take a taxi to cover the 44 miles to their hotel.

Jensen was viewing plans of the Bluebell on a Ministry of Defence tablet. He then looked up at Roger sitting opposite him and spoke.

"I can see from the yachts plans that the bow and stern have double hulls with inspection hatches, but I don't fancy spending a day or two cooped up in either of them until the yacht drops anchor."

"Anyway, there's no way of getting on that yacht while it's in the marina! The ship to shore walkway is the only access and I'm pretty sure that while berthed, someone on board is watching it most of the time through the security cameras."

Roger cut-in, "So, we board at sea, when the yacht is anchored!"

"Any thoughts of how we get past the crew once onboard?" said Jensen.

"Yes, I've an idea," said Roger. "The surveillance team have been taking photographs of the crew, so we can disguise ourselves to look like two of them with similar builds. I just hope that we don't run into them, or someone stops to talk."

"OK, sounds interesting and amusing," said Jensen, "Do we have any backup?"

"There's good and bad news there," said Roger "The Ministry of Defence has promised to help us out, but their plans are as yet a little sketchy."

"Well, that sounds a little worrying at this stage Roger! I'd better have another good look at these plans, for possible hidden places on the yacht."

Roger looked back at Jensen, "My colleague Lucy is doing the same task back in London."

Roger then took out a duplicate Ministry of Defence tablet from his briefcase, to also look over the yacht's plans. "Hopefully one of us will strike lucky!"

CHAPTER 14 - **Pursuit**

April 5th 6:30 a.m.

It looked like the beginning of a bright day in Limassol, the temperature was around 50 degrees Fahrenheit, and normal for the time of day. Fortunately, the onshore winds were producing a light breeze.

Since the yacht's return to Limassol, it had been placed under around the clock surveillance. The maintenance team came onboard, did their necessary lubricating of the engine, checking gauges and electrical systems, and then left. Alekos expected that there was a possibility of foreign surveillance, but nothing was found at the villa, and his team had not reported anything suspicious.

The Bluebell slipped away from the marina with a full working crew of 12, along with Cheryl. The voyage was expected to take no longer than four days.

The Bluebells departure was transmitted to Jensen and Roger. Within thirty minutes they boarded a small yacht on standby at the marina. It was manned by three men, a skipper and two of his sons. The moorings and cross-spring lines were unfastened and the motorised yacht headed out into the bay.

Because the Bluebells radar would be able to pick up any pursuit ship on water, the Ministry of Defence diverted HMS Astute, a submarine in the area to assist Jensen and Roger. They met up with the submarine just over two miles offshore. They thanked the captain of the yacht and then boarded the submarine. Shortly after boarding, the submarine gently slipped beneath the undulating waves.

April 6th 5:30 p.m.

The Bluebell came to anchor 15 miles offshore from Alexandria. Unlike the previous day, the sea was now producing choppy waves, which buffered against the yacht and forced the crew to use the handrails.

Alekos picked up a handheld transceiver and contacted Adisa.

"When can we meet my friend?" said Alekos. "I'm now at our agreed location."

There was a slightly crackling reply. "My Eclipse will be with you in about half an hour."

"I'm glad that we can do business again," said Adisa. He was wearing a slight grin, but he knew Alekos would be feeling some pain at his new price.

6:10 p.m.

A periscope rose from the sea and turned to point at the Bluebell and a nearby schooner. The view became unclear as the motion of waves washed over it, then cleared again as the periscope was raised higher.

#

Fenders were secured to the outer upper hulls of both yachts. The Eclipse then came alongside the Bluebell. Then ropes were thrown for securing the boats. Because it was too dangerous to open up the lower deck boarding platform, instead several rope ladders were dropped to Adisa's schooner.

The choppy waves forced the boats to rock back and forth against each other, in turn causing difficulty in passing the 15 disguised fruit cans containing heroine.

When they had finished, Aleko's had exchanged 25 1-kilogram bars of gold worth 'One Million 425,500 Euros'.

6:35 p.m.

Adisa was onboard the Bluebell, saying his farewells to Alekos. He handed over a small packet of 10 uncut diamonds estimated at €29,750. As before, Alekos checked the diamonds and then exchanged a 500-gram gold bar.

Adisa then spoke, "I'm sorry the sea is so choppy today. It makes it impossible to celebrate our new business deal. My men will be happy to meet with their women again now! We meet up again on the 14th of this month, when hopefully the weather will be kinder to us! It was a pleasure doing business with you Alekos."

"Until the 14th of the month", said Aleko, but he was grateful that he did not have to entertain any of Adisa's crew.

Alekos showed little emotion as he gave a firm handshake to Adisa. He realised that if the Financiers in Trondheim could find him a new supplier, then this handshake would be the final time.

Adisa climbed over the handrail back onto the Eclipse. The ropes and ladders securing the two ships were unfastened, and shortly after, the schooner powered away into the night and shortly out of sight.

11:25 p.m.

Alekos walked slowly on the aft deck. He had waited long into the evening until the chopping of the waves subsided. The decks on the Bluebell could now be walked throughout without any use of handrails. The night sky was clear of cloud, and the temperature was warm and welcoming at about 60 degrees Fahrenheit.

Looking east he could just make out the lights coming from Alexandria. He wondered what he would be doing if the weather had been less severe and he had finished earlier. The yacht would have most certainly been docked in the port.

The night sky was filled with constellations, their names had been taught to him from childhood.

In the southeastern sky he could see the constellations of Centaurus (Half Man Half Horse) and Libra (the Weighing Scales). Above them was the constellation of Virgo (the Virgin).

In the southwestern sky, the constellations of Monoceros (the Unicorn), Canis Minor (the Lesser Dog), Gemini (the Twins), and Cancer (the Crab), were slowly setting into the horizon.

In the western sky, Betelgeuse the massive red giant was the only remaining star to set in the Orion constellation.

In the northern sky, he could see the constellations of Cassiopeia (the Vain Queen), Cepheus (the King of Aethiopia), Draco (the Dragon), Ursa Minor (the Smaller Bear) and to the east of Draco, Hercules (the Mythological Hero).

#

A periscope gently rose out of the sea and turned to pinpoint the Bluebell. The yacht was about a half of a mile away at anchor.

Jensen's and Roger's faces, necks, hands and feet were dyed in more suitable Mediterranean colours. They were then kitted up in wetsuits which covered their fake crew outfits, their hair styles were altered and dyed to match two of the Bluebell's crew.

Each were equipped with:

1. An underwater sea scooter, with oxygen tank and feeder to the diver's mask.

2. Specialised transceiver equipment with miniature camera and earpiece attachments.

3. Capsules containing tracking devices for the submarine and their own communication equipment.

4. Beretta 92FS semi-automatic pistols.

The conning tower slowly rose above the sea, and 20 seconds later the top of the hull broke the surface. The submarine was covered in special black rubber tiles that absorbed radar. However, Commander Steve Ryan did not want to stay on the surface too long.

Jensen and Roger climbed out of the mid-hull hatches, and then were handed the sea scooters by several of the midshipmen. Then they jumped into the sea. Within seconds they disappeared beneath the warm water.

Commander Ryan standing inside the conning tower gave the men five minutes to clear his submarine. He then returned into the submarine and closed his hatch. He then gave the order "Close all hatches". Then after seeing a green light indicating that all hatches were sealed, ordered "Dive, Dive to 100 feet."

#

11:45 p.m.

In the Bluebell's concealed control room, Alekos sat alongside Nicolás and Cheryl. One of the laptops was linked through a transceiver to a router, which then linked to the satellite dishes.

Nicolás took control of the laptop and through a software interface, unlocked the V-SAT antenna from the C Band. It had linked the Bluebell to the internet, then with a touch of another software switch, his computer took over control of the antennas, and they began to scan the night sky.

#

Jensen and Roger arrived at the underside hull of the Bluebell. The sea scooters were equipped with switchable ON-and-OFF magnets that were powered from the batteries, so were easily parked against the hull. They then slowly hauled themselves up the port and starboard anchor chains.

When they reached the Main Deck platform, they pulled themselves slowly over the side onto the bow. They then removed their wetsuits, revealing their faked crew uniforms. They hid their wetsuits behind the sofas near the bow.

Jensen and Roger then split-up and began exploring the Bluebell.

The Bluebell plans had shown it had five levels. There were two levels below the Main Deck, a Basement Deck containing the storage room, fridge freezers, laundry room, engine room and fuel tanks. The next level above it contained the crew sleeping quarters and tender garage.

The Main Deck contained the bow, VIP bedrooms, dining area and Saloon. There were two Side Decks which were narrow walkways, which linked the Bow Deck and Stern Deck. Above the Main Deck was the Fly-bridge Deck that contained the captain's area, Bridge, office and his sleeping area. It also contained Alekos's domain, his office and sleeping area. Above the Fly-bridge was the Sundeck, containing a bar, grill station, gym and a relaxation seating area.

Jensen had agreed with Roger that if they found anything interesting then they would send two buzzes through the earpiece, which was activated by a small button on their transceivers. Three buzzes sent by both would indicate that it was safe to talk. As agreed earlier, Jensen made his way to the storage area, while Roger headed for the engine room in search for any access to a hidden room.

From the plans, the Bluebell had five double cabins for the crew. There were another five guest cabins available, presumably three were occupied by the owner, captain, and Cheryl. Two cabins might have been left as spares, or given over to senior crew?

Because it was very quiet Jensen assumed that most had turned in for the night. He found it was easy to be able to walk past those on duty without them realising anything was wrong.

Jensen walked down two sets of stairs, opening and closing watertight doors before he reached the basement storeroom. It was dimly lit, but he managed to find a switch panel, and after pressing a few switches, the whole room lit-up.

Jensen spent a good fifteen minutes searching through the storeroom, checking fridges, cold storage freezers, and container bags. He sniffed the bags for any drug residue. Heroin smelt like vinegar or animal urine, and would taste like vinegar. Cannabis had a strong pungent smell. However, his search proved fruitless.

He then buzzed Roger three times. But there was no reply, not even one buzz to indicate that it was unsafe to speak.

Jensen took the Beretta from his holster and climbed the stairways to the Main Deck.

On reaching the Main Deck, he could see through a portal window that his colleague was standing in the Saloon with a man pointing a pistol at him. He could see the man was asking him questions, but from past-experience he knew that Roger would give him a tough time.

Jensen thought carefully. Should he rescue Roger now, or try to locate the bio-chips? He thought, as Roger was still alive, there was still a chance of doing both.

Back in Whitehall, Roger's colleague Lucy had analysed the Bluebell's plans and came up with possible locations for the secret control room.

The Bluebell was designed with two large fuel tanks giving a range of 7000 nautical miles instead of the normal fuel tank, that would provide a range of 3800 nautical miles at 11 knots. So, the yacht was designed to cruise to the Caribbean during winter and to cruise to the Mediterranean during the summer months.

Lucy tracked down the maintenance logs database to a local firm in Limassol. She discovered the yacht had never travelled to the Caribbean. So, she informed Roger that one of the fuel tanks could be a fake, and had been secretly converted as a Citadel Room (a safe hideaway room), by another manufacturer?

11:55 p.m.

Jensen walked down a stairway to the engine room. As the yacht was anchored for the night, there was nobody about. A generator was still working to generate the lighting. So, he put on a set of earmuffs and walked past the engine control panel and the two Caterpillar engines that powered the yacht.

Passing the engines, he found a watertight door which he remembered from the plans. He opened it and walked through into an unlit room. He found a light switch next to the door and closed the door behind him.

He could now remove the earmuffs as there was soundproofing insulation built into the area, which was unusual. There was also another recently built stairway, they were not in the plans he had viewed, and it looked like it led directly to the Main Deck.

He walked down a three-foot stairway and saw two huge fuel tanks in front of him. They were built directly on top of the hull, one lying behind the other, leaving walkways on the port and starboard sides.

Jensen then began to examine the two fuel tanks for any concealed entrance. He pulled on a chrome pipe connected to one of the tanks, and an instrument gauge, but nothing happened. He tried the chrome pipe and instrument gauge on the other tank, again nothing happened.

Unaware to Jensen, inside the first tank nearest the stern, three people sat on leather swivel chairs viewing a large LCD screen. The LCD screen was connected to an output from one of the two computers in the room.

On an electronic panel connected to the computer, a green L E D lit up suddenly and then turned to blue.

Nicolás pressed several keys on his computer which sent thousands of possible self-activating routines and codes from the bio-chips to the computer. The codes travelled from the computer to the antenna-transmitters, and then sent into space to hopefully hook into any spy satellite passing overhead.

At first, nothing happened for 20 seconds, then the second green L E D lit up and turned blue.

Inside, the large screen lit up, Alekos eyes became fixed on it. A satellite had accepted an uplink signal and was now busy downloading data. "Excellent work Nick," said Alekos.

On the outside of the fake fuel tank, Jensen struggled to find hidden levers and switches. There were several instrument's recording quantity, temperature and pressure of the fuel inside.

He could see the readings of the gauges on the instrument's gently moving up and down. But noticed that the readings on both tanks mirrored each other. He then realised that some of the readings were likely fake!

Inside the first tank, Nicolás flicked a switch. "Sir, that's all the data from that satellite. Can I try the erase program now?"

"Yes Nick, give it a try."

Nicolás pressed a couple of keys on his computer and his program was delivered to the satellite. He then waited for five minutes while his program self-activated.

"That's done it," he said. "I'll try a download now." Nicolás pressed a couple of more keys on the computer. To his delight the data received was a series of zeros.

"Sir, my program has erased all the intelligence data held by the satellite. At the satellite base station, they will assume a technical fault and send the satellite on a repeat assignment."

"Excellent work Nick. But we will use your program sparingly."

Alekos then turned to Cheryl, "Now, let's see if we can find that strange spacecraft again, using your new algorithms."

Cheryl handed Nicolás a set of cable leads with attached interfaces. One interface connected to the computer, the other to a new batch of bio-chips. Nicolás adjusted the interface to link with the existing bio-chip containers. He then typed into the computer the co-ordinates of the satellite from the earlier photograph.

The ship's antennas began to scan through the night sky to pinpoint the location. Within 30 seconds the first green L E D lit up and turned to blue.

Nicolás pressed several keys on his computer, sending thousands of activation codes to the satellite. He was hoping it would be the mysterious spacecraft, and one of the activation codes would trigger a data download.

Again, nothing happened for 20 seconds, then the second green L E D lit up and turned blue.

The large LCD screen in front of them, sprang into life again.

Text appeared on the screen which displayed: "INTERCONNESSO" in Italian, then in English "INTERCONNECTED". It then scrolled the exact texts down the screen.

In the blackness of space, the spacecraft 200 miles above in the Thermosphere, held its exact location with the Earth's rotation by firing it rockets. The computer onboard automatically linked-up to a base station onboard a giant ship in the Indian Ocean. Within minutes, the instruments onboard the spacecraft had pinpointed and analysed the yacht. In a couple Computers within the giant ship had searched, accessed and validated the Bluebell's original registered design schematics.

All three in the hidden room were excited. "We have found it!" voiced a jubilant Nicolás. "I have the frequency and the activation code! But it thinks we're Italian!"

"That's where the yacht was designed and built," said Alekos, but was now concerned at the recognition of his yacht's origin.

40-seconds of silence passed, while the spacecraft waited for several parameter values to be sent to it. Those values would contain the coordinates of the host station. If the coordinates were sent, the spacecraft was then programmed to trace the signal and verify the coordinates, before accepting any further commands.

As the giant ship acted as the only host station, and no coordinates were received in the 40-seconds, the spacecraft traced the signal and slotted in the coordinates of the Bluebell.

The text on the large LCD screen changed to a large print, and spat out "VIOLAZIONE" in Italian, followed by "VIOLATION" which scrolled rapidly down the screen, repeating its endless warning in a loop!

In fright, Alekos, Cheryl and Nicolás recoiled backwards in their seats!

In space, an alarm was activated, the bulbous front of the dark vessel opened up like a car ferry. A twelve-foot dark rod moved and protruded from the opening of the spacecraft. It was a stealth missile.

Then the screen message changed to further startle them:

"IL CONTO ALLA ROVESCIA INIZIA TRA 60 SECONDI!" Then, "THE COUNTDOWN WILL COMMENCE IN 60 SECONDS!"

"Countdown! What Countdown?" muttered Alekos.

The screen then answered his question.

"ABBANDONA LO YACHT ORA! DISTRUZIONE IN 30 MINUTI!" Then, "ABANDON YACHT NOW! DESTRUCTION IN 30 MINUTES!

Then "30 00," appeared under the text, then "29 59", "29 58", "29 57".

Nicolás cried out! "It's counting down!"

Alekos looked at his watch, it showed 12:15 a.m., he shouted, "Shut everything down Nick". He then picked-up an internal phone and contacted the Bridge, "Alekos speaking, get the yacht out of this area as fast as you can!"

Outside the front of the fake fuel tank, Jensen could see a hatch opening. He swiftly moved to the rear of the tank and out of sight.

Alekos, was first to leave, followed by Cheryl and Nicolás. Alekos moved swiftly to the Bridge to explain to those on duty, why he instructed them to move the yacht.

Just before Nicolás left the room for the stairway, Jensen caught a glimpse of him pushing a fake thin fuel line to close the hatch.

Jensen not knowing what had caused the three to leave, now saw a golden opportunity to investigate the room.

The anchors fully retracted within five minutes, then the engines of the Bluebell sprang to life. Jensen could feel the movement of the yacht beneath his feet, as it started powering away.

He pulled the fake fuel line gently backwards. A hidden entrance hatch then opened up. He quickly walked inside.

He could see that there were three swivel chairs behind a large desk. There was a control panel and two computers linked to a transceiver. In front of the desk was a large switched-off LCD screen. To the right of the computers were glass boxes containing translucent liquid and miniature cables, linked to what he had originally thought to be overgrown grubs or kidney beans.

They were not grubs; they were the same revolting memory bio-chips that he had seen at Gene Solar Ltd. An interface cable led from the glass boxes and connected to a hub, and from there it led to a computer.

Jensen took out his transceiver with inbuilt camera and took several pictures as he quickly thought through the problem. This was not the time to grab the glass boxes as there were 12 of them. The laptops could be easily replaced on a large vessel as the Bluebell. No doubt there was backup copies of the software too! However, the transceiver might not be easily replaced. It was not worth destroying the equipment now, as they would surely take it out on Roger. Peter had told each of them to find the evidence then leave it to the Navy to finish the job. First, he needed to liberate his colleague!

#

Alekos walked back into the Saloon to find two of his men, Lukaz and Yego, pointing pistols at Roger.

Yego spoke, "Sir, what should we do with our uninvited guest?"

Alekos, gazed at Roger, but under stress was not sure what to do with him.

Alekos shouted, "Who are you? What are you doing on my yacht?"

Fortunately, Roger had disposed of his earpiece and transceiver just before he was caught, as they were small items and easily discarded behind machinery. The Beretta semi-automatic pistol was another matter and could not be easily explained away. It was also a standard weapon issued by the UK military.

"I'm a Detective," said Roger. "My client suspects that you are having an affair with his wife and are smuggling contraband into Cyprus."

"Ridiculous," said Alekos, he then looked at the Beretta, which Yego was now holding up to his sight.

"You're a Government Agent! Where are your colleagues?"

"Just me."

"Do you take me for a fool!" Alekos then turned to Yego, "Yego, show him some manners!"

Lukaz's pistol was still pointing at Roger, making him powerless to do anything to protect himself. Yego then punched Roger in the stomach, winding him. Roger gave out a yell. Yego continued to batter Roger with the pistol butt, until he collapsed in an unconscious state on the deck.

Alekos looked down at Roger and was pleased with the punishment that Yego had given out, "Yego, Lukaz, take our guest to a vacant cabin and lock him inside. We are too close to Alexandria here; we can always dump him overboard tomorrow in the middle of the Mediterranean!"

A thought raced across Alekos mind, "Nick, go back to the control room and check it again, NOW!"

"Yes Sir" said Nicolás, the same thought had crossed his mind too! He raced back to the control room.

Nicolás found the control room as he had left it, it appeared that nothing had changed. He closed the insulated panel door behind him and checked the computer and transceiver. He thought, if there were other intruders onboard, then it was unlikely that they had found the room. He picked-up the internal phone and pressed button '2', hoping to contact Alekos in the Saloon.

"Alekos here! Nick is that you?"

"Yes Sir, it's all clear down here!"

"Excellent Nick!" Alekos then looked at his watch, it was 12:49 p.m.

"Nick, the screen message was just a bluff, we have lost time, so we'll resume in half an hour."

"Yes Sir."

However, Alekos's watch was running fast.

A support platform extended the twelve-foot stealth missile until it was clear of the spacecraft. A small section at the front of the support platform then manoeuvred, changing its elevation from the horizontal position to the vertical, which in turn pointed the missile towards the ocean below. Twenty seconds later the rear nozzle on the missile fired and sprang to life. The missile released itself instantly from the platform and headed under the control of the internal computer to its target and destruction.

As the missile picked up speed, the thermal tiles wrapped around the tungsten armaments exceeded 2000 degrees Fahrenheit. 106 seconds later at 47,520 feet, the missile passed from the Stratosphere into the Troposphere. Five seconds later, the missile travelling near 8.5 Mach, tore through the upper decks of the Bluebell with a deafening explosion.

The shock-wave sent the crew flying. Most of the windows in the upper decks shattered, as the screeching missile sliced through them, then sliced into the bottom deck and into the fake fuel tank. The blast wave threw Nicolás against the inside wall. Fire consumed the room and its now dead occupant. The huge downward force of the missile cut straight through the fake fuel tank floor, along with the steel hull beneath.

The air throughout the decks was now toxic with an intense smell of burning oil and rubber from broken fuel pipes, door seals, and burning leather from furniture.

In the belly of the yacht was a gaping six-foot hole and the sea was gushing through it. Several watertight doors initially held back the sea, but under the strain, seawater started squirting through the outer seals, and then the pressure built up, and in a succession of explosions, burst them open.

The yacht's engines came to a halt as the fuel lines were cut. Parts of the upper decks blew-out with deafening explosions, taking some of the crew along with them. The exploded sections transformed into fireballs 20 feet above the yacht. The crew tried to stagger back to their feet, but faced further difficulty through the swaying of the yacht.

Alekos looked down through the broken decks in despair to see seawater gushing and slowly rising from inside the hull. As he recovered from the shock, he realised the hopeless situation, and then shouted, "Abandon the ship! Deploy the life-rafts!"

In the meantime, Jensen managed to find his balance and continued searching for his colleague. In the confusion no one was paying attention to him. He activated his transceiver and set the band to his colleague's tracker capsule. The transceiver bleeped away and led him to a locked door in the guest quarters. He fired into the lock and found Roger inside. Roger was relieved to see Jensen, but bloodied from his previous beating.

"I think we have overstayed our welcome," said Jensen. "Let's get out of this hell!"

"No argument there!" said Roger.

As they passed down the corridor a thought raced through Jensen's mind.

"Roger, I'll have a quick look for Cheryl, she might be in one of these cabins. See if you can find an inflatable life raft inside a container on the Main Deck. They are generally painted white and stored in drum like barrels, or large suitcase package containers."

Jensen searched the remaining four cabins in the corridor without success. He then found Roger outside on the Main Deck.

A high-pitched shrieking noise broke out from the decks below, followed by several more high-pitched shrieks and explosions from several more watertight doors bursting open under the pressure. The Bluebell's hull shuddered as life began to drain away from it.

Roger spotted Cheryl on the starboard side, firmly holding onto a side rail. She looked traumatized and was stumbling on her feet. He pointed her out to Jensen, "There's our girl!"

Roger had found a drum with a life raft inside it. They released it from its securing, then walked over to Cheryl's side. Jensen pulled out a rope from the centre of the container and tied it to the side railing. Jensen and Roger then picked up the barrel and threw it over the railing into the sea.

Cheryl turned to the men, she stared at Jensen, his facial disguise was no longer safe, "Don't I know you?"

Jensen grabbed her and took her screaming along with himself over the side.

Roger gave the rope connecting to the floating drum a strong tug. Seconds later the life raft inside ejected from the drum and inflated on cue. He then jumped into the sea after them.

As the Bluebell slowly drifted away, the three hauled themselves into the raft.

Cheryl, now at wits end yelled, "What the hell do you think you are doing?"

Jensen replied, "Cheryl, just sit tight for now and pipe-down!"

She was further shocked, "Oh my God, it's you!"

The Bluebell's communications officer found Alekos and updated him. "Sir, I've spoken to several people at the harbour, they will be here within 30 minutes to an hour."

Alekos searched the yacht until he found Captain Balaskas. "Nicolás is missing and we have injured and dead crew."

Alekos continued, "I can replace the yacht, but it's going to be difficult to replace my men with their specialised skills. I do not think it wise for us to return to Cyprus now!"

"Sir, the Bluebell will be underwater soon! We have to save as many of the crew as we can! That's our priority now!"

The fire onboard the Bluebell lit up the night sky. Jensen realised it might be some time before the submarine picked them up.

Jensen turned to Roger, "What if they had used a different control room and that fuel tank was no fake but full of fuel?"

"Yes," said Roger. "Everyone on board would have been incinerated!"

On hearing Roger's reply, Cheryl realised how close to death she had come.

She was sitting in the bottom of a life raft in soaking wet clothes. The raft was bobbing up and down in the Mediterranean Sea, in the early hours of the morning, and sitting next to her was her ex-university boyfriend and a stranger. She was in a state of shock and bewilderment at the same time!

CHAPTER 15 - **Package**

April 7th 2:00 a.m.

A periscope rose through the rolling waves. The conning tower followed the rising periscope, it then broke the surface and within minutes was standing 30 feet above the waves. After 18 minutes, the radio engineers onboard HMS Astute managed to locate Jensen and Roger through their homing beacons.

Commander Ryan manoeuvred the submarine until the life raft was riding up and down the waves against its hull. Two hatches opened up on the top of the hull and several sailors climbed out holding rope ladders. The ends of the ladders were secured to the hull, the rest of the rope ladders were thrown overboard into the life raft.

After being taken onboard, they were given towels, allowed to shower, and given dry clothes before meeting up with the commander. An hour later they were face to face with Commander Ryan in his meeting room.

Commander Ryan was sat down in a comfortable leather chair at the head of a metal table. He was a big man with piercing green eyes, silver hair and slightly reddish cheeks.

He waved his hand to beckon Cheryl, Jensen, and Roger, to sit down on the green leather seats at both sides of the table. He looked sternly at them as they sat down.

He spoke with a slightly detectable Irish accent. "Inspector Jensen, do you know what set the yacht alight?"

"No," said Jensen. "I was below deck searching for Roger when it happened."

Commander Ryan then turned to Cheryl. "Do you know, Dr. Brenton?"

"Yes, I was on the Main Deck when a fireball shot out of the sky, I thought it was a satellite that had fallen out of its orbit."

Commander Ryan raised a smile, "That's no doubt what the initial insurance claim will state!"

Commander Ryan looked at Jensen and Roger, "The radio reports that have come in within the last thirty minutes, indicate that an unidentified object in space was overhead at the same time."

"It did not appear on radar, but the Americans could see it from one of their own satellites using advanced optics. A canopy at the front of the spacecraft was open. Although they were unable to detect any missile launch, this craft is the most likely culprit!"

Jensen then turned to Cheryl. "Cheryl, I know what you were up to onboard the yacht!"

Cheryl thought for a few seconds, then demanded, "I want legal representation!"

Jensen gave Cheryl a long hard look. He had loved her once and still had strong feelings. He now feared she faced years in prison.

"Don't look at me like that, you bastard! I'll be free in days, you'll see!"

Roger then turned to the captain. "Commander, what's going to happen now?"

Commander Ryan looked sternly at the three, then spoke. "We intercepted the yacht's communications officer's request to the harbour for help. There is sensitive equipment within this submarine and we do not have any room onboard for these people. So, we notified the Egyptian higher authorities too. They are sending several coastal patrol vessels to this area. Anyone they find alive will be detained for questioning."

"In the meantime, I have orders to drop you all off at Gibraltar. As I have other assignments to perform, it will take about four days to get there."

"A private jet will take you from RAF Gibraltar to Heathrow airport. The flight time to Heathrow is about three hours. Inspector Jensen, you will hand over Dr. Brenton to M I 5 at Heathrow."

"Dr. Brenton, until we reach Gibraltar, you will be staying onboard under the protection of Inspector Jensen."

CHAPTER 16 - **Assessment**

April 14th 1:00 p.m.

Jensen was in a Ministry of Defence meeting with Peter Mathews, Raymond French and Roger. The room they were in was huge and grander than any of the other rooms he had been in at Whitehall.

Peter started the meeting, "Earlier today, I've spoken with the M I 5 Chief Rosemary Yates, and the M I 6 Chief Jon Barton. The Alexandria harbour police only managed to arrest three of Alekos's men. But there were no signs of him or his captain. They could have gone down with the yacht of course, but I doubt that's what really happened."

"So far, the divers have reported a couple of motor-launch tenders missing, somebody part incinerated inside a fake fuel tank, and three more dead crew members floating in the sea. Several boats got to the scene before the harbour police, so until the yacht is thoroughly searched by the divers, we do not know how many of the crew are actually missing, dead, or have died since of injuries?"

"Do you have any update on Cheryl, Sir?" said Jensen to Peter.

"Yes, she's done a deal through her solicitor with the government. One interesting point that she mentioned is that one of the Financiers of the operation is Harald Haugen. Harald lives in Trondheim Norway. Jensen, that's your next assignment. Pay Harald a visit!"

Roger cut-in, "Sir, is there any more info on the spacecraft?"

Raymond interrupted. "Unfortunately, it's moved to another orbit. The CIA can no longer find it. There's nothing we can do about that for the moment. The '1967 Out of Space Treaty', signed in Washington, London and Moscow, banned the use of conventional nuclear weapons from space, and prohibited military bases being setup on the Moon."

"To quote an absurd statement by a professor of Space Law:"

"In law, space is like international waters. No one owns it, no one can colonise it, but you can fish in it!"

"The CIA just managed to get pictures of the front of the spacecraft opening. Until we catch the craft deploying missiles, we can do nothing about it. For now, it's up to a country or an organisation to claim ownership before we can act!"

CHAPTER 17 - **Copenhagen**

April 16th 1:00 p.m.

Jensen was walking alongside Rebekah Petersen in the Copenhagen Tivoli Gardens. They had met 10 years earlier on a train travelling from Stockholm to Copenhagen.

He had found an empty seat opposite her and shortly after made some conversation. On that day as the present, she had worn a thick faux fur coat. She was about five feet six inches in height, long medium-brown coloured hair, bright blue eyes, and slightly reddish cheeks.

To Jensen, she had radiated style and eloquence, and he wanted to know more about her. He had fond memories of that first meeting together.

Back then, her father was alive and the Autumn was turning into Winter. Her father had phoned her mobile, Jensen only understood a little Danish at that time, but was quietly amused with her frequent replies every few minutes to her father in English, "Yes Papa, or No Papa." She must have had Papa captivated by his sweet little daughter too! Smart girl!

Today she earned a living as an investigative journalist, and specialised in tracking down people.

Rebekah and Jensen walked slowly around a boating pool passing a Chinese Tower to their right. She caught a glimpse of the Roller Coaster in the background, which brought a smile to her face.

"I love the Tivoli Gardens David. There's only a light breeze today, and not a cloud in the sky. It's going to be a warm afternoon. David, we've lots of catching up to do. The last time we had a good natter was last year, way back in May."

"I'm sorry Rebekah," said Jensen, "I've been caught up with police work, and now I've been reassigned to Whitehall for a short time."

"I thought you jacked-in all that crazy stuff years ago?"

"I thought so too, but a girlfriend from my university days has got herself mixed up in bad company, and I was asked to track her down."

"So, what's happened to her?"

"She's awaiting trial in the UK, and using plea-bargaining. That's how we got to know about Harald Haugen in Trondheim."

"There are 10 Harald Haugen's in Trondheim, but from Cheryl's description, and the time spent with a face profile artist, plus the following Norwegian passport search for a proof check, then only one person fitted the bill."

"So, he's the main reason why you contacted me, the last romantic - hey!"

Jensen, felt a little flushed, guilty, but amused. "Rebekah, since we first met on that train to

Copenhagen, you've got married, then divorced, and today you mentioned earlier on the phone that you have temporarily split with your latest boyfriend!"

Rebekah smiled, "I'm only joking David, my relationship with Karl is sort of ON and OFF. OFF at the moment. I just need some space from him."

"David, getting back to the subject, Cheryl was unusually cooperative? That's not the behaviour I'd expect!"

"Yes, I thought the same too! "She clearly did not anticipate or want help from Harald, or from Alekos. M I 6 could not find anything on record for Harald."

"OK, I've done a little delving into your friend Harald."

"He's no friend!"

Rebekah continued, "I've been able to trace his family line back to the 2nd World War in Trondheim. There are other questionable records to show his family line originating from Oslo in 1910."

"Meaning?" said Jensen.

"His great grandfather does not appear in any Trondheim records until July 1940. The German invasion started from April the 9th 1940, in all ports from Oslo to Narvik (that's 1200 miles). Narvik is about 560 miles north of Trondheim."

"Although the records in Oslo show his past family tree, however, they could be forgeries too?"

"You mean, Harald might have Nazi descendants?"

"Jack-pot, David. I'm coming to Trondheim with you. I can feel a good story brewing!"

"This will be dangerous Rebekah. But even if I was to say 'No', you would go there anyway."

"Too right!" said Rebekah. "We can sort out the flight and hotel this afternoon."

She then wrapped her faux fur coat arm around his arm and continued walking with him.

"But first take me for a ride on the Daemon Roller Coaster, and then we can have lunch after at the Søcafeen restaurant."

CHAPTER 18 - **Trondheim visit**

April 17th 1:00 p.m.

Jensen and Rebekah had booked themselves into the Radisson Blu Royal Garden Hotel in Trondheim.

Jensen had stayed there several times before on business for Whitehall. The building had an almost glass exterior shell which was extended at its southernmost side. The eastern side overlooked the Nidelva river.

The river was wide enough at that point to have a marina on the opposite side of the riverbank. The marina was filled with small and medium sized motorboats that were mostly used for weekend getaways. Thirty minutes after arriving, they sat down to lunch at the hotel restaurant with a table overlooking the marina.

Jensen wore a traditional dark blue suit with open neck shirt, whilst Rebekah wore a green plunge satin midi dress, with a drape.

Rebekah loved seafood dishes. She ordered a mixture of peeled prawns, scallops, cod, hake and trout mixed up in spaghetti with a rich sauce. Jensen, went for a traditional Norway Stew, called Lapskaus, which was made of boiled beef and vegetables, diced together and cooked into a stew. Rebekah ordered a Chardonnay to go with the meal while Jensen stuck to a bottle of Norwegian Ale.

When the waiter was out of sight Rebekah spoke. "What's the plan for Harald?"

Jensen took out his mobile, and opened up the photograph section. He then selected a photograph of Harald's home and pushed the mobile across the table.

"Whitehall sent me several photographs of his property. He lives in Trondelog Road, it's off the Brekavegen Road."

"You can flip through the photographs. His house overlooks the fjord. He has several buildings on the site, including a barn. The main building consists of two floors, mostly glass front windows which face to the road and fjord."

"Near the house is a smaller separate cottage, presumably for visitors and relations. All the buildings have typical wooden outer wall panels painted white."

Rebekah smiled, she showed Jensen a picture of the visitor's cottage, "I don't think any sane person would want to stay there!"

Jensen continued the conversation, "Whitehall tried to phone the property several times this week without success."

Rebekah cut-in, "So, do you think he might have abandoned the place?"

"Maybe? He would know what happened to the Bluebell and has probably gone to ground for a while. I still think it's worth having a good look around."

Rebekah looked concerned, "Harald might have left a few traps?"

"Yes, there might be a few surprises waiting for uninvited guests?"

"I assume the house is loaded with intruder alarms. As I'm a police inspector, if I was caught breaking into the premises, it would create an international incident, and I'd be fired. So, I think I'll play safe and have a word with the local bobbies."

"Rebekah, I want to see the place this afternoon, fancy coming along?"

"Sure!"

The waiter returned with their meals and drinks on a trolley cart.

"That looks delightful!" said Rebekah to the waiter, bringing a smile to his face.

5:21 p.m.

A white Mercedes E estate police car drove past Harald's property and stopped a short distance away.

Sergeant Sven Larsen switched off the engine. Police Inspector Erico Johannessen opened the glove box and took out two walkie-talkies.

Johannessen, and his sergeant, wore full uniform. To Jensen, Johannessen looked to be in his mid-forties. He looked professional and not the type to trifle with. His Sergeant looked younger, possibly late-twenties or in his early-thirties. Fortunately, they had earlier visited a judge, and had all necessary papers to enter Harald's premises.

Johannessen turned in the front passenger seat to face Jensen in the rear. He handed him one of the walkie-talkies. Rebekah and a hired locksmith Eric Pedersen, were also sat in the rear seats.

"The channel is fixed on one frequency, just switch it on," said Johannessen.

Johannessen continued, "Assuming there's no one in, I'll go ahead and search the main house with Sergeant Larsen. Jensen, you search the outhouse."

They got out of the car and walked up to the main house.

As they walked closer to the buildings, Jensen noticed several surveillance cameras. They had anticipated them. If they tripped any alarms, and the local police station was contacted by a security firm, the on-duty police were instructed to notify the security firm to cancel the alarm while they investigated the site.

Inspector Johannessen walked up to the main door and rang the bell. He waited several minutes and tried again. After no response, he turned to the locksmith and gave Eric Pedersen a nod.

Pedersen was in his mid-fifties. He wore a tweed coat and a tweed cap, possibly to cover his balding head. He examined the lock, then smiled as he recognised the mechanism.

He took out a leather pouch from his pocket and removed two of his lock-pick tools. One tool was used to locate and pick each tumbler rod, and the second to turn the lock to the open position.

As the tumbles did not sequentially fall into place, he moved a lock-pick tool up and down, and back and forth the lock several times. It was all done within six minutes and the door opened.

The room inside was richly decorated. It contained green and blue satin wallpaper and furniture that looked as if it had been ordered from London's Harrods or an equivalent store in Norway.

"OK," said Johannessen, "It will take some time to search the main house. Eric, go with Inspector Jensen and Rebekah and see if you can open the door in the outhouse building?"

Inside the main house, Johannessen located the alarm control panel near to the front door, and switched off all the silent alarms. He could see that Harald liked his water scenes, the walls held many oil paintings, mostly focused on fjords, sea bays and river scenes. Harald, also liked crystal glass tables, leather furniture, and thick luxury-carpets.

Johannessen found an office room, it contained a large mahogany desk containing several draws. The draws were not locked and only held an empty notebook and a pen, and brochures for house and garden furniture.

Johannessen and Larsen walked up a crystal spiral staircase to the top landing. There were four bedrooms, all having roughly the same dimensions. Each bedroom had a king-sized bed, side cabinets, dressing table, built-in wardrobes, and an ensuite bathroom with a shower, wash basin and toilet.

Each of the bathroom cabinets were supplied with essential toiletries. Behind a picture of a water scene in each bedroom was a small safe. The safes were left for Eric, he would have to try to break the combinations later. Harald's bedroom contained suits, shirts, trousers, underwear, and other items of clothing.

As Jensen approached the visitor's building, Pedersen overtook him. The door had an electronic keypad lock. Pedersen smiled again as he recognised the mechanism.

Pedersen undid the screws securing the keypad panel, then secured and locked a tamper proof spring beneath the lock with another special tool from his leather pouch. He then took out a flat wire paperclip and bent the metal so that one end would be curved and able to reach inside and make contact with the last of four wire connection points. The other end of the wire was straightened so that it could make contact with the inner side of the outer panel, making a circuit. This time he opened the door in under four minutes.

Jensen and Rebekah were disturbed by how easy it was for the master locksmith to break into both buildings.

Jensen then spoke, "Rebekah, Eric, stay outside for a moment, I've no idea what's waiting inside!"

Jensen walked carefully past the opened front door onto a four-foot pathway, which looked like it encircled the entire inside of the building. Across the pathway and front of him was a closed inner door. The closed window curtains which reached in sections around the entire building, were just there to bluff those viewing the building from the outside, and were to disguise the true purpose of the inner meeting room.

Jensen opened the door and the room lit up. It was in the style of Art Deco. The room was circular, about 60 feet in diameter. The walls had teak panelling, with engravings into them of Venice and Milan buildings, and views from Santorini.

A circular carpet stretched outwards from the centre. It was coloured in sections of light and dark purple and white, with white and dark swirls running through it. On top of the carpet were two rectangular crystal glass tables containing bottles of various alcohol spirits, along with clean glasses.

Behind the tables were two large circular sofas, and four single chairs. They were all coloured in off-white. The room was lit-up by several pillar-styled lamps placed around the room, and secondary by three circular bands of smaller lights placed in a darkened red plaster ceiling.

Jensen was initially startled, then on spotting a brandy bottle on the table, walked over and poured himself a drink. He then looked more closely at the glass, thought twice about what he had done and put the drink down to one side of the table.

Jensen did a thorough search of the room and pressed firmly on the panels. On pressing one panel, it swung inwards revealing a TV remote control inside. He removed the device and pushed the ON switch.

A panel opened up in the teak panelled wall to the side of him revealing a large LCD TV. Jensen then pushed a red button on the device. Another panel opened revealing a safe, and a further door opened up in the floor revealing a spiral stairway, that roughly led down 15 feet to a lit-up corridor.

The large screen initially showed white static, then came to a focus showing a figure of a woman. It was not a real woman, but a CGI image of a female wearing traditional Scandinavian dress.

The CGI had long flowing blonde hair running down past her shoulders, with a red two tapered inch band holding her hair in place. She had blue eyes, and a ruby and white satin dress, with a thick striped belt, in red, white and black, which hung around her waist. Two elaborately decorated broaches were attached over the dress embroidery.

The CGI girl appeared to recognise his presence, and then smiled, then said, "Si 'Eva' og still et spørsmål?"

("Say 'Eva' and ask a question?")

Jensen knew that Eva in Norwegian was Eve in English.

A smile appeared on Jensen's face; Harald had his own version of Alexa, with a CGI AI Avatar. He had to try to answer her!

"Eva, hva er på NRK1-kanalen i kveld klokken 9."

("Eva, what is on the NRK1 channel this evening at 9 o'clock.")

"ANTIKKDUELLEN"

("The Antique Duel.")

Knowing he was dealing with an AI; and his Norwegian was a little rusty, Jensen asked the following question:

"Eva, do you understand English?"

"I can speak seven languages. Norwegian, German, Italian, Spanish, French, Portuguese, and English."

Jensen was taken aback by the answer, however it gave him the opportunity to try something, "Eve, where is Harald Haugen?"

After about a pause of 20 seconds, Eve spoke, "Harald Haugen is in Malta."

"Eve, what is the address in Malta where Harald Haugen is staying?"

"The address is not available!"

"Eve, why is the address not available?"

"The property is registered by a Maltese company. No further information is available."

"Eve, what is the name of the Maltese company?"

"That information is not available!"

A white static screen replaced Eve. The panel to the safe started to close. Jensen dashed to the safe and put the controller facing upright, blocking the closing panel.

Jensen heard a click coming from the direction of the inner door; it now looked closed. The room lighting slowly diminished and changed to a reddish colour.

A panel opened in the ceiling. He could see a camera positioned within a metal box mechanism, with a five-inch tube protruding from it. His ears picked up as he detected the faint sound of gas being pumped into the room.

The camera and mechanism followed his movements. Two popping sounds came from the mechanism. A needle like dart landed in his chest; another went into his right leg. On pulling the darts out he began to feel weak, and then he experienced intense pain.

His chest then tightened, followed by another excruciating pain which travelled up and down his chest, and up to his left arm. His right leg then started to ache, then he lost all control and feeling in it, and collapsed on the carpet. Jensen could see the camera was still pointing at him. He dragged himself across the carpet and pulled himself under one of the crystal-glass tables.

Another dart fired, missed him and bounced off the table. Jensen took a minute to recover. Pulling the table along with him, he dragged himself to the opening of the spiral stairway. When he got to the stairway, he pushed the table away and descended the steps on his stomach to the corridor below.

Down the corridor he found further doors leading to two bathrooms. He then realised that the bathrooms had a dual-purpose. If any uninvited visitor got hit by any of the poisonous darts, Harald did not want them to make a mess on his luxurious carpet, on the floor above.

Jensen dragged himself to the nearest bathroom and forced himself up onto a toilet seat. He then pushed off the water closet lid. After a while the pain began to ease in his chest and right leg. Jensen then took out his handkerchief and soaked it in the water closet.

On climbing up the stairway, Jensen covered his mouth and nose with the handkerchief. Now able to handle the crystal table and use it as a shield, his only priority was to get out of the room alive.

As Jensen nearly reached the door, he heard two more popping sounds from the mechanism. One dart bounced off the crystal table, but the other hit his left leg. Jensen let out a large yell and collapsed for the second time on the carpet.

6:15 p.m.

Several large bangs came from the passageway door. Pedersen had heard Jensen's yell and tried to rescue him, eventually forcing the inner door open. Pedersen and Rebekah walked slowly past the door. To the right of them, Jensen was on his knees, his back was against the wall and using the table as a shield in front of him.

On seeing them, Jensen shouted, "Don't come any nearer, that camera fires lethal darts."

Jensen made a dash for Rebekah and Pedersen, taking them and himself hurtling across the passageway floor.

Jensen took in a lungful of fresh air, and then slowly looked down at Rebekah lying underneath him. They were lying halfway out of the room into the corridor. "Thank God for that, but where're the policemen?"

Rebekah said loudly, "You really should have said, 'Thank you Eric!'"

Eric found his feet, then stretched out his arms and pulled up Rebekah and Jensen onto their feet.

Jensen was grateful, "Thanks Eric, you're a life saver!"

Rebekah continued her conversation in a quieter more controlled tone, "The police are still at the main house. We knew you were in trouble when you yelled, but I couldn't get the inner door open, so, Eric broke it down."

They walked out of the building. Jensen then contacted Johannessen through the walkie-talkie.

When the police turned up ten minutes later, Jensen updated them on the TV, the camera, and dart gun. He explained the building was a death-trap for unwelcome visitors.

Johannessen walked over to the Mercedes, and then brought out a Heckler and Koch MP5 sub-machine gun from the boot. He then loaded the retractable bullet stock into the weapon. When he felt the stock was secure, he removed the safety catch, walked over to Jensen and handed it to him.

"Inspector, would you like to make that building safe?"

A smile appeared on Jensen's face, the sub-machine gun manufactured in Germany, was standard issue for the Norwegian police, "OK, everyone take cover behind the car."

Jensen fired five rounds into the building. They travelled through the corridor, into the meeting room and pierced the TV screen, smashing it into pieces.

"Bye-Bye Eva!" said Jensen, and then dashed back to the car and ducked behind it, alongside his colleagues.

Twenty seconds later, broken electronics ignited in the gas build-up, and blew the building apart.

He then turned to Rebekah, "That's going to wake up the neighbourhood and bring in the fire crews. Harald will not be welcome back here again!"

Rebekah started laughing, "True, and you won't be welcome back here too! But I think we need to get you to a hospital now!"

CHAPTER 19 - **Central Police Station Trondheim**

April 20th 10:00 a.m.

Jensen and Rebekah sat around a table on the second floor in the Sentrum Police Station located at Gryta 4. At the head of the table sat Station Chief Superintendent Eivind Strand. He was wearing a dark greyish suit, white shirt with matching dark blue and black striped tie. He looked to be in his early-sixties.

"I thank you both for helping us with Harald Haugen's colourful background." He then laughed. "Especially his amusing Eva CGI. He should have marketed it. Now, during this week, we are undertaking a thorough investigation of his properties in Trondelog Road. So far, I have the following information for you."

"The darts that hit you Inspector contained a poison which acted similar to a severe wasp sting."

"It was twofold:"

> "Firstly, to paralyse part of your body on contact through the delivery of neuro-active peptides. These toxins were matched with our database, and found to be extracted from cone snails, which are found in tropical and sub-tropical waters. You were fortunate, the toxins from the big ones would have killed you outright."

> "Secondly, to deliver excruciating pain. It contained the allergy inducing-component Antigen 5 that can cause anaphylactic shock. The amount was sufficient to kill an unhealthy person, or someone allergic to a single wasp sting."

"From analysis, the gas used was 'Dimethyl ether', which was there to finish the job. If Harald could not have properly disposed of your body, you would have been dumped in one of our local forests."

"When they would have discovered your body, the pathologist would have diagnosed death by anaphylactic shock resulting from wasp sting. It would not have occurred to the pathologists to investigate your lungs for toxic gas."

"Although, 'Dimethyl ether' is relatively cheap to manufacture, fortunately, it's also highly inflammable, as you discovered."

"I understand that Inspector Johannessen loaned you one of our sub-machine guns. Good, you were correct to destroy the building, I wouldn't want any of my men walking into that hellish place!"

"Because of the severity of this case, we are getting the Etterretningstjenesten involved, known to you both as the Norwegian Intelligence Service."

"Eric was able to open the safes in the bedrooms. Three were empty, but the one in Harald's bedroom contained 525,000 Norwegian Kroner, the equivalent of about 44,300 Euros. He was unable to open the safe in the outhouse, but we contacted the manufacturer, and have manage to get it open."

"There were several documents inside, some linked to Tax Free Havens. I suspect that Mr. Haugen has many other properties and businesses spread around the world. We are investigating where his wealth originated from?"

Rebekah cut-in, "The Nazi Party?"

The Chief Superintendent paused for a few seconds while he looked directly at Rebekah. "Indeed, we suspect that too! There was also a laptop in the safe."

Jensen cut-in, "Anything interesting?"

"Yes, we were able to bypass the password screen, but the information in the disk drive is encrypted and will prove difficult to break. Inspector, I will provide you with a copy for your GCHQ. If you do manage to decipher it before the NIS, then contact us immediately."

"Certainly," said Jensen. "But I'd be grateful for two copies. I'll take the other copy to a woman awaiting trial. She's an expert on cracking encryptions and might just be willing to help us to reduce her sentence?"

Rebekah turned to Strand. "As you are aware, I'm an investigative journalist and have several contacts in Norway, and I've worked in this country several times. I'd like to stay on in Trondheim for a while."

Strand got the message!

"Miss Petersen, you have a formidable reputation. I've read up on Jakob Rosdahl, who defrauded dozens of Norwegians. Your investigations into his activities and your magazine article led to his arrest and conviction. Yes, you have my permission to work with our Central Police Department."

Rebekah then turned to Jensen. "Sorry David, I need to stay on in Trondheim for a while to look further into Harald's background. I suspect he might have accomplices here too!"

"OK Rebekah, but take great care!"

Jensen turned to Strand.

"This will be a dangerous investigation, if Rebekah has to investigate any buildings in Trondheim that are connected with Harald Haugen; can an armed policeman work alongside her?"

The Strand looked at Rebekah and then back at Jensen. "Yes, it will be done! She will be temporary assigned to my department!"

Rebekah turned to Jensen, "David, I'll keep in contact."

Jensen looked at Rebekah, "There's usually a regular flight to Stanstead or Gatwick in the morning, and sometimes a direct flight to London City Airport. I have your mobile phone number, so I'll keep you in touch with updates!"

"Good luck in Trondheim Rebekah! But we still have one more evening here. Now where can we visit?" Jensen thought for a few seconds. "I've an idea, have you ever been to 'Heidi's Bier Bar'?"

Rebekah looked at Jensen with amusement and started laughing, "You mean, full of non-lethal real-life Eva's, serving from behind the bar!"

Strand raised a smile and a giggle.

CHAPTER 20 - **HMP Bronzefield**

April 22nd 1:00 p.m.

It was a cloudy overcast day and it looked like rain was heading Jensen's way. He drove a hired Mazda 3 into HMP Bronzefield. Bronzefield is an adult and youth offender female prison located on the outskirts of Ashford, in the county of Surrey in England. It was also the largest women's prison in Europe. The prison is located about 19 miles west of Whitehall and operated privately by the Sodexo Justice Services.

After a security check at the entrance gate and again inside the building, Jensen was led to a meeting room where he found Cheryl sitting on a chair at the far side of a plain wooden table. She looked a bit glum, was wearing plain grey clothing and looking a little strained and frustrated with her predicament.

She looked up and across at Jensen, "And what can I do for you? Bastard!"

"Enjoying the peace?"

"What do you want David?"

"I want you to help me decipher some files that have been copied from a hard disk drive?"

"Bastard! And you want me to help you!"

"I'm hoping you can unscramble several addresses and accounts on a USB Memory Stick?"

Cheryl thought for a while, "So, what's in it for me?"

"When you go to trial, helping me will reduce your sentence!"

Cheryl fixed her deep brown eyes on Jensen's eyes and then looked a little amused. "That's if I go to trial dear, I've still got a few cards to play!"

Jensen froze a little, she was clearly holding back on something.

Jensen buried the thought and smiled back. "Your records show that your deciphering skills at Gene Solar were excellent. If you are prepared to help, I can take you away from here to a lovely place in Cheltenham."

"The government has several secure houses down there spread across the town with hidden labs. Gene Solar will provide you with bio-chips, and I can borrow some of your old work chums to aid you, if that helps?"

"No, there's no chance I'd risk my life working with any of that bunch again! If I agree, what's the catch?"

"You will be sharing a house with two women. One is a computer scientist from GCHQ. Her name is Andrea Parkinson. She's been familiarising herself with your work at Gene Solar."

"Due to the nature of your work, the other woman Flight lieutenant Angela Carter, will be an armed officer from the Cranfield UK Defence Academy in Shrivenham. If you accept the deal, you will all be playing the roles of lodgers in a leased property."

"That's cosy, so I'm swapping this prison for a gilded cage!"

"A specialised team has been put together at GCHQ, just down the road from the house, so you will be asked to collaborate with them too."

"OK, deal, now get me out of here!"

"Good Heavens, Cheryl!" said Jensen "I did not realise you were so keen to leave this wonderful place!"

"Cheeky bastard!"

"Cheryl, a couple of things have been playing on my mind. Was it you who decided that Aberavon Beach was the best place to dispatch the bio-chips from?"

"Firstly, I did not know you were in the police force. You grew up in the area, and we went to your local beach several times during our university summer breaks. To avoid any unforeseen events involving custom officers, my people wanted a flat sandy beach that went on for miles, and it had to have an access road to it, so I suggested Aberavon Beach. It was meant to be a quiet operation, until the contractor's car hit a policeman; and that changed the outcome."

"Contractor? Do you know who the contractor was?"

"No, not really! I just knew my contact was called Andrés. Two contractors were hired on that night. One was hired to drive the car down from Swindon, after I handed the bio-chips over, and the other was a backup, positioned on the pier. He had a rifle with an infrared optical sight. He was hired to keep an eye on things if they did not go to plan, and to pick-up the other contractor after he ditched his car."

Jensen remembered, "Yes, I thought I saw a glitter of red light coming from the pier."

"How did you get involved with Alekos?"

"I was in Cyprus on holiday, when I saw an advertisement for a Cyber Security Expert. I knew that Cyprus was a hub for international money dealings including money laundering, so I thought I'd give it a try and arrange an interview."

"But you had a dream job back in Swindon?"

"Well yes, but I had an excellent offer from Alekos too. So, I could work for Gene Solar Ltd. for the next 20 years to get a good pension, or work for Alekos for a couple of years, and make enough money to comfortably retire, and then see the world!"

Jensen was stunned! He then recovered his composure and continued the questioning.

"How did you manage to smuggle the bio-chips past the security at Gene Solar?"

"They're bio-chips, we created dozens of them over the past year. They should all be labelled and given IDs. The gold internal interfaces are miniaturised and too small to be detected by the security equipment at Gene Solar. The silicon chips and external interfaces would trip alarms, but can be easily removed and replaced with others, that's provided you knew where to buy the equipment, and I did!"

"The date was set for the 26th of February, because the tied at Aberavon Beach would be at its lowest at 10:30 on that evening. In the four days before the pickup, I smuggled out three bio-chips each day in a polythene pouch, and stored them later in a thermos flask. Provided the bio-chips are bathed in solutions of nutrients, there's no harm done!"

"After I finished work, it was just a matter of driving past the contractor's car. After we both recognised each other from photographs, I then drove to the prearranged rendezvous at the Shaw Forest Carpark in Swindon. I handed over four thermos flasks to him. There're no security cameras over there looking at you, as in other car parks such as ASDA and Sainsbury."

Jensen then realised fate and the passage of time had transformed Cheryl into a cold-blooded ruthless bitch. She was no longer the girl he had fallen in love with. Jensen was more disappointed with himself. On reflection, he wondered whether he'd been the catalyst for this transformed personality, which probably began when they split-up just after university?

"Cheryl, I've got a few phone calls to make before your release. I can return your possessions you turned in on entering this prison. I'm driving down to Swansea today. So, I could drop you off at Cheltenham?"

"OK, but I'm famished, so don't leave until I've had my lunch. Have you had a meal yet?"

"Not yet."

"Then you're in for a treat, prison grub is lovely!"

Jensen smiled. He pictured himself as the only man in the dining room filled with hundreds of women prisoners. They would give him a field-day!

He realised he was being teased, "Wouldn't you prefer me to find a nice restaurant around here instead?"

"No need! I love pasta and seafood food. One of the girls mentioned that there's a Harvester restaurant less than a mile away!"

CHAPTER 21 - **Central Police Station Swansea**

April 23rd 8:30 a.m.

It was a damp day with a slight taste of salty sea in the air. The rain had been drizzling on and off throughout the weekend.

Jensen drove into the Central Police Station carpark at Grove Place and parked his Audi A4.

The Police Station was situated three quatres of a mile from the seafront and marina. It was a modern, pinkish brick coloured building. The upper three floors contained many offices. It also contained an armoury on the second floor, and a basement with twelve temporary holding cells.

Viewing from the outside, the ground floor consisted of inlays of greyish slab blocks, which contrasted to the pinkish bricks of the main building, and the band of blue brick tiles which just managed to curve around the left side of the building. The blue bricks rose to the third floor. The police station is the area headquarters for the Western Division of the South Wales Police.

Facing the police station on the other side of Grove Place Road was the Magistrates Court, and just up the road from there stood the Swansea College of Art.

Jensen said his hellos to colleagues he had not seen for several months, then walked into his office to be greeted by a pile of paper that had accumulated from the previous day. He realised that in his absence, other colleagues had been assigned to take over his duties, and his paperwork.

He was always happy that Swansea is generally a safe place to live and to work in, and for tourists to visit.

Jensen had been assigned there for four years. His job covered the policing of a vast area, taking in

Swansea, Neath and Port Talbot. When off duty, he would divide his time between visiting the Gower Peninsula, Oxwich Bay, Caswell Bay, Langland Bay and Three Cliffs Bay. There were also museums, restaurants, and nightclubs.

There was a knock-on Jensen's office door.

"Come in."

"Hi Geoff, how are you?"

Jensen had known Geoff for over three years. Like himself, he was a plain clothed police inspector in his mid-thirties. Geoff also had additional duties as a meetings coordinator.

"I'm fine. Glad your back to save me from doing your damn paperwork again!"

"Very funny," said Jensen.

"Did you get it all done?"

"No, I'm stuck for addresses that are encrypted on a USB memory stick. There're a lot of people working on it to unscramble the information."

"What happens if they unscramble it?"

"I'm not sure Geoff, they might reassign me!"

Geoff, joked sarcastically, "Well, lucky-you boyo if you're off again, I only get to see Ibiza once a year, for a couple of weeks."

"Geoff, did they manage to clear the wreckage of the Mercedes and drone?"

Geoff smiled, "Yes, all done! The Merc was stolen from London, and fitted with cloned plates from an identical car from the Stockport Borough area in the Southeast of Manchester."

"The 157th Welsh Regiment and our Forensic Department, both reported the drone was built from parts available from most hardware and electronic suppliers, probably within Europe. The fragments of the missiles we found, were unidentifiable, possibly bought over the dark web. By the way, you have a catchup meeting with the Chief at 11 o'clock in his office."

"OK, I'll be there! But Geoff, what's wrong with the nightlife in Swansea, or the bays around the Gower anyway? With Oxwich Bay, Port Eynon and Rhossili. What more could anyone ever want?"

Geoff gave Jensen a joking hard stare, then mouthed a silent rude expression while leaving the office.

CHAPTER 22 - **Swansea Bay**

May 8th 6:30 p.m.

Jensen was enjoying an evening walk across a local sandy beach when his mobile phone rung. He took out the phone from his inside breast pocket and answered the call.

"David Jensen."

"Hi, I'm Andrea Parkinson calling from Cheltenham. Cheryl's managed to do the job!"

"Excellent!"

"Could you see me tomorrow at the house, say around 12?"

"I'll need to check with my Chief first, but it shouldn't be a problem. How are Cheryl and Angela?"

"Angela's fine, she's talking to Cheryl in the garden. Cheryl's a little full of herself after completing the job. However, there's been a further development concerning her. Whitehall have asked me not to say anything further over this line as they are verifying the information. I'm sorry, I cannot say any more. See you tomorrow, Inspector!" The phone call ended abruptly.

Jensen then called his Police Chief, Alex Jones. He explained his reasons for travelling to Cheltenham the following day.

He then walked through the golden sands on the beach for a further half-hour, then headed for his favourite, 'Fiona's' cafeteria, and ordered a coffee.

The cafeteria had a balcony outside and contained several tables and chairs providing spectacular views of the bay. He found an empty table and watched the sailing dinghies pass by. He was a little troubled with the abrupt nature of the message.

After finishing his coffee, he headed back to his nearby flat, which was on the top floor of a compartment block, off the Mumbles Road.

CHAPTER 23 - **Cheltenham**

May 9th 9:00 a.m.

Preparing for possible trouble, Jensen first called into the Swansea Central Police Station and filled in the paperwork for a fifth generation Glock 17 pistol. Jensen liked the weapon; it was lightweight and allowed for 17 bullets in the standard magazine. It was trusted by law enforcement officers and military personnel around the globe because of its unsurpassed reliability. Fortunately, the station had over a dozen models of the pistol.

12:20 p.m.

As Jensen approached Cheltenham along the A40. He had suspected that for a while his Audi was being followed by a grey Jaguar car. To check this out he drove into Tennyson Road, about a mile from GCHQ, then turned into Spenser Road and then drove down to the bottom of Spenser Avenue. Having lived in Cheltenham for eighteen months, he knew this road would lead to a dead end. He turned his car around at the bottom of the road, and then drove up the road another 30 feet and parked the car.

A minute later a grey Jaguar car pulled up at the top of the street. Jensen thought that these people were hoping he'd lead them to the secure house! Jensen picked up his mobile phone and made a quick phone call. He then left the Audi, and checked under his jacket that his pistol was loose to draw from its holster. He then walked towards the parked Jaguar.

A minute later, Jensen tapped on the driver's window and displayed his police ID. The engine was still running.

There were two men in the car. The driver rolled down his window.

"Can I help you Sir?"

The driver's accent and skin colour possibly indicated he was from somewhere in the Western

Mediterranean, but his passenger looked paler and probably English. Jensen could sense the tension of the man in the passenger seat. His left hand was hidden from view and down the side of the seat next to the door. Jensen looked back at the driver.

Jensen drew his pistol, "You, keep both hands on the wheel!" Jensen waited several seconds until it was done.

Jensen then pointed his pistol at the passenger. "Nice an easy now, drop the pistol and put both hands on the dash."

He could feel the tension in both men.

"I have no pistol, Sir."

"Raise your left arm and put it on the dash with your other hand, or I'll shoot you in your seat right now!"

The man slowly raised both hands and put them on the dashboard. Jensen walked around to the passenger door, and opened it. A pistol dropped from the side of the passenger's seat, making a clunking sound as it made contact with the pavement.

Police car sirens broke the silence, and distracted both the driver and Jensen. The driver took full advantage, snapped his foot down on the accelerator and sped off. However, he realised too late that the road led to a dead-end. He spun the car around, screeching the wheels, and headed back up the road towards Jensen.

Jensen shot at the front tires and then the driver. He dashed out of the path of the car into a gap between two hedges leading to a small garage. The car breaks screeched as it collided with a police car now blocking the road. Airbags inflated and deflated rapidly in both vehicles and the Jaguar's engine cut-out.

The policemen quickly left their vehicle. The driver in the Jaguar car was groaning, Jensen had wounded him in his shoulder. He was holding a blooded handkerchief against the wound and applying pressure. Jensen picked himself up and pointed his pistol at the men. Displaying his ID to the policemen, he then walked around the car and picked up the pistol on the pavement and handed it to one of the policemen.

The policemen walked around the Jag and shouted, "OK, both of you get out now!"

Jensen kept his eye on both men, and pointed his pistol on each of them in turn.

Jensen then turned to the police officers. "These men are probably assassins. Arrest both, but get an ambulance for the wounded man before he bleeds all over the pavement. Watch him, and do not let him out of your sight. You can lock him up with the other man, after he's been patched-up!"

1:20 p.m.

The secure house was located in Canterbury Walk Road, about two and a half miles from GCHQ. It was sufficient distance away from the intelligence centre as not to cause any suspicions to neighbours. Jensen pulled up behind a White Mercedes parked outside the front of the house. He was immediately concerned!

The Mercedes was an S-Class Coupe, which reminded Jensen of the blown-up car on Aberavon Beach a few months earlier. It did not feel right! Jensen got out of the Audi and walked up to the front door. He looked up and down the street for anything else that looked out of place. Satisfied that all was clear, he pressed the doorbell which emitted the familiar 'Ding-dong' sound.

Andrea opened the front door.

"Come in Inspector."

Jensen sensed tension in her voice. Andrea led him into the living room.

Jensen had a nasty shock. Sat on the sofa was Richard along with his sister Cheryl and Angela. Angela was looking a little embarrassed. Cheryl was smiling.

"Hello again Inspector," said Richard.

Jensen looked straight at him and forced a reply, "Hi!" He then turned to Cheryl, "Cheryl, what's your brother doing here?"

"Richard's a diplomat for the People's Republic of China, now working in Malta, and he's on official business. He flew into the UK yesterday."

Jensen turned to Richard, "Why are you here?"

"I'm here to congratulate Cheryl on becoming a diplomatic advisor for the People's Republic of China in Malta, and to see that no harm comes to her while she leaves your country!"

"What?" said Jensen in a loud voice, taking his pistol out for a second airing of the day.

Andrea grabbed Jensen's arm. "I'm sorry, but it's all official Inspector!" She then gently pushed his pistol arm down.

"The government was informed yesterday of Cheryl's posting; we have no option but to let her leave!"

"This is ridiculous Cheryl. You told me you grew-up in Singapore!"

Cheryl, looked back at Jensen, and raised a further smile.

"My father moved to Hong Kong to work as a translator for an Asian Corporation. He met and married my mother there. Richard and I were both born in Hong Kong, and I lived there until I was twelve. Father found a well-paid job in Singapore as a translator, and worked there until he recently retired. So, I became a national and have a Singapore passport. But I've worked for the Chinese government since I completed my PhD. The CCP have of course granted me Chinese citizenship for this posting."

Jensen realised Cheryl had deliberately conned him, and had 'taken him for a ride' at HMP Bronzefield.

She had told him the reason for joining Alekos's team was purely a money matter.

Ironically in a flash of memory, it occurred to Jensen that she was probably recruited by the CCP, while doing her PhD. at Hong Kong University. This would be around the same time that he was being recruited to work for the IBID in Whitehall.

Before him now was a CCP trained agent. But was she unable to see through the madness of its political system? Or, was she participating in a deadly game by playing in both fields?

Richard took over the conversation, "Inspector, Alekos's men turned up at my doorstep a few days after you left. You gave me your contact details, so, I let them know you were a police officer from the Swansea Bay area looking for Cheryl. They have been watching you since that time, and have kept me informed of your progress."

"That information was also passed up the chain to the Party Secretary Wang Leji, and from there to Qian Yi, who is the Foreign Minister of the People's Republic of China. He contacted your Foreign Secretary of State Sir Henry Gibson, and after discussions with your Prime

Minister Richard Harris, I was allowed to fly into the UK to pick up Cheryl."

Cheryl started smiling, "I just wanted to see the look on your face darling, before I leave!"

Cheryl then went into her bedroom and brought out two white suitcases.

Richard opened the front door, picked up the suitcases and walked over to the Mercedes and loaded them into the boot. He then got into the car, rolled down the driver's window, and tuned the radio to Radio 4.

Cheryl walked over to Jensen and planted a kiss on his cheek. "Bye Ex-Darling. For your own safety, let's hope we never cross paths again!"

She then walked through the open door, got into the front passenger seat of the Mercedes and blew a kiss to Jensen as she and her brother drove off.

Jensen turned to Andrea, "I'm stunned! No wonder I could have been killed an hour earlier. Do we have all the deciphered information and addresses?"

"Yes, all done! The GCHQ and NIS have them. But by now the CCP might have all the information too!"

Andrea looked at Angela and Jensen, "I think we should all make our way over to the Doughnut building and call a meeting."

Jensen gave Andrea a stern look, "I'm not looking forward to that!"

"Ugggggg! Me neither!"

5:00 p.m.

Jensen was driving along the M4 to his flat in Swansea Bay. Half an hour earlier he had left Holland House, a police station in the Lansdown area of Cheltenham. He was there to file a report on the two characters he had met in the grey Jaguar car.

In the earlier GHO meeting, he had contacted his colleagues at Whitehall, NIS, NSA, Britain's Intelligence Surveillance Base in Cyprus, and the British High Commission there.

Breaking the encryptions with the help of bio-chip memories from Gene Solar was quite an achievement, but achieving it by using the labour of a communist spy, and her probably holding fake passports from several nationalities too, had not impressed anyone. Too many security checks must have been bypassed while she had moved from country to country.

One of the tasks for the intelligence agencies was to inform the various tax havens, which Harald Haugen was investing his millions into. They also had to convince them to freeze his assets. As many of these places relied on illicit dealings to make their own money, it was going to be an almost hopeless task.

Jensen's orders from Whitehall were to pack his suitcase and get on the next available flight to Malta. He had to find Alekos and Harald and destroy their organisation, before they found the opportunity to start it up again.

Jensen also needed to stop any interference from Cheryl and her brother. As this mischievous pair had the full backing of the CCP, it was going to be another almost impossible assignment. But he had to try! At GCHQ he was given a small 10.2-inch iPad, which contained background information on Malta. This trip was going to be no holiday!

8:00 p.m.

Back home, Jensen was sitting on his living room sofa and reading information from the small iPad. He wanted to find out as much background information on Malta as possible.

In the early-1950s, Malta was a Crown Colony of the UK and served as a strategic hub. Pressure at that time from the USSR and the USA was forcing the UK to give up the colony, leading to Malta's independence.

However, in 1956 a referendum organised by the then Prime Mister of Malta, Don Mintoff, showed that 77% of voters from a 59% turnout, wanted Malta to be part of the UK, with the same rights as Northern Ireland. However, the UK had serious doubts, and if allowing this proposal to go through, would only provide a small budget for the island.

The reasons behind this decision were that by the mid-1950s, defence needs had changed, and the Naval Base at Malta was not as important as it once had been. The UK therefore would end up subsidising the island for little return, and if allowed to continue would open the door for other Crown Colonies to apply for full membership. Don Mintoff rejected the small budget offer, resigning in protest. So instead, Malta was granted independence on September 21st 1964.

Malta is a small rocky island which can be driven across by car in forty minutes. Today its population is in excess of 442,500. In recent years the island has become a hub for online gambling, fuel smuggling from Libya and offshore banking, with many wealthy and well-known suspects linked to money laundering.

A former Prime Minister Joseph Muscat had to resign over the death of a journalist Daphne Caruana Galizia's, from investigating corruption in his government. A former police finance officer investigating bank corruption was also fired on suspicious grounds that he was getting too close to the truth.

The police force in turn was constantly under suspicion for corruption. 37 of its 50 traffic cops had been detained on suspicion of using station fuel for their own cars.

You could also be fast tracked into citizenship within weeks, provided you had enough money to pay into the state coffers. William Somerset Maugham, had said of both the French Riviera and Malta - "a sunny place for shady people." After the UK Times posted a Brit's guide to buying a home in Malta, many commenters were discouraging, as many held the same view as William Somerset Maugham.

Jensen then viewed several YouTube videos on Malta. Each expressed the modern Malta, and how it was an excellent investment opportunity for those wanting to move to this central hub, in the Mediterranean.

Opportunities existed to set up a business there, or go there to live or retire. The videos brought a smile to his face, but Jensen realised that from viewing foreign news broadcasting stations, such as the Indian stations 'WION' and 'VANTAGE', that they held similar accusations of corruption against the British Institutions.

Jensen thought of Rebekah in Trondheim, and worried for her safety, while they both investigated this dirty game!

CHAPTER 24 - **Malta**

May 11th 11:00 a.m.

Alekos and his wife Sarah, were lying on sun loungers, enjoying the sun on a candy-coloured roof terrace. They were on the top of one of Harald's penthouse suites in Kalkara, South Malta. A four-foot elaborately patterned white painted wrought iron fence surrounded the edge of the roof terrace. The edge overlooked Triq Marina street and the Kalkara Marina where many motorised and sailing boats were docked. Beyond the maria, there was plenty of activity from small sailing crafts passing by.

The terrace overlooked a yellow-brown candy-coloured steep harbour wall on the opposite bank. The sun was strong and a large fan on the terrace provided a light breeze, making it very enjoyable for the relaxing couple.

The penthouse had six bedrooms. Two of Alekos's men, Markus and Seth, both electronic engineers, along with their wives shared the accommodation.

On the roof terrace the men and their wives were seated around a large crystal glass table enjoying the morning, and engaged in conversation. The men were relaxing, drinking from cans of local Cisk lager, while their wives supped on Antonin Blanc wine from Gozo, at 44 Euros a bottle.

#

Five thousand, two hundred, and thirty-one miles away, a large screen in Beijing was being viewed by two intelligence officers. The screen showed the output from a CCP spy satellite scanning over tops of buildings in Kalkara. The scanning image came to a halt at a set coordinate above West Street.

The image was then zoomed-in and focused to perfect clarity. It showed Alekos, his wife, and his colleagues. A link to the image was then sent to the

Chinese Embassy in Malta, which was located just four miles away in Lapsi Street.

#

11:45 a.m.

A 'Ding-dong' sound came from the front door. Seth, left the crystal glass table and walked down two flights of stairs to answer the call. Seth checked the video link before opening it. He was surprised and pleased to see it was Cheryl.

After he opened the door, his joy was short lived when Cheryl pulled out a small calibre pistol from her handbag and pointed it to his heart.

"Hi Seth," said Cheryl. "Move a few paces backwards dear, while I let my boys in."

Behind Cheryl was her brother Richard, and behind him was six-armed men from the Chinese Embassy. Once they were all past the door, Richard quietly closed it.

Cheryl moved the pistol to Seth's head, "Now my sweet, take me to your leader!"

Seth, looking shocked, reluctantly led the group back to the roof terrace.

As the group walked through the white patio doors, four of Cheryl's men surrounded the three sitting at the crystal glass table, and pointed their pistols at them, resulting in a stunned silence all around the table.

"Sit down with your buddies Seth," said Cheryl. She then walked over to an equally stunned Alekos and his wife.

Alekos was taken aback with Cheryl and her henchmen. She pointed her pistol at him. He slowly sat up on his sun lounger, followed by his wife on hers.

"Cheryl, I was sorry you disappeared from our lives in Alexandria, but there's no need for this! Put that gun away!"

Cheryl took a long look at Alekos, then cast her eyes on his wife, now trembling.

"Alekos, I didn't know you had a girlfriend."

Outraged, Alekos shouted back in anger at her, "This is my wife, Sarah!"

Cheryl gave his wife another look. "Hi Sarah."

Cheryl then turned back to Alekos. "I want to make you an offer that you shouldn't refuse! I want you and your men to come and work with me for the CCP!"

"I don't understand?" said Alekos. Now in anger, and raising his tone, "You were working for meeee!"

"Alekos, Harald's tax haven accounts are now visible to the security services. His monthly pay cheque into your bank account will shortly be drying up. How did you think I was able to find this address?"

"Then we should inform Harald at once!" said Alekos.

Richard cut-in, "Thank you, but no! We don't want any competition!"

Richard continued, "Either you agree to work for us, or, we'll end your career right now?"

"The CCP, are you mad? Do you think I would volunteer myself and crew to work for a bunch of political thugs?"

"Thugs?" said Cheryl, "I don't do drugs and I don't deal in conflict diamond smuggling!"

Sarah turned to Alekos. "She's lying, tell her dear!"

Alekos looked sternly at his wife, "Quiet woman!"

He then turned back to Cheryl.

"Do what you must, I'll not work for the communists!"

Cheryl added, "Alekos, don't worry for now! In-time, you'll come around, especially, when faced with the alternative!"

Cheryl then took out a second pistol from her handbag and fired a drugged dart into both Alekos and his wife. Alekos tried to get up off the sun lounger, but lost his balance and fell unconscious onto the terrace floor. Sarah tried to reach Alekos, but quickly fell unconscious, falling over his body. Cheryl pulled Sarah away, separating them.

Cheryl then walked over to the crystal glass table. She could feel the tension and fear in the air from everyone sat around it.

"Now boys, with the Bluebell sunk I thought you'd all be missing work. So, you can work for me instead. Now, unless you agree to help me, you will all be taken to a lovely prison cell in North China. A cell where you will be given daily exercise, provided of course that you smile first." She laughed. "But much healthier than lounging in the sun here!"

"Boys, as you are aware from seeing the news on TV, the CCP have work camps to correct your thinking! All of you boys will be smiling and singing the party song in no time, along with your wives. Nobody will miss you here in Malta, or in Cyprus. Nobody will be concerned!"

Seth sprang forward to grab the dart gun from Cheryl, but a henchman standing over him, hit his head with the butt of his pistol, and knocked him flat-out. His wife Zoey, in fear for her husband's life, left her chair, and knelt down beside him to check his injury.

Cheryl, looked down at the woman, "This is no time for sentiment dear!" She then looked up at the other couple. "Let me know if Alekos decides to change his mind, or if any of you boys want to?"

Cheryl then fired drugged darts into the four captives, and soon they fell unconscious.

Several minutes Richard turned to his men, "OK lads, one couple at a time. Take your time, we do not want to draw any attention to ourselves."

At the top lift entrance, three large laundry baskets were eagerly waiting for each couple. In the underground carpark, a large laundry van was parked with two occupants onboard. The driver and his colleague were eagerly waiting for the deliveries.

#

2:30 p.m.

Jensen's flight arrived in Malta International Airport after a three-and-a-half-hour flight from London. Roger Phillips was waiting for him. After passport control, Roger led Jensen to a loaned British Embassy Jaguar car. Roger opened the car boot and took out a Glock 26 pistol and shoulder holster, and handed it to Jensen.

Roger updated Jensen during the route. "The Maltese Police did not find anyone at Harald's flat in Kalkara this morning. But in three of the bedrooms, they did find empty suitcases, several men's suits, dresses and casual clothing, underwear, and pairs of footwear. So, there was some sort of hasty departure."

"So, it looks like a tip-off, or Cheryl and Richard got there first!" said Jensen.

Roger continued, "We are now heading for the northwestern part of the Island where Harald has a villa. It's in the Mellieha area."

"The Maltese Police have gone ahead, so they should have surrounded the place by the time we get there."

Thirty minutes later they pulled up at the villa. The villa consisted of four floors built into the side of a hill. The first and second floors were built from multi-shaded grey granite blocks.

There were window inlays and terraces with small four-foot walls with additional stone white balusters. The third floor consisted of several white arches set about eight feet apart, with window inlays. The top floor looked about 12 feet in height, with mostly glass window surrounds. A garden of olive trees encircled the villa.

Outside the villa, Jensen and Roger met up with Superintendent Adam Losco. Losco was in full uniform and stood about six feet in height.

"I have been asked by Government House to assist you," he said.

"Excellent, welcome," said Jensen, shaking his hand. "We have several questions for Harald, and an arrest warrant from the Norwegian Police, but it's probably not valid on this island!"

The Superintendent smiled. "This one is a pretty cool customer; he must have been aware of my men surrounding his villa for the last thirty minutes!"

Losco rung the bell. A camera above the door activated and focussed on them. Shortly afterwards the front door was opened by a maid servant.

"Please come in. We have been watching you for some time, and waiting for you to call."

The maid then escorted the three men into a living room containing three cream-coloured sofas. The sofas surrounded a large wooden table which stood on a red and brown carpet. The room was brightly lit with off-white walls and white netting curtains.

Jensen knew Harald was an art lover of the sea and rivers, from what Johannessen had told him about the pictures decorating his Trondheim home. Here too he had hung several paintings on the walls depicting harbour scenes, along with portraits.

"Please sit down, Mr Haugen will be with you shortly."

"Would you like some refreshment while you're waiting?"

"No thank you," said Losco. The exact words were repeated by Jensen and Roger.

Ten minutes passed then Harald appeared with a colleague. Harald was a big built man in his 50s and looked just over six feet tall. He had short cut silver hair, and blue eyes. He was heavily suntanned indicating that he must have been in Malta for several weeks. He wore a white open neck shirt and brown slacks. His colleague was much paler in complexion, so perhaps had not been on the island that long. He had brownish hair and green eyes, and wore a blue shirt with dark blue trousers. He looked far more intense, whereas Harald kept his feelings hidden.

"Good afternoon gentlemen, what can I do for you?"

Losco started the inquiry, "Sir, from investigations in Norway leading to the recovery of financial information, concerning your property portfolio here, we would like you to accompany us to the Police General Headquarters to discuss these matters further."

Svein Thorsen had since updated Harald on the destruction of his Trondheim outhouse, on the 20th of April. Harald gave Jensen a long hard look.

Harald then turned to Losco, "Inspector Losco, I'm a citizen of Malta. As far as I'm aware Malta has no treaty with Norway with the exception of the 2013 Double Taxation Relief treaty. I assure you that all my dealings and accountancy transactions in Malta are ethical and are in order. I'll ask my accountant in Fgura to meet us at your police station."

Harald then walked over to a phone and dialled a colleague.

"Hi Tumas, I'm in the accompany of several police officers. They are having a little difficulty with my financial dealings. As you manage all my financial assets in Malta, can you meet us in half an hour at the Police General Headquarters in Floriana? There was a short pause. You can! Excellent! See you soon."

Tumas was not an accountant, he slowly put down the phone while he thought carefully over the call. He then picked the phone up again to phone a different number. The phone rang in another villa that was less than a mile away from Harald's villa. Several more men working for Harald were staying there.

Harald put on a light green jacket and was escorted by Inspector Losco to a waiting Ford Focus police car. Harald looked surprisingly relaxed and remained silent. Roger and Jensen followed the Ford Focus in the Jaguar. The cars headed down the Triq tal-Prajjet road then turned into the Triq il-Mellieha road and headed for the Route 1 highway, which ran the length of the eastern side of the country.

After travelling several minutes, the cars passed a quarry on their left. Seconds later the police driver pulled up sharply, forcing Harald and Losco to lurch forward in their seatbelts. Behind them, Roger slammed on his breaks. The road ahead was blocked by two Range Rovers.

Two drones hovered above the Rovers. The drones looked familiar to Jensen and were equipped with missiles, that were now pointing at the cars. Two men got out of one of the Rovers. They were holding pistols and wearing body armour, and approaching the police car.

The police car driver reacted immediately. He reversed the car, pulling up at the side of the Jaguar, then he swung the driving wheel around, and drove it into the quarry, hoping to find another exit.

Roger followed the police car, while Jensen took out his pistol, rolled down the window and fired several rounds at the gunmen. One man fell to the ground, but like his accomplice, he was also wearing body armour, so, was only left temporary breathless from the impact of the bullets.

On entering the quarry, the policeman swung the car to the right and headed northeast along a narrow road. He passed a truck and a tractor, and then drove past several small buildings. An earth bank appeared directly ahead of them.

The police car driver realised that he'd made a mistake, so spun the car around and headed back in the direction he came from. A missile fired from one of the drones exploded ahead of his car, deeply cratering the road.

The police driver swerved out of danger, then decided to drive up the northwest quarry road, hoping to find an exit on the other side of the quarry. He put his foot down on the accelerator. Roger followed in the Jaguar.

The second drone then caught up with the first, and fired ahead of the police car. Its missile hit a wall, blasting it into pieces. The police driver swerved to dodge the falling bricks. With its tyres screeching, the car reached the boundaries of the northwest side of the quarry. The car then headed east on an outer rim road.

The police driver accelerated the car again, surging it forward. Both drones were flying overhead, then the second drone sped ahead of both cars and fired two missiles into the road. The first drone then hung back in the sky and positioned itself behind the two cars below.

Both cars were engulfed in mud, smoke and dust. The police driver could not avoid the deep crater and the car lunged into it and stalled. Roger's Jaguar followed the car into the crater. The impact on the cars winded and disoriented everyone inside.

After several minutes when orientation and normal breathing returned to the men, they managed to get out of the cars. They found themselves looking up to a five-foot crater edge with Harald's men looking down on them pointing pistols.

"We only want Harald," said the leader. "The rest of you stay put, and put your hands up where I can see them!"

A rope was thrown to a pleased looking Harald, and he was pulled free.

The two drones were still airborne and hovering 20 feet above the crater. One was still armed with a missile.

"Now gentlemen," said Harald, looking stern, and pointing to the remaining armed drone, "Stay exactly where you are for 30 minutes or that drone will finish you off!"

Harald then got into a Range Rover with four of his men and was driven away. The drone with spent missiles followed the car.

Two of Harald's men stood at the edge of the crater, one held the drone controller.

In a very quiet voice Losco asked "Do you think they will let us go in 30 minutes."

"No, no way," said Jensen, "They'll kill us as soon as Harald is safe. We'll shortly be mincemeat!"

Just then several quarry workers plucked up enough courage and started to approach the two men.

A quarry man shouted, "X'infern qed jiġri hawn?"
("What the hell is happening here?")

On hearing several voices and realising that the two men on guard would be momentarily distracted, Jensen dashed inside the car and grabbed his pistol. He turned and shot the man holding the drone controls and then fired several shots at the drone.

The man controlling the drone buckled and collapsed. He just managed to press the missile launch button as he fell. The drone spun as it launched its missile. The missile blasted into a grey brick block building, demolishing it.

Above the crater, the shock wave blew all the men, backwards and upwards, then downwards falling hard on the ground. The man holding the drone controls was dead. His colleague was still alive but unconscious. When he came around, he found himself surrounded by angry quarry men.

Jensen, Roger and Losco and the police driver down in the crater, were spared the full blast of the explosion. They climbed up the rope left for Harald, met up with the quarry men that had saved their lives and thanked them. Losco handcuffed the prisoner and then phoned the local Mellieha police near the Santa Maria Estate.

Fifteen minutes later, police sirens could be heard approaching the quarry. Covered in dust and mud. Jensen could sense what Roger and Adam Losco were thinking. He turned to look at them.

"Yep, when our superiors read our reports, we are not going to be very popular!"

CHAPTER 26 - Bab Sharq Police Department

May 14th 10:30 a.m.

It took two stops and over 12-hours of air travel to get to Alexandria. Jensen booked into the Arabian Nights Hotel because of its proximity to the city centre, good reviews, and its great name.

Jensen contacted the harbour police and was directed to the Bab Sharq Police Department. A meeting was arranged for later that afternoon.

4:30 p.m.

Jensen took a taxi to the police station. The sandstone-coloured building was two and three-storey in places. It had a prominent clock tower, mostly glossy green in colour, with what appeared to be a light wooden pointed top section containing a clock. A giant stature of a golden eagle was affixed to the lower quarter of the clock tower.

On arrival at the Main Reception Desk Jensen was escorted to an office at the rear of the building. Twenty minutes later a female forensic scientist walked into the room.

"Good afternoon, Inspector, I'm Professor Jannat Rashied."

The professor looked to be about 5 feet four inches and in her mid-thirties. She was a Muslim and dressed in Islamic clothing. She wore a dark red headscarf covering all her hair, and a long flowing dark green dress which stretched nearly to her ankles. The dress had long dark green sleeves stretching nearly to her hands. Embroidered on her dress near to its full length, and near to the full length of her sleeves, were dozens of dark golden flower patterns.

"Inspector, I have been informed that you are enquiring about the Bluebell, which was sunk on the 6th of April."

"Yes, Professor Rashied, what has your investigation come up with?"

"The yacht went down in 150 feet of water, about fifteen miles off our great port."

"The missile did not carry explosives, but relied on speed of impact that generated a shock wave to do the damage. The missile impact tore through all the decks, and pierced the hull of the yacht. I've been informed that you were on the yacht at the time?"

"Yes professor, that's correct!"

The professor continued, "On the seabed near the yacht, our divers located several interesting items. One item was a four-foot tungsten and steel rod combination, made from a central rod with eight rods welded around it."

"Each rod was made up from eight six-inch sections that fitted together through a four-inch steel connector socket. Heat and cooling were used on the connector sections to lock the rods firmly together. The six-inch tungsten rods nearest the nosecone were pointed, and designed to cut clean through metal. This was a kinetic energy weapon of considerable destructive force!"

"After reconstructing all the pieces, the missile was approximately twelve feet in length. The outer casing consisted of a large thermal tile (now partly burnt through), which neatly fitted over the tungsten rods and liquid propellant. There were small navigable flaps within the tailfins. The tailfins and flaps were also made from the same thermal material. The thermal material also contained particles of a radar absorbing paint. The liquid propellant section was encased within an alloy tube. The nozzle was connected to a gimbal for moveability. Presumably, just before launching, the onboard computer was fed with the target coordinates. After launching, the onboard computer guided the missile by its nozzle through the gimbal and the tailfin flaps to its target."

"Professor, can you tell me where any of these material parts originated from?"

"Well, yes, Tungsten is mined in many places, for example, Rwanda, China, Canada, Russia, Vietnam and Bolivia. It is extracted from two types of minerals, Wolframite and Scheelite."

"At present, China is the largest producer, accounting for over 80% of world production. Minerals have slight differences in impurities, so we'll search our database to see if it can be matched to a specific region."

"The tile casings were specifically designed to lower the outer skin temperature to 350 degrees Centigrade or less. Normally silica fibres are mixed with water and chemicals, and then poured in moulds. The moulds are then processed in microwave ovens at temperatures of 2,350 degrees Centigrade to fuse the fibres. This made-up about 85% of the missile's thermal heat protection."

"In this case the remaining 15% consisted of a Carbon Carbon Composite (CCC), which made up the nosecone, and rocket engine nozzle. This is not uncommon; it's mostly used for missile nosecones. Before the American Space Shuttles were retired, you would have found the same material in their nosecones."

"The paint is a radar absorbent material, usually referred to as RAM. The most common type of RAM is iron ball paint. This contains tiny spheres coated with carbonyl iron or ferrite. Again, we are doing an analysis of this to check if anything matches, but we are dealing with state secrets here, so we are unlikely to be successful!"

"The electronic components controlling the tail-fin were mostly shattered into small parts, but we managed to locate several square centimetres of a mounting board on which part of a processor was found. We may be able to trace part of a printed name on it to a manufacturer."

"As we were aware of your visit and enquiry, we should have some results within the hour, but our databases are not infallible, and we might be unsuccessful in pinning down the origins of several products! You are welcome to stay in this office while you wait."

"Thank you, Professor Rashied, I'll wait for the results. Before you leave, earlier in the evening, at around 6:10 p.m., a schooner was tied-up next to the yacht for about 35 minutes. Did you find anything else?"

Professor Rashied had been informed of the docking by M I 6, "No, nothing relating to that has been reported. Anything of value was probably taken onboard the missing tenders. However, should we discover any additional illegal activity, such as narcotics, smuggled alcohol, ivory, jewellery, armament's, etcetera, then you will be notified. If any of these items are found, they will be confiscated by the Egyptian government!"

"I'll get one of my assistants to bring you in some refreshments."

"Thank you."

The professor then left the room.

5:30 p.m.

Professor Rashied returned and gave Jensen a detailed analysis of the components. She looked pleased with what her team had achieved.

"Inspector Jensen, the bad news first. Unfortunately, the liquid propellant rocket component was damaged and burnt throughout on impact, and its components untraceable."

"However, we have identified the composition of the tiles to a manufacturer located just outside Tokyo. In English they are called Emperor Tiles." She then showed Jensen the Japanese name for the firm (皇帝タイル).

"The absorbent paint components, as I feared are impossible to trace, due to state secrets. The tungsten alloy composition is not too far removed from a product manufactured by Wolfram Wire Ltd., it's located to the north of Taipei in Taiwan, I suspect the raw tungsten ore was mined in Vietnam and was imported into the country."

"The electronic components which controlled the tailfins and gimbal originated from Takagi Electronics. They have a manufacturing plant at Seoul in South Korea, but there is no indication that the unit was designed and assembled there."

It suddenly dawned on Jensen, Japan. South Korea, Vietnam, Taiwan. Could these countries be secretly working together or was there some mega rich mastermind or masterminds behind it all?

Jensen kept his thoughts to himself, although he could see from the professor's facial expressions that she too was uneasy with the findings and suspected the same. Anyway, he now had several leads, his first lead, was the tile manufacturer on the outskirts of Tokyo.

"Thank you, Professor Rashied, for your help and time." Jensen reached out and shook her hand.

"You're welcome, Inspector Jensen."

7:30 p.m.

Back at the hotel, Jensen contacted Whitehall to get permission and finance to visit the tile manufacturer in Japan. He knew the Japanese had a thriving space industry and that the Taiwanese had several space start-up industries. Jensen asked Whitehall to investigate any personnel that had left their posts in these industries during the last five years. But that was going to be a tall order.

Jensen then phoned Roger to get an update on Malta. Cheryl had been seen entering and leaving the Chinese High Commission, but there was nothing further to report on Alekos and his men, or on Harald. He thanked Roger for the update and closed the connection.

He sat back on his sofa and watched an English TV channel until 10 p.m.

He had a two-day flight ahead of him and needed to quickly learn about heat dissipation tiles, CCCs, and of course a brief history of Japan. Whitehall would arrange his company visit. He would be acting as a UK government representative, investigating possible markets in heat dissipation tiles for missiles. This was the same type of research he once did for the International Business Innovations Department before it was axed.

CHAPTER 27 - **Flight to Japan**

May 16th 9:00 a.m.

During his flight Jensen researched several articles on Japan including Wikipedia. He viewed several videos including a UNESCO Heritage video about the origin of foreign trade with Japan.

In the mid-sixteen hundreds, Japan had been a closed society from the outside world. Captured foreigners from shipwrecks were badly treated and could be executed. Japanese people at that time were limited to only exploring the Japanese islands. If they travelled any further, they could face a death sentence on returning home.

The United States President at that time, Millard Fillmore (13th President), wanted trade with Japan so assigned a naval Commodore, Mathew Perry, to bring his idea to fruition. The commodore realised that Japan was on the same latitude as California, where many of his naval and commercial ships were harboured. On the 8th of July 1853 the commodore entered Tokyo harbour with four ships, two of them were steam powered.

To play safe, the fleet sailed under a white flag. The commodore wanted to pass a letter written by the US President to the emperor, and to show off the advanced US technology. However, at that time, he was unaware that the emperor had little power. The real power was wielded by the Tokugawa Shogunate government.

After four days of trying to see the emperor and failing, Commodore Perry was requested to leave. The commodore was not a person to give up though, and insisted that if the letter was not delivered by himself, then the American President would take the reaction as an insult, and that he would not account for the consequences. So, the Shogun government reconsidered and then allowed the commodore to visit the emperor.

The emperor received the letter and many gifts, including a model of a steam powered locomotive, a telegraph, and a telescope. However, accepting the letter was one thing, but this did not indicate that the Japanese were happy to trade with the United States, despite the benefits that the commodore had explained.

The emperor was also given a visit to the commodore's ships. There were four warships, including two steamships. The steamships were known as the black ships by the Japanese because they had not seen steam ships before.

The emperor was shown around the ships which were equipped with cannons and handguns. As the US were technologically advanced, the commodore discouraged the Japanese from starting any war with them, as this would result in the destruction of the Japanese fleets.

After the visit Commodore Perry informed the emperor that he would be back in one year with the expectation of signing a trade agreement. He then loaded up supplies and provisions and set sail for Hong Kong.

Much sooner, in the following February, Commodore Perry returned with a fleet of ten warships and 1600 men. This time the Shogun government caved-in and signed a trade agreement. The agreement contained a special clause, which stated, "should Japan trade with any other nation, then they must also trade the same goods with the United States."

Trade benefited both countries. Fifteen years later the Shogunate government collapsed and the emperor had his full powers restored. In 1873 Japan followed Perry's example and acquired a fleet of steamships and soon became a formidable power in the Pacific.

Both the US and Japan recognised Perry's contribution, and have memorials in both countries. In the US there is a memorial in Rode Island Naval Academy, and another in Japan where he first landed.

Japan has also an annual festival called the 'Black Ship Day', to mark the day that Perry arrived. Both countries have also museums to commemorate him. Tokyo today owes its worldwide technological development through the opening-up of its commerce to the world through this one man.

Jensen felt that somewhere between the articles he studied, and the videos he watched, laid the real truth. Jensen thought about the similarity between the Opium Wars fought between China and Great Britain, between

1839 to 1842, and from 1856 to 1860, and how the power of the gun had determined trade, no matter how disgraceful the tactics used. He then fell into a light sleep for thirty minutes.

10:00 a.m.

Jensen awoke to review his notes on Carbon Carbon Composites.

A composite is when two or more different materials are combined to make a superior material. In the case of building a nosecone and rocket nozzle, a preform, consisting of a carbon high strength heat resistant fibre with low density, would be sandwiched over a low-density carbon material with good shear properties (that is, resistance against a load).

The composite of these materials was known as a matrix, and if necessary, it could be cut to size. The end-product would be a compound material made of high strength, high stiffness, good shear properties and low density, and able to withstand temperatures up to 3000 degrees Centigrade.

Japan's carbon fibre consumption was about 15% of the global market, with North America at about 35%, Europe 30% and the rest of the world at about 20%.

Carbon fibre is used in a host of products, including high performance braking systems, turbo-jet engine components, missile nosecones, rocket nozzle's, heat shields, aircraft brakes, biomedical implants, engine pistons, electronic heat sinks, and automobile and motorcycle bodies.

There are basically four methods of processing CCCs.

1. Thermosetting Resin-Based Processing.

The resins are dissolved in an organic solvent or furfuryl alcohol with a catalyst and curing agent. The resin is then heated in the range of 350 to 800 degrees Centigrade, to decompose it. Then hot pressuring begins up to 10 megapascals (a pascal is defined as one newton per square meter), along with temperatures in the range of 150 to 350 degrees Centigrade for up to 10 hours. This improves the density of the compound during the curing process. Finally, the composite is graphitized at temperatures in excess of 1000 degrees Centigrade.

2. Thermoplastic Pitch-Based Processing.

Pitch is produced through the distillation of carbon-based materials, such as plants, crude-oil, and coal. The impregnated preform is subject to carbonization in an inert atmosphere to convert the compound to coke, and a high-temperature treatment, in the range of 1000 to 2700 degrees Centigrade, for the graphitization of coke. This densification process is carried out at atmospheric or reduced pressure to obtain the correct density. This is a more efficient process than the first method.

3. Chemical Vapour Infiltration Processing.

This entails the infiltration of a gaseous precursor into the reinforcing fibre structure (the structure being the preform).

The precursor is just a gas which participates in a chemical reaction to produce another product. The process is driven by either using diffusion (a high-density movement to a lower density), or achieved, through an imposed external pressure.

The deposition fills the spaces between the fibres, forming a composite material in which the matrix is the deposited material.

This process is the most expensive, and can take several weeks, although leads to a very pure product. Isothermal CVI is the most widely used process. This involves using a large furnace and repeating the cycles of gas infiltration which can take up to 355 hours. This method is ideally suited to rocket nosecones, and rocket engine nozzles.

4. Chemical Vapour Deposition Processing.

The preformed carbon carbonate is shaped to the desired structure. Then densification of the composite begins by infiltration from pressurised hydrocarbon gases (for example, Methane or Propane).

The pressurisation of the gases is achieved in the range of 990 to 1210 degrees Centigrade. Gas is decomposed from deposition on the fibre surface. This process is dependent on the thickness of the preform. Heat treatment is continued until the modulus elasticity and strength is achieved. Modulus elasticity is also referred to the resistance to being deformed.

#

Jensen remembered from the talk given by Professor Jannat Rashied. She said, the nosecone on re-entry was designed to dissipate most of the thermal heat from space. So, the remainder of the missile would have different thermal protection with less heat dissipation.

The professor had explained that the thermal protection for these tiles would be made from silica fibres, with an epoxy resin, and then filled-into a fibreglass honeycomb. The fibreglass honeycomb would have been manufactured to fit snugly over the central tungsten rod core, fuel tank, rocket nozzle, gimbal, tailfins and onboard computer.

CHAPTER 28 - **Tokyo**

May 17th 10:00 a.m.

Jensen felt good to be back in modern Tokyo. He'd visited the city several times when working for Whitehall. Most of all, he liked the inbuilt discipline of the Japanese. The pavements and undergrounds were clean, and unlike many cities that he had visited in other parts of the world.

The disciplined training started at a young age. As children they are assigned duties for the upkeep of the schools, which included sweeping floors after lessons and even cleaning toilets before returning home. Most objects in the homes were meant to last a lifetime, so were given a spirit status, "Do not kick the table again dear as it hurts the table." He thought, that might be taking things a bit too far, but it still worked in their present-day ideology.

What he did not like was the work ethic, that led people to working extra-long hours in the evening, generally for no pay to please their bosses. Like Hong Kong, in Tokyo, most people could only afford to live in small rooms, so spent most of their time working extra hours, eating out, or being mentally forced into having to party with their bosses late into the evening. Internet cafés refugee, Manga café refugee or Cyber-homeless was another big problem. These are a class of homeless people who do menial work during the day for payment from as little as 1400 to 2400 yen, (about 8-14 pounds), in order to afford to sleep in internet booths during the night.

The latest trend through employing 'cute girls' to work outside the shops in order to coax customers into them, and having to work the girls all hours, was also a big safety concern, but clearly brought some income into their families.

Tokyo has six major districts:

1. The Shibuya District, which has the world-famous busiest road crossing,

and several thousand people can cross the road in about 30 seconds.

2. The Chiyoda District of former Tokyo City, in the eastern mainland. The central area of this district also contains the Imperial Palace.

3. The Chuo District, similar to Manhattan, with high rents and over the top coffee cup prices. It's also known for its shopping district Ginza.

4. The Minato District, which is famous for the nightlife and the famous Tokyo Tower. It's also known for Roppongi Hills. This is a large property development.

5. The Shinjuku District, known for its nightlife and entertainment district Kabukicho, where the locals go to hang-out in the evenings. Visitors from out of the city would find the last trains leaving at 12 o'clock. So, on weekends, most revellers stayed at the nightclubs which were open until 5 o'clock the following morning. This would be the

time that the new day's rail service would start-up again.

6. Finally, the Taito District, best known for its shrines and temples, but it also contained the National University of Fine Arts and Music, and the Ueno Gakuen University, which is a private university that specialises in music.

Jensen hired a Mazda 3 at the airport as he was aware of the overcrowding on the underground trains. He headed to his reserved room at the Shinagawa Prince Hotel, in the Minato district.

Fortunately, Japanese drivers also drove on the left side of the road. Jensen had an International Driving License, but if anyone planned to stay longer than a year, they would require a full Japanese license. The British would find it easier to get a full license if they already possessed a British one. People from other parts of the world would be expected to take a written exam.

After booking in and dropping his bags off in his room, Jensen left the hotel and went for a long walk. He had an appointment with a manager from Emperor Tiles the following day and had a lot to think about.

Tokyo is built near a fault line which cuts across Honshu (the main island of four), and runs north to south, just west of Tokyo. Minor tremors were not uncommon. The big tremors used to pull buildings down, but most buildings today in Tokyo are built out of concrete.

To make the buildings more attractive, colourful tiles are used as decorations on the outside of walls. It was a thriving industry.

Emperor Tiles did both the decorative and thermal insulating tiles. The Whitehall arranged visit for him, also included a tour of the factory.

Jensen also needed to see the despatch yard, to find out where the nosecones, nozzles and thermal protection tiles were heading?

Whitehall provided him with specifications for nosecones and rocket nozzles, which hopefully would impress the management at Emperor Tiles.

2:00 p.m.

Jensen went for a test drive to locate the tile manufacturer on the outskirts of the city. The journey took approximately 45 minutes. Satisfied that he could navigate through Tokyo's traffic and get to the meeting on time the following day, he returned to the Shinagawa Prince Hotel.

    Jensen parked the car in the hotel carpark and then went out for a further walk around the district. He walked through the Hamarikyu Gardens, a public park containing a medium sized lake. It was built around the site of a 17th-century Shogun villa.

    He walked past an ice-cream van and small shop selling hot food until he reached the marina. He was delighted to be looking across water again. Opposite on the far bank were many tall buildings, some of them skyscrapers.

    The temperature was about mid 60 degrees Fahrenheit and a light breeze was coming from the river. He passed the time by watching people fishing on a nearby riverbank, and spotted several camera enthusiasts taking photographs of tourist boats passing through to the Sumida River in the Northeast.

CHAPTER 29 - **Emperor Tiles**

May 18th 11:30 a.m.

At Emperor Tiles Jensen found the visitor's parking bay. He collected a briefcase from the boot of his Mazda and locked the car. On finding the Reception Room, he then walked over to the receptionist.

Jensen explained that he had an appointment and announced himself as the potential buyer working for the UK government. He was then asked to take a seat while Mr. Niko Mizushima attended a customer. He waited for twenty minutes until a man approached him.

"Good morning, Mr. Jensen, I'm Mr. Mizushima, would you come with me to my office please!"

Mr. Mizushima was slim built, about 5 foot 6 inches in height. He had greyish hair and looked to be in his late-fifties. He wore a Navy-Blue suit with matching tie. His face looked stern, but he raised the occasional smile while directing Jensen to his office.

On entering his room, he avoided his desk, which had business papers spread all over it. Instead, he requested that Jensen sit down on one of the two red leather chairs surrounding a small mahogany table. He walked over to a kettle, and asked if Jensen would like a cup of green tea to refresh himself. Jensen thanked him, and two cups were poured. Mr. Mizushima then put the two cups down on the table and sat in the opposite chair. Jensen remembered that Japanese tea was always served scalding hot, so would be careful.

Mr. Mizushima passed one cup to Jensen, leaving his own to cool down.

"Can I first ask you this question Mr. Jensen. Why does the British government have an interest in our thermal nosecones and rocket nozzles, when the American market would supply identical products in the same price range?"

Jensen picked up his cup and took a quick sip, then focused his memory on the articles he studied the night before.

"Since we have left the European Union, the UK government is striving to create new markets around the world. Trading with America will obviously bring benefits to both countries, but also trading within Asia has the potential to open far more doors."

"After all, did not Commodore Mathew Perry sail from America to Japan in 1853 to open up trade between the two great nations, leading to greater things!"

"Indeed Mr. Jensen, you might be aware that we celebrate Commodore Perry, in a three-day annual festival in May. It's called the 'Black Ship Day' and held in Shimoda City, about 1000 kilometres southwest of Tokyo."

Jensen added, "Yes, the festival commemorates his landing in 1853 on the 8th of July. The 'Black Ship Day' refers to the two steamships he brought with him, along with two sailing ships."

Mr. Mizushima smiled, "Ahh, you have done your homework Mr. Jensen. Do you have the specifications for your rocket nosecones and nozzles?"

"Yes," said Jensen. He opened his briefcase and then passed the specifications over to Mr. Mizushima.

"These are just the measurements for several types of missile nosecones and nozzles my government is interested in. Your company's part, is to inform us of the most economical way you can produce them. This information must be kept highly confidential by your company."

"Do you favour any processing method Mr. Jensen?"

Jensen recalled his notes, "The Americans use the Chemical Vapour Infiltration method. But this I understand requires a huge capital outlay. You're the experts, and I look forward to reading your recommendations."

"Quite so Mr. Jensen!" Mr. Mizushima smiled, "Mr. Jensen, we have the equipment to do the Chemical Vapour Infiltration method. We'll keep your specifications and recommendations highly confidential."

"I understand your government has requested that you would like to be taken on a tour of our facilities?"

"Yes Sir, that would be excellent."

"If you have a few hours to spare, I have arranged for a guide to show you around our facilities for making CCC products, and as a bonus we will also show you around our domestic tile facilities. Just in case the British government might want to brighten up the exteriors of their Whitehall offices?" "Ha-ha!" He laughed at his own joke.

"I could not think of a more interesting way to spend the afternoon!" said Jensen.

Mr. Mizushima smiled, allowed Jensen to finish his green tea, then escorted him back to the Reception Room.

12:30 p.m.

Jensen was introduced by the receptionist to the tour guide, Mrs. Sara Matsuo. She was slim and pretty, looked in her early-forties, and wearing a red and gold embraided dress. She was very eager to show him around the Carbon Carbon Composites manufacturing section. She informed him that Emperor Tiles was well equipped to handle the four main methods of making CCCs, but they first needed to put on safety equipment.

After an hour's tour, they met up with a group of business people from several countries, and were shown around the domestic tile manufacturing plant, beginning with the raw materials and ending with a multitude of the finished tile products.

Mrs. Matsuo then addressed the party, "Thank you for coming with me on our tour. I hope I've answered all your questions? Before we break for a meal and refreshment, is there anything I have not covered?"

This was Jensen's chance. "Mrs. Matsuo, how do you manage to organise the transportation of your products to many parts of the world?"

"Mr. Jensen, as you would expect from Emperor Tiles, the process is all highly automated. I can show you around our dispatch bays. This will not take up much of our time."

The party then left the tile finishing section and headed to the dispatch bays.

They were led to, and then taken inside a huge warehouse building. Inside automated carriers were busy lifting orders from holding shelves, and then moving them into dispatch bays. They were then shown around the computer department, that was organizing and controlling the dispatches.

On leaving the department, Jensen turned to Mrs. Matsuo.

"Mrs. Matsuo, how do you ship the CCC products?"

"Ahh, the products for the Japanese and Taiwanese Space Programs. They are in the next warehouse; I think there's just enough time to show you all around."

Ten minutes later, they were shown around a smaller warehouse stacked with metal crates. To Jensen, some of the crates looked about fourteen feet in length, while others were smaller, about ten feet in length. Jensen observed the crates were stacked in three locations:

In the first location, they were clearly labelled for the Space Centre at Tanegashima JAXA (Japan Aerospace Exploration Agency). Jensen knew this site was originally established in 1969 from three space institutions, and was now in the hands of JAXA.

There are two space centres, one located at Tsukuba Science City in Ibaraki; the other is located on the Southeastern coast of Tanegashima, an island approximately 25 miles south of Kyushu. Which itself is an island off the west mainland.

In the second location the crates were addressed to Advanced Rocket Research Center (ARRC), National Chiao Tung University, Taiwan.

In the third location the crates were just addressed to Airforce Research Division.

After showing everyone around the dispatch bay, Mrs. Matsuo checked her watch and realised it was time to take the party back to the Reception Room. She was aware that one member of her group was missing. She thought possibly it was a call of nature as they had passed a toilet block earlier, or he might be caught up in a conversation with an employee.

Jensen had spotted a toilet block in the warehouse and thought it a perfect excuse to slip the party. When they walked out of sight, he looked around for any cameras. On not spotting any, he found a crowbar and opened up one of the crates destined for JAXA.

The 10-foot crate contained two small rocket nozzles. The nozzles were too small to power a large spacecraft into orbit but big enough to fit into the rear end of the missile that sunk the Bluebell. He then closed the crate and tried another. The crate contained the same nozzle types as the previous crate, so he closed it up again.

The sound of an automated mobile stacker heading his way forced Jensen to made himself scarce and to hide behind a stack of crates. The mobile stacker went over to the JAXA crate that he had just closed. The mobile stacker made off with it to the loading bay No. 2 drop-off point, and gently unloaded it there.

On returning from stacking the crate, the mobile stacker moved to the crates labelled Airforce Research Division. It read the barcode, picked up the larger 14-foot crate and transferred it to loading bay No. 3. It then returned and found another crate with the same destination barcode and picked it up.

As the mobile stacker travelled away from the crates to loading bay No. 3. Jensen walked over to examine the barcodes on several of the remaining crates. Above the barcodes in very fine print was an address, they were destined for the Okinawa, MCAS Futenma,

Airborne Division 25th Wing Unit. He had to see inside one of those crates.

Jensen opened a crate and swiftly removed the artificial fibrous straw. He found a recognizable nosecone and three thermal heat protection tile surrounds. He realised a four-foot tungsten bar would fit comfortably inside. Removing more fibrous straw, Jensen uncovered six tiled tailfins with flaps, and two small rocket nozzles. He heard the transporter returning, so quickly closed the crate, and then hid out of sight.

Okinawa island was in Japan's southernmost island chain, which stretched for over 600 miles. Jensen knew that the southernmost part of the main island was heavily populated, and the US maintained a heavy presence there. There were large docks and two US airbases on the island. Also, it was about 500 miles from Taiwan, which also was to be his next port of call.

The mobile stacker returned to the JAXA crate area and selected another one, it then picked it up and moved off. When it was out of sight, Jensen left the warehouse and headed for the Reception Room.

At the Reception Room desk Jensen was then directed to the dining area. Mrs. Matsuo looked up and put on a false smile as he entered the room.

Jensen spoke his rehearsed lines, "I'm very sorry, but I needed to visit the Gents. When I returned you had all gone, so I headed back, but unfortunately, I got a little lost."

Mrs. Matsuo did not believe one word of his account, but gave a pleasant smile."

"I'm happy you're in one-piece Mr. Jensen; factories can be very dangerous places if you do not know the territory!"

The group was given a 5-star lunch. Final pleasantries consisted of a short talk from Mr. Mizushima and a gift of pens from Mrs. Matsuo.

In the Reception Room, and before departure, the business-men and women were given the opportunity to arrange further meetings with managers. Jensen had his meeting earlier, so he said his farewells and left.

When all the business people had left, Mrs. Matsuo went to Mr. Mizushima's office. On looking through the glass panelling around his office, and seeing that he was not occupied with anyone, she knocked three times and entered the room.

Mr. Mizushima looked up.

"How did it go Sara?"

"It went as well and as successful as last week's group. But we need to check all our camera recordings in the warehouses! One member arrived later at the dining area, and claimed he got lost, but eventually found the Reception Room."

"Ahhh Yes! That would no doubt be Mr. Jensen!"

"Correct!"

7:30 p.m.

The rain was drizzling against the windows in Jensen's hotel room, but he needed to get some exercise, so decided on an evening walk.

Earlier, following his visit to Emperor Tiles, he had visited the British Embassy to update them. Since the discovery of the spacecraft, all UK embassies in Europe and Asia had some of their departments working 24/7 on trying to identify people which either had the wealth or knowledge that might be associated with the enterprise.

This time he armed himself with a pistol given to him earlier at the embassy, as he did not want to take any unnecessary chances on his last evening in Tokyo. He thought that if he was followed that evening, he still would be relatively safe. He could rely on his cover story of possibly placing orders for the UK government. Money talked!

Jensen had checked earlier for any news from Roger in Cyprus and Rebekah in Trondheim. Roger was still in pursuit of Harald and Alekos, Rebekah had been luckier and found a financial connection between Harald in Trondheim, a man named Svein Thorsen and a woman called Anne Westrum.

During 2015 and 2016 Svein and Anne, had both bought villas and development land in the Seychelles. She had traced their transactions from the same Seychelles fund that was linked to Harald. It was beginning to smell!

Jensen walked again through the Hamarikyu Gardens, past the ice-cream van, now closed, but the small shop was still selling hot food. This time, there were nobody fishing on either side of the river bank, or any amateur camera enthusiasts. He relaxed and walked over to the river bank and for a while watched the small tourist boats passing.

In his late twenties, Jensen had enjoyed the Tokyo nightlife. He wondered whether the nightclubs he had visited were still there, or had they been knocked down now and replaced with something more outrageous, such as the insane Robot Restaurant in the Shinjuku district.

He knew that after a few drinks the Japanese youth were not the stiff shirts as most westerners thought! They let their hair down and had fun weekends dancing to pop music, as most did in the cities around the world.

Jensen headed back to the centre. He was determined to visit Tokyo Tower once again before he left the city. On realising he would be searched at the tower, he decided to risk-it and dropped off his pistol in his hotel room. He then walked on towards the big red tower.

Tokyo Tower was Japan's answer to the Eiffel Tower. It was 1092 feet in height, and the second largest tower to Tokyo's Skytree Tower. Skytree Tower stood 2080 feet in height, which is one of the tallest towers in the world, and built in 2010. Tokyo Tower was older, and built in 1958. There were two observation decks, the Main Deck at 490 feet, and the Top Deck at 820 feet.

Jensen found a restaurant at the foot of the building. It was called the 'Terrace Dining TANGO'. It was an Italian restaurant which mixed food from the homeland with Japanese food.

After a quick meal he went to the foot of the tower and bought himself a 1,200 Yen ticket for the Main Deck, which he knew was around seven to eight English pounds. If he had the time, he would have taken the stairways. However, at 600 steps, it would have taken a good hour to reach the floor, which he did not have the energy for, so took the lift instead.

The observation platform on the Main Deck was about 15 feet wide, which encircled the tower. There was an inner platform area which contained a lift, a small shop, a restaurant and a stand. The stand and two seats were placed in front of a brilliantly lit miniature Tokyo Tower. It was there for you and your loved one to be seated in, and to have your pictures taken.

The Main Deck also contained Club 333. When open from 5 p.m. to 7 p.m., this was where you would be entertained with local singers and comedians.

The walk-around platform provided magnificent 360-degree views of Tokyo. These views were spectacular by day, but much more intense at night as the whole city was lit up by a multitude of neon lights.

On one side of the platform, which looked out to views of Shiodome, a mile away, and Ginza, a mile and a quarter away, he discovered very thick see-through glass panels, that were built into the floor. They allowed brave sightseers to stand on them to view directly below. Jensen walked around the platform several times. He thought that he might regret it if he did not step on one of the glass panels, so finally, he did. Indeed, flying in an aircraft was one thing, but this he found nerve-racking.

A man walked right up to Jensen. The man was positioned just behind a pathway that Jensen was standing in. The pathway was closed-off by several three-foot silver posts, and a two-inch red belt, that connected through the tops of the posts.

"That's quite a spectacular view, is it not, Mr. Jensen?"

Jensen looked up at the spectacled Japanese man. He was wearing a raincoat, and holding a rolled-up umbrella. Its tip was firmly placed on the edge of the glass panel that he was standing on. He had seen similar umbrella-like devices before. They usually concealed a deadly mechanism hidden inside it. He loosened his jacket if he needed to grab the umbrella from the man.

"And, who are you? I know that umbrella is also a firearm, with enough power to bring down a Grizzly Bear, and easily enough power to shatter the glass that I'm standing on."

"My name is Mr. Riku Kato, I work in security for the Japanese government." He pointed to the restaurant. "Can we talk over there please?"

Jensen slowly moved off the glass panel and walked over to a free table at the restaurant and sat down.

Mr Kato then went over to the counter and ordered two drinks.

He returned to the table, "I hope you do not mind, but I've ordered two coffees."

Mr. Kato spoke in a quiet tone. "I'm aware that you are working for the British government, but you have also been reported as conducting a little private enterprise?"

Jensen looked bemused, "Can you expand a little on that?"

"Emperor Tiles reported to us this afternoon that you were seen on camera examining several crates that were destined for the American Airbase in Okinawa."

"Mr. Jensen, Emperor Tiles are a powerful company! I suspect that the only fact that has ensured your safety so far, is because you are working for the British government."

Jensen was unsure of what this man knew and whether to trust him.

Jensen lowered his voice, "Mr. Kato, do you have any ID on you?"

Mr. Kato then opened up his wallet to show a government security ID. Jensen hoped that it was the genuine article.

"Do you have transport?" said Jensen.

"Yes, I have my car parked nearby."

"Mr. Kato, I'm hoping to be travelling to Taiwan tomorrow, but I think your department needs to be informed of what I believe is happening. One or several members of your many security departments might already be aware of it, but have been told not to divulge any information for now?"

"Will you come with me to the British Embassy in Chiyoda City? They will prove to you that I've not been moonlighting on the job and the situation is far more serious than you might have suspected."

"I also need to go back to my hotel first to retrieve an item and drop it off at the embassy!"

Two coffees arrived at the table. Mr. Kato smiled, and thanked the waitress, then picked up a cup and raised a further smile. "This will be a lovely change from drinking green tea all day. Mr. Jensen we can leave shortly."

CHAPTER 25 - **Blast-off**

May 12th 12:30 p.m.

Seven hundred and forty-five miles off the Antarctic coast, a huge transporter ship came to a stop. The Seven Seas Adventurer had originally been designed for the transportation of brand-new cars for dealers around the world. However, the ship's interior had been completely redesigned to equip something vastly bigger.

The ship's location was well off the shipping lanes. It dropped anchor 12 miles offshore from Macquarie Island.

The island was 21 miles long and 3 miles wide, and located in the Southern Western Pacific Ocean.

Macquarie island was 932 miles south-east of Tasmania, and part of that state. The territory belonged to Australia. It rarely had any human inhabitants. It was however a haven for penguins, seals and walruses.

Twenty minutes passed, then the bow doors of the great ship started to open. Seawater was pumped into tanks near the bow, lowering the bow by 10 feet and giving rise to the stern. The engineered dip, made it easier to eject its core craft.

A large jet-black craft slowly came out from the bow. The craft was horizontally loaded on the top of a floating platform. It took another 40 minutes for the platform to disengage from the ship. The great ship then slowly returned to its normal horizontal position, as seawater was pumped out of its bow tanks, and the bow doors slowly closed.

The ship then restarted its engines and withdrew to a quarter of a mile from the platform. A large motor at the rear of the platform was then activated and slowly started to pump seawater into a vast rear compartment.

The compartment served as a counterweight for the craft. As the seawater was pumped into it, the craft began to rise from its horizontal position to the vertical.

It took a further hour for the craft to come to the vertical position.

A tender with four engineers onboard was then lowered over the side of the ship and sent to the platform. The engineers spent an hour on the platform performing pre-launch flight checks before returning to the ship.

6:00 p.m.

Several loudspeakers positioned around the ship, spang to life. "All crew, All crew, with the exception of launch personnel, you have permission to leave your stations and come to the upper decks to view the launch."

The night air was cold and crisp, energizing and refreshing. As the crew waited for everyone to assemble for the launch, many passed the time by looking up at the night sky.

The moon was three quarters full and glistening in the northeast. The spacecraft and platform were just visible by the moonlight, but as a cloud passed the moon, it was blacked out from view. The spacecraft and platform slowly drifted away from the ship.

Above the spacecraft the constellation of Orion was just visible, but from the latitude looked as if it was drooping to about 65 degrees, with the sword pointing to the sea and horizon.

Rigel the seventh brightest star and a binary star, along with Betelgeuse, were dominant in the night sky. The belt consisted of three smaller stars, Mintaka, Alnilam and Alnitak, which pointed to another binary star, Sirius. Sirius the brightest star in the night sky, formed the bottom end of the constellation of Canis Major (the Greater Dog).

Further to the east and above Orion was the constellation of Monoceros (the Unicorn). Further again to the east was Canis Minor (the Lesser Dog) with its dominant star Procyon, which is the eight brightest star in the night sky. Procyon is a binary star, the main star Procyon A, with a faint white dwarf companion Procyon B, that would not be visible in the night sky except by the use of binoculars.

After fifteen minutes passed, the loudspeakers sprang to life again.

"Attention! Countdown is about to start! Attention! Countdown is about to start!" Fifteen seconds of silence passed, then:

"10…9…8…7…6…5…4…3…2…1, Blast-Off!"

A blast of blue and yellow flame surged from the spacecraft engines. The salty smell of the sea-air was replaced by the taste of vapourised liquid fuel, then followed by intense noise, and heat. The spacecraft slowly started to rise from its platform, followed by a gigantic roar of its engines as they reached full power and radiated intense heat. Cheers of approval and clapping of hands sprung from the crew.

The spacecraft shot out multicoloured flames and smoke as it picked up momentum. A minute later only a small flame could be seen as it streaked into the lower atmosphere. The first stage separation went as planned, and the final stage fired. The first stage fell back to Earth, and its engines reignited again to enable it to make a perfect landing on the launch platform. The spacecraft controllers onboard the ship, monitored the flight throughout a 30-minute period, whereby it reached a set altitude of 22,230 miles.

The loudspeakers came back to life. "Main engines cut-off. Spacecraft in geostationary orbit!"

Everyone onboard was quiet. Then a minute later the loudspeakers came back to life again.

"Navigational engines now fired. Spacecraft heading to specified location."

The crew cheered and clapped in celebration. Onboard were representatives from South Korea, Taiwan, Vietnam, Japan, India, Indonesia and Australia.

After the cheering died down the loudspeakers came back to life.

"Main crew, now return to your duties. Recovery launch platform crew, proceed to assigned tasks."

Several minutes later the ship's engines were started up and the ship slowly approached the launch platform. The ship's engines then shut down and a reverse operation began to recover the platform and the recovered spacecraft's first stage.

The bow doors began to open and sink at a downward elevation as the stern began to rise. A tender with four engineers onboard was then lowered over the side of the ship and sent to the platform. The engineers onboard secured the first stage, and then activated several motors to drain the seawater tank compartment.

After 40 minutes the launch platform container was drained of seawater. It had returned to its vertical position, and the recovered first stage, had returned to its original horizontal position. Onboard the platform propellers guided by radio control, brought it near to the front of the ship and the open bow.

The engineers on the tender then attached mooring lines to the platform. Once the platform and rocket stage were secured and winched inside the ship, the bow doors closed. Seawater was pumped out of the bow tanks, and the ship slowly returned to its correct horizontal elevation. After passing all safety checks, the ship started up its engines again, and then headed to warmer latitudes.

#

9:30 p.m.

Jensen was in his hotel bedroom at The Marriot Hotel at St. Julian's, where Roger was also staying. He was reading through his report for the 11th of May when his mobile phone rang.

"Hello, David Jensen."

"Hi David, it's Roger. Lucy has just phoned. She's been contacted by the CIA. Another spacecraft launch has occurred!"

"Can you describe what happened?" said Jensen.

"Two of their spy satellites recorded unusual heat trails heading for space just outside the Antarctic. The spacecraft that they originally discovered was coated in some type of radar evading stealth paint, so it's probably a second launch of the same spacecraft design."

Jensen interjected, "You can bet that it's no longer in that orbit! OK, do we have any more details on the sinking of the Bluebell?"

"Sorry, there's no update from Whitehall on the Bluebell. I'm staying on in Malta for a couple of weeks to help the police here. They have people searching for Harald at the airports and harbours. Harald's proved to be a tricky devil! We are also interviewing people who we detained at his villa."

"Good luck with that one, Roger!" said Jensen, laughing and sensing the reluctance of these people to provide any information on their millionaire employer.

"So, it looks like Alexandria is my next port of call, literally!"

"Roger, if you haven't eaten yet, I'll see you down in the hotel restaurant in fifteen minutes?"

"I'll be there," said Roger.

CHAPTER 30 - **Taiwan and Taipei**

May 19th 2:30 p.m.

The flight to Taipei with China Airlines left Tokyo at 9:25 a.m., and arrived three hours forty-five minutes later.

Jensen had booked into the Regent Hotel. It is located on the eastern side of the Tamsui River. He took a taxi from the airport to the hotel, found his room and put his luggage away. He then sat back to relax, and to light sleep for several hours in a comfortable blue armchair in his room.

Later he reflected on the meeting with Mr. Kato at the British Embassy. Mr. Kato was indeed unaware what the British and US intelligence services had uncovered, but gave him permission to travel to Taipei provided he kept him updated on any development.

#

Jensen had never been to Taiwan before. So, he relied on background information provided by Whitehall, Wikipedia and YouTube videos. He was relieved to discover, that unlike Japan, most people in Taiwan spoke English.

One comment from watching a YouTube video amused him, the narrator explained that he was British and currently teaching English in Taipei. The narrator explained that bartering for goods was common in Taiwan. He said that locals will eventually get ripped-off by the deal, but foreigners will get more ripped off than the locals. Jensen raised a smile, as he had heard similar stories from many parts of the World.

Taiwan's recent history had been turbulent. After WWII ended, a power struggle continued between Director-general Chiang Kai-shek, and Chairman Mao Zedong. Chiang Kai-shek led the Kuomintang Party (KMT), in the then Republic of China (ROC). The opposition leader Chairman Mao Zedong, was the leader of the Chinese Communist Party (CCP).

The ROC, weakened from fighting in the Second Sino-Japanese War (1937-1945), throughout 1949 faced a series of CCP advances. This led to the retreat of the ROC and the setting up of the People's Republic of China on the 1st of October. Chiang Kai-shek fled with his people to Taiwan and made Taipei the temporary capital.

After fleeing, over two million people from the mainland consisting of military, intellectuals and business people were added to the six million population of Taiwan. This created friction with those brought up on the island.

To retain order, the KMT imposed martial law on the island population in May 1945. The martial law continued up until 1987. No serious political opposition could be created over this period. In all, more than 140,000 people were imprisoned, or executed for assumed anti-government or pro-Communist behaviour. Even pro-democracy demonstrations were put-down during this time.

When Chiang Kai-shek died on April 5th, 1975, his son Chiang Ching-Kuo took over and began democratic reforms until his death on January 13th, 1988. Lee Teng-hui born in Taiwan, and was Chiang Ching-

Kuo chosen successor. He became Taiwan's first president, after Chiang Ching-Kuo's death, and took over the political reforms. In 1996, he was the first to be democratically elected as President of Taiwan and considered to be the 'father of democracy'. He died on 30th, July 2020.

In May 2016, the Democratic Progressive Party (DPP) won victories that enabled the KMT to lose its legislative history, for the first time. Tsai lng-Wen of the DPP, became the first female president of Taiwan and was re-elected in 2020.

#

Taiwan's capital city was a magnificent sight, and dominated by the Taipei 101 Tower, which has 101 floors above ground and five basement floors. The lowest above ground floors house a luxury atrium shopping mall. Most of the space above the mall are devoted to offices. Above ground, it resembled a huge bamboo structure made out of glass, with eight large blocks. Each block sloped inward to its base. Each block had eight floors, eight was a lucky number in Taiwan.

The tower contains many businesses that deal in banking, finance, communication, motorcars, and restaurants. It also contains several observation decks and a gym. Most people can visit the observatories on floors 88 to 91. There are two indoor observatories on floors 88 and 89. Floor 91 is an outdoor observatory.

Like Tokyo Tower it also contained a club. The top floor on level 101 is a VIP club named Summit 101. However, this club was generally open to celebrities, but ordinary people can also access the club if they spend more than one million Taiwanese dollars shopping in the Taipei 101 Mall, at the base of the tower. This is equivalent to £24,936 or $35,677. As gratitude to these people, Summit 101 provided spectacular views of Taipei.

Taipei 101 had sixty-one lifts; some take you up to floors where to get to higher levels, you have to exchange lifts. However, there are two lifts on the 5th floor, which take you directly to the top observation tower within 37 seconds. The whole building stands at 1,667 feet in height, including the spire, and was the world's tallest building until 2010, when it was superseded by the Burj Khalifa in Dubai, which now stands at 2,717 feet.

Taipei 101 was earthquake proof, and had a massive metal ball which was painted yellow and suspended from its highest floors. The metal ball is used as a vibration dampener to counter any movement of the building in a typhoon or an earthquake. The ball is open to view by the public. There're are 2,046 steps from the ground floor to the 89th floor observatory deck. These steps inspired the annual marathon to the top.

Taipei had many other attractions, notably the Chiang Kai-shek Memorial, the National Palace Museum, the Zhongshan Hall, where the Japanese surrender ceremony was held in October 1945. There were also Confucius and Yinshan Temples, and the Botanical Gardens.

Jensen went for an afternoon walk through the local Kangle and Linsen Parks. As he met the evening rush hour at 6 p.m., he was immediately aware that Taipei was a scooter city. Later that evening, realising that he was about three miles from the Taipei 101 Tower, he decided to flag down a taxi and visit the site for an evening meal, and later pay the TND $600 admission fee, this was about £16 to go to the top 89th indoor observation deck.

CHAPTER 31 - **Wolfram Wire Ltd**

May 21st 9:00 a.m.

Jensen arrived at the factory, which was located Northwest of Taipei. The journey took about a 10-minute ride in a super train, and a further 10-minute ride in a taxi to get to the factory gates. Whitehall had arranged his visit and a tour of the plant. He was to join a party for potential international buyers.

There was no initial meeting with a manager this time though. At the Reception Desk Jensen was introduced to a party of four, three men and a woman. The guide introduced himself as Mr. Lee Niuu.

As Jensen anticipated, Mr. Niuu informed the group that the tungsten ore had already been processed into powder by another firm, which was located in South Vietnam. This made sense, as there were ample supplies of the wolframite ore there. Nui Phao in the Thai Ngugen province was about to become the second largest tungsten mine in the world.

An Austrian company Hazel Resources, had its ferrotungsten plant located there and already in production. Another company which was based in Munich, H.C. Starck, the world's leader in technology metals, was also building a tungsten chemical plant in South Vietnam.

Mr. Niuu explained that ores are crushed and roasted or processed through a variety of chemical reactions, precipitations and washings. This process produced ammonium paratungstate (ATP). This is then sold, or processed further to produce tungsten oxide. This oxide could be further roasted in a hydrogen atmosphere to create a pure tungsten powder.

They put on safety equipment, then Mr. Niuu then took the party around the six stages of production at Wolfram Wire Ltd. The normal end product was Tungsten wire, which is used throughout the world for filaments in light bulbs.

The six stages of production consisted of:

1. Pressing.

The powder was sifted, mixed, and a binder added. The powder was then weighed and loaded into a mould, and then further loaded into a press. The mould could be of various sizes. The powder was then compacted into a bar. But in this state, it's in a fragile condition. The mould was then removed, leaving the bar.

2. Presintering.

The bar was placed into a metal boat and loaded into a furnace with a hydrogen atmosphere. The high temperature consolidates the material together, reducing it to 60-70% of full density.

3. Full Sintering.

The bar was placed in a special water-cooled treating bottle. An electric current was then applied to the bar generating heat. The heat caused the bar to densify about 85% to 95% of full density and to shrink about 15%, and a rod of six inches in length and a diameter of up to 1.250 inches (depending on the order).

4. Swagging.

The rod was reheated between 1200-1500 Centigrade and passed through a swagger. The swagger applies hammer blows to the rod in the region of 10,000 blows a minute, reducing the diameter by a further 12% on each pass. This continues until the rod was reduced to between 0.25 and 0.10 inches.

5. Drawing.

The rod was then passed through dies of tungsten carbide or diamonds to reduce it to a specified diameter. This can be as fine as 0.0005 inches.

6. Wrapping.

Finally, the wire was wrapped around spools of various lengths. The cost of a spool was dependent on the order containing the diameter and length of the wire. Prices ranged from TND 460 ($125) spools, to the top range costing TND 463500 ($150,000) per spool.

After the tour the party was introduced to managers for potential talks over bulk purchases of spools, that ranged from 0.01 to 0.0005 inches in diameter.

Jensen did not stay long. He made an excuse that he had another appointment that afternoon and that he would be in touch later. He did not have the time to establish whether the six-inch rods produced at the end of the Presintering Stage, were being sold on, or welded together at the factory to produce the four-foot rods, and then sold separately. He recognised the same parts and that was sufficient.

2:30 p.m.

When Jensen returned to the Regent Hotel, he telephoned Whitehall. He knew the Taiwanese government would be contacted shortly after. Further diplomacy would be in the hands of the UK government. If the Taiwanese government already knew what he suspected, then there would be urgent communications between the two governments. Otherwise, if the Taiwanese government were unaware of the situation, then all factories in Taiwan dealing in tungsten ore, would have to be visited by the Taiwanese government Inspectors, to crackdown on any illegal resale of six-inch tungsten rods.

#

Jensen's next move was to pay a visit to the US Airbase Airborne 25th Wing Unit. He spent the next two hours researching Okinawa Island.

Okinawa was one of several islands off the Southwest coast of Japan. It had a subtropical climate, with sunshine most of the year. Today, there were over

30 American bases stationed on the island. They were there to show an American presence, and to counter any communist threat from mainland China.

The reason for the American presence dated from WWII, resulting from a major battle in the Pacific that was fought on the island and surrounding sea. The battle, was between the American Allies and the Japanese.

The Americans landed on the 1st of April 1945, and were only met with minor resistance. However, a 98-day battle followed from the 26th of March until the 2nd of July. The strategic importance of the island was that the Allies had originally planned to use the airfield at Kadena, to mount an invasion on the mainland 340 miles away.

At that time, sections of the Japanese Army based on the island were ordered to return to the mainland to defend it in what was anticipated to be the coming invasion. So, to defend the island all local men, women and boys of 14, or older, were conscripted and given orders to fight to the death. Many of the locals did not possess military weapons, so had to make them out of sharpened bamboo sticks.

At sea the Japanese Navy and Airforce were outnumbered by the Allies, which led to Japanese officers being ordered to sacrifice their lives for their country. Consequently, Kamikaze pilots would crash their aircraft into the wooden decks of the American aircraft carriers, damaging and sinking several of them.

The Japanese Navy had officer's willing to man miniature submarines and speed boats loaded with explosives, and would ram the American and Allied Battleships, taking many lives. The Japanese troops were reluctant to surrender in the last few months of the war, preferring to fight on until death. That greatly troubled the Allies!

On land the Japanese resorted to guerrilla tactics, hiding in caves by day, and killing by night. So, tanks equipped with flame-throwers were used to destroy any last resistance. This left many mental scars with survivors who had witnessed their colleagues being burnt alive, and ending in a dreadful death. The 98-day battle was thought of as 'living through a *Hell on Earth*'.

At the end of the battle, it was estimated that 95,000 Imperial Japanese troops and over 20,000 Americans were killed. This led to the construction of a memorial stone in Okinawa, named 'The Corner Stone of Peace'.

The memorial stone, located at the Peace Memorial Park in Itoman City, lists over 149,000 persons from Okinawa, that were killed. A quarter of the civilian population of the island, were either killed, or took their own lives, or died in the Pacific War. The stone list all the names of those who were killed in the Okinawa battle. As of June 2021, 241,632 names are engraved on the memorial.

One study by William Shockley (an American scientist), for Henry Stimson an American statesman, calculated that if the Allies invaded, the war would last another 18 months and there were several estimates for casualties. One estimate would result in between 1.7 to 4 million American casualties, with 5 to 10 million Japanese casualties. It was this alarming figure that made the Americans rethink their plan to invade the Japanese mainland. In the end they decided that to drop the atomic bombs on Hiroshima on the 6th of August, and Nagasaki on the 9th of August, would result in fewer Allied deaths. The bombs would however kill between 129,000 and 226,000 Japanese.

#

4:30 p.m.

It then dawned on Jensen that Cheryl would have reported to her masters on what had happened to the

Bluebell. He wondered how far behind the CCP would be? Jensen took out his mobile, contacted Whitehall and requested to continue the conversation through a scrambled line. He asked them to check on the Bab Sharq Police Department and Emperor Tiles.

Whitehall recontacted him thirty minutes later. The phone call proved his fears. He was informed the computers in the Bab Sharq Police Department in Alexandria, and Emperor Tiles in Tokyo had been hacked. The hacking had been traced back to the Ministry of State Security (MSS), a CCP Intelligence Unit based in Beijing.

He was further informed that following tensions in 2013, there were competing claims by the Peoples Republic of China on the mostly uninhabited Senkatu Islands, which are to the west of Okinawa Island. However, the Peoples Republic of China also laid claims to Okinawa.

He had to visit the MCAS Airborne Division 25th Wing Unit and find out how great was their involvement in the missile and spacecraft operation, and whether millionaires, or governments were involved in this black project? He had to put a stop to it before Okinawa would become under attack from an enemy and became '*Hell on Earth*' again, or was the island just another link in a very long chain?

CHAPTER 32 - **Okinawa**

May 23rd 9:30 a.m.

It had been a short one-and-a-half-hour flight to Okinawa Naha Airport from Taipei. Naha, was Japan's busiest airport. From the airport, flight schedules run to Hong Kong, South Korea, Thailand, Singapore, mainland China, and of course back to Taiwan. Jensen spent most of the flight completing his research on the island.

Okinawa Island is approximately 66 miles long and on average seven miles wide. It covers a land mass of 466 square miles. The island is 400 miles south off the main island of Kyushu and the remainder of Japan, and 300 miles northeast of Taiwan.

Okinawa has a sub-tropical climate, with a population in the region of 1,400,000. The area surrounding Naha has a population of roughly 800,000 residents, while Naha City has a population in the region of 320,000 inhabitants. As a consequence of the Battle of Okinawa during WWII, the island hosts 26,000 US military personnel. These people are contained in 32 bases and 48 training sites accounting for 15% of land area.

There are two US air force basis on the island, the Kadena Air Base and the Marine Corps Air Station (MCAS) Futenma, at Ginowan. The Japanese government pays large amounts of compensation to the island residents due to the environmental impacts of the bases.

Environmental impacts include noise and chemical pollution, and health issues resulting from aircraft accidents and forest fires caused by live ammunition exercises. This has also led to soil erosion and earth tremors on the island. The existence of the US bases constituted an obstacle to economic development in the island. However, the Japanese government was prepared to put up with these obstacles than leave itself vulnerable to any potential attack from its neighbour China, and any threats from North Korea.

Today the Kadena Air Base, is a United States Air Force base and home to the USAF 18th Wing, the 353rd Special Operations Group, reconnaissance units, 1st Battalion, 1st Air Defence Artillery and many other associated units. Nearly 18,000 American servicemen, family members and 4000 Japanese employees and contractors work, or live at the base. Besides the airbase there are over 30 other USA bases spread over the island.

The MCAS is part of the Marine Corps Installations Pacific command. The base includes an 8990-foot runway by a 148-foot width. It is home to approximately 3,000 Marines of the 1st Marine Aircraft Wing and other units. The air station operated a variety of fixed wing and tilt rotor aircraft.

#

The missile crates at Emperor Tiles were addressed to the MCAS airbase, Airborne Division 25th Wing Unit. Whitehall informed Jensen that a Lieutenant general Richard Maximilian oversaw the 20th to 25th Wing Units.

Maximilian's rank contained three stars, and required being nominated by the President followed by a majority vote of the Senate.

Maximilian was 58 years of age and had joined the air force when he was 21. He had graduated from the Massachusetts Institute of Technology.

Jensen hired a Toyota Corolla at Naha Airport and headed down the 332-motorway until it connected to the 58-motorway, which headed towards Ginowan. He left the motorway and turned right at the Oyama junction, which was next to a YAMAHA motorcycle shop, where the Pipe Line Road began. He followed the road for a third of a mile to the MCAS Futenma Main Gate. The roads along his journey were a little busy but he managed the ten-miles in about 25 minutes. After showing his credentials at the Main Gate he was directed to a car parking area.

After parking his car, Jensen was escorted by a security guard to the Admissions Office. There he was told to look up at a camera, then photographed. He was then questioned by a male personnel. When the man's questioning stopped, some thirty minutes had passed.

Jensen was then introduced to Captain Alex Harris, and then led away with him. He passed through a further security gate that required him to enter a four-digit code that was given to him in the Admissions Office.

Jensen was then led to an office door that required a further four-digit code from Captain Harris to open it. It led to a very unspectacular office which just contained a wooden table and three chairs.

Sat down on the furthest chair was Lieutenant general Maximilian. His uniform jacket hung around the back of his chair. He had a similar slim athletic build to the Defence Secretary Peter Mathews back in Whitehall. He wore steel rimmed spectacles, through which penetrating dark brown eyes stared back at Jensen.

"Sit down Inspector Jensen. Alex, I want you here too, please sit down!"

"Your credentials have been verified Inspector, now, what do you want from me?"

Jensen observed Maximilian looked at ease, as if far too relaxed.

"Are you aware that CCC missile nosecones and jet thrusters are being delivered secretly to your 25th Wing Unit?"

Maximilian gave an amused look and laughed. "Inspector Jensen, you're in the middle of a military airbase, what else did you expect?"

"CCCs from a commercial company, Emperor Tiles, based in the outskirts of Tokyo?"

The smile on Maximilian's face slowly disappeared. He then turned to Alex and gave him a look as if to confirm the statement.

Captain Harris gave a strained look of bewilderment, "We receive deliveries from many countries, Sir, but that's unusual for a missile nosecone, as we would normally use an American defence contractor. I'll look into it!"

"Then do it quickly and discreetly!" said Jensen. "In all likelihood you have a rogue unit in your division."

"Whitehall and I also believe there's a military unit, most likely consisting of mercenaries working for the CCP, and they're on their way here to locate and destroy these missile parts! They will tear this airbase apart to get at the weapons!"

"How come?" said Maximilian.

"It's a long story, I'll put you in the picture now!"

"Doctor Cheryl Brenton, a researcher, working at Gene Solar Ltd. based in Swindon UK, stole 12 specialised computer chips from the company."

"She later used the chips to unscramble spy satellite data. She was working from a super-yacht, that was anchored 15 miles offshore from Alexandria, Egypt."

"However, on the next mission, offshore again from Alexandria, a spacecraft controlled by an unknown organisation, deployed a missile that destroyed the super-yacht. I was onboard the yacht at the time the missile hit it. As the yacht sank, a British M I 6 agent and I managed to capture her. She was originally sent to Bronzefield prison awaiting trial; but being a decryption specialist, I put her to work in Cheltenham with a team tasked with deciphering encrypted files from a criminal organisation, for GCHQ."

"This unknown organisation has no nationality, but appears to have connections throughout Southeast Asia. The CCP have hacked the computers in the Bab

Sharq Police Department in Alexandria and Emperor Tiles in Tokyo, and discovered that unauthorised missile parts are being delivered to the 25th Wing Unit on this base, for this organisation."

Maximilian rose from his chair and looked in anger at Jensen. "That woman is more trouble than she's worth! You should have left her to rot at Bronzefield Prison!"

Jensen felt the earbashing, but said nothing.

Maximilian then picked up a phone and ordered that security on the island should be stepped up on all bases, the civil airport and ports. He then turned to Captain Harris.

"Alex, put tracking devices in all crates in the 25th Wing armoury holding bay, and we'll see how many of them stray?"

"Yes Sir!"

CHAPTER 33 - **Hachijo-jima**

May 25th 8:30 a.m.

An American Bell Boeing MV-22B Osprey, gently lifted itself off the MCAS Futenma air force runway at Okinawa. The Osprey was designed for multi-mission. It had a tilt-rotor, enabling both vertical take-off and landing. It was also equipped with short take-off and landing capabilities.

The Osprey had both the functionality of a helicopter and the long-range flight of a turboprop aircraft. The aircraft carried two pilots. They were from the 25th Wing Unit. Allowing for headwinds, the destination of the aircraft was a four-hour flight to Hachijo-jima Island, 846 miles northeast.

Hachijo-jima is a volcanic island in the Philippine Sea, and was 178 miles south of Tokyo. The population is over 7,500 people, living on 24 square miles of land. It has the second heaviest annual rainfall in Japan with an average of 120 inches of precipitation per annum. The climate is humid subtropical with an average temperature of 70 degrees Fahrenheit.

9:00 a.m.

Jensen was relaxing in his room at the Vessel Hotel Campana when his mobile rung. He was informed by Captain Harris that the flight to Hachijo-jima island was on schedule and the tracking devices had indicated that several unauthorized crates were in transit.

1:00 p.m.

The Osprey came to a vertical landing on Hachijo-jima Island airport. Within minutes from landing, the 25th Unit based on the island wearing civilian clothes, unloaded the cargo. They wore civilian clothing to avoid any attention when travelling throughout the island.

The unit loaded the cargo into two Japanese Hino trucks, painted blue and cream, avoiding military camouflage. The trucks also had false company logo's, consisting of a thick golden band forming a triangle, with red lettering within the band, displaying 'Investigative Landscape and Properties Holdings'.

They drove east for just over a mile to the Hachijojima Oriental Resort hotel. The hotel building was situated about a tenth of a mile from the Philippine Sea, and appeared as if long abandoned.

The hotel was designed in luxury French baroque-style and built during the 1960s tourist boom. When completed in 1963 it was called the Hachijo Royal Hotel. The hotel was once one of the largest hotels in Japan, and the jewel in the crown of the island. It attracted holiday makers from all over the country.

In 1996 the hotel was renamed as the Pricioa Resort. It closed again in August 2003, to reopen again in 2004 as the Hachijojima Oriental Resort. The hotel was again closed-down in 2006, when a reduction in tourism resulted in the business running out of money.

The island was once famous as a diving area, but today hardly anyone visits. This very fact came to the attention of the 25th Wing Unit in Okinawa.

In the hotel and grounds, nature had taken over with overgrown vegetation. A footpath with three feet high stone baluster walls on each side of it, led from the 2 1 5 highway, some 200 feet to the hotel. The path too was overgrown with vegetation. Most of the vegetation in the grounds surrounding the hotel had grown to over four feet, and badly required attention. Luckily, the entrance road which wrapped around the hotel and led to the back basement entrance was sufficiently wide enough for the trucks to drive through.

Unaware to the local community, the hotel had been secretly leased to the US government. In several parts of the buildings making up the hotel, the walls and ceilings were crumbling away. However, the huge basement was intact and ideal for the 25th Wing Unit to set up an electronic surveillance centre.

On the roof, the large dome and the smaller dome above it were replaced with fibreglass copies and then painted to retain their former look. Inside the domes were high-powered antenna-transmitters. The fibreglass domes now allowed radio transmissions to pass through them with ease, and would enable communication with satellites and other listening posts.

The base served as one of the uplink stations for the US intelligence networks in South East Asia. Unknown to the other intelligence networks, it had a dual purpose of partnership with a huge ship, which was capable of launching a spacecraft when at sea.

The trucks reached the basement carpark. Any curious sightseeing groups visiting the hotel for YouTube videos of abandoned buildings, would take them to be the staff of a speculative investment company, evaluating whether to reopen the hotel at some time in the future. Inside the crumbling building, the 25th Wing Unit only worked from the basement which was equipped with a modern ventilation system. Many areas of the hotel had stagnant air, so when not on duty, the unit shared two nearby luxury houses.

CHAPTER 34 - **Battle stations**

May 26th 2:30 a.m.

A Type 039C Yuan Class Chinese submarine, gently broke the sea surface off the Kuba area, on the eastern side of Okinawa. Fifteen minutes later a mercenary unit climbed out from three hatches on the deck.

The mercenaries hauled out four dinghies from the submarine and inflated them. Petrol motors were passed through the hatches and attached to each dinghy. The mercenaries ignored the motors, took out the paddles and then headed to the shore.

4:00 a.m.

Gunfire and explosions broke the night peace at the Yoshiura Thermal Power Station plant. The sound was audible from the Ginowan Police Station and Vessel Hotel.

Jensen woke from his sleep, along with many of the hotel guests. Minutes later giant explosions ripped through the power station. Seconds later Ginowan City went dark. Jensen found his pocket torch and quickly dressed. He then put his Glock pistol in his jacket holster and left the hotel.

The local police sent several armed units to the power plant. Shortly after, they were followed by Fire Brigades with blaring sirens. Jensen got into his hired car and drove to the plant. He met up with a police sergeant just outside the plant and showed him his ID.

After seeing Jensen's ID, Sergeant Yamashiro updated him. "Two men working here have been killed Sir. We think the saboteurs are still here in the plant."

"OK sergeant, let's get in there and finish this, but I'll stick with you as I don't want anyone taking me for a saboteur."

Two large gas towers had been blown apart and fire was climbing 50 feet from the remains of the structures.

The armed policemen carefully entered the plant, followed by several military units from the airbase.

Together, they searched through the buildings, and rubble from the destroyed administration block. It took a further half an hour to cover the site; but the saboteurs had disappeared.

It dawned on Jensen what might be going on. He found a military unit lieutenant.

"Lieutenant, I think this is a diversion. You need to step-up security on the airbase and get your navy to check shipping in the area. Check for an enemy submarine offshore too!"

The lieutenant realised the danger, and communicated the warning. While he was talking, distant gunfire and explosions were heard from the direction of the Ginowan MCAS Futenma Airbase.

Jensen dashed to his car and drove off. On approaching the airbase, he realised that the rear 'Back Gate' was nearer, so headed in that direction. On arrival he found himself in the aftermath of an earlier fierce battle. Two security men that had manned the rear gate lay dead, and were sprawled on the road in front of his car. Their office and the entrance barrier were blown away. He realised the men must have been blown out of their office from several hand grenades or a bazooka rocket. Jensen drove across the base and the runway towards Maximilian's office.

Jensen stopped his car short of the office, took out his pistol and started walking. The night air was heated from the burning buildings. The foul smell of oil and petroleum, played a deadly game with his eyes and throat, which made breathing difficult. Spontaneous gunfire broke out, as US military units were engaged in fighting, with what appeared to be an invisible enemy.

Inside the office he found Captain Harris slumped over the wooden table. He was holding a pistol in his right hand, but lifeless! A bullet hole in his head, another in his chest and a small pool of congealed blood on the table, meant that he had been dead for some time.

Jensen got back in his car and headed again down the runway and airfield. Gunshots were coming from the furthest hanger. Recklessly, he drove the car straight into it.

Inside two Osprey aircrafts were on fire, the dual engines and oversized propellers on one craft were blown away, and on the second craft damaged, and spitting fire. Brown smoke and spluttering electronic noises were coming from the cockpits.

Two bullet rounds fired at Jensen; his windscreen shattered; the bullets narrowly missed him. Jensen could not see the enemy. On realising he was too close to death, so, quickly put his car in reverse and headed out of the hanger. He reached a nearby office which was lit-up inside. He saw a figure of a man in the centre of the room, so he left his car, checked his pistol, and then made a dash for the building.

Inside the office, he found a man wearing a USAF officer's uniform, but pointing a pistol directly at him. He was a big man, possibly over six feet. Cold piercing brown eyes stared back at Jensen. Cabinets had been opened, and papers which had been removed from the metal draws were piled up in the centre of the room, along with video tapes. The pile was soaked with the liqueur from a half-empty bottle of brandy; the man looked as though he was about to set it alight.

The uniformed officer spoke with a cool commanding voice. "I'm Captain Gray, the Lieutenant general is directing combat against the mercenaries. I've been left in charge of this office. What can I do for you?"

"Put that pistol down, I'm Inspector Jensen, I'm not your enemy!"

"Oh yes, I've heard about you!" Gray kept pointing the gun, he looked tense, as if he was deciding whether to kill Jensen or not to.

Jensen looked hard into the man's eyes. "Does the unit in Hachijo-jima, know what's happening here? They might be the next target?"

"Yes, Captain Harris informed the unit earlier. Fortunately, the base is hidden and there's a secret entrance, so the mercenaries might not find it!"

"The two Osprey's in the hanger, are only fit for the scrapheap now. The loading bays for the crates are in there too. That's where the gunfire is concentrated, but as you can see, all the information concerning flight details is on the floor in front of you."

"Really?" said Jensen. "Harris was killed earlier by the mercenaries. You still haven't put down your pistol Gray. Are you responsible for shipping the unauthorised missile crates to Hachijo-jima?"

Gray removed a box of matches from his coat pocket with his freehand, then looked directly at Jensen, "Unfortunately, it looks like all their flight information will be lost too in the fighting."

Jensen then realised the Gray was far more dangerous than he first had thought.

"Gray, how did they manage to smuggle those crates into this base past security? Wasn't there any checking? What's your part in this little adventure?"

"Questions, questions Jensen, I'm the one holding the pistol here!"

Gray continued, "However, I'll put your mind at rest. This, by the way, won't help you, because you'll be found dead shortly!"

"All missile parts are firstly unloaded at a depot hub in Ginowan City, by an agreement with the 25th Wing Unit and the depot company. During pick-up by the unit's transport lorries, the crates get re-labelled US product, it's that simple!"

"Five years ago, an organisation was created to protect the South, Southeastern, and Eastern Asian

Countries from interference or possible invasion by the CCP. It is known as the South East Asia Anti-Totalitarian Affiliation (SEAATA). If Taiwan goes, Japan will be next. It's run by billionaires. Government's have been too slow to react to the threat!"

Jensen was not impressed, "That sort of paranoia is going to spark another World War!"

"Come, come, Mr. Jensen, I have access to intelligence reports that you would never get clearance for!"

"I wouldn't be too sure about that Gray!"

Jensen could see Gray's face tensioning; he was going to shoot. Jensen dived for the floor as a shot was fired. Jensen quickly removed his pistol from his holster and shot-out all the lights in the room.

"Jensen, that's four rounds you've wasted!"

Jensen found a chair and flung it across the room. Gray fired two blind shots in the direction of the noise.

Jensen found a waste bin at the side of his right foot, and threw it into the air hitting the ceiling. Gray fired a further two blind shots, but Jensen was now within reach of him and forced Gray against a wall. Jensen grabbed his pistol hand and repeatedly hit it against the office wall forcing Gray to let out a wail!

A further two bullets fired from Gray's pistol, shattering a wall mirror and a large window-pane. Finally, the pain in Gray's hand was too intense, forcing him to release and drop the pistol. Jensen then punched him several times in the face, forcing Gray to fall backwards onto the floor. Gray got up and fought back, found a chair and threw it at Jensen.

Jensen, covered his head and deflected the blow from the chair. His retaliation was immediate. After landing several more blows to Gray's head, Jensen grabbed him, picked him up and flung him through the shattered window. Gray landed on the grass verge outside the building. He was motionless.

On hearing the window being smashed, military police headed for the office and broke into the building. They shone torch beams into the room, locating Jensen.

A security guard shouted, "Get down on the floor, hands and legs apart or you will be shot!"

Jensen did as he was ordered. Lying face down, he allowed himself to be handcuffed. Soon, he was forced upright on his feet and led away by two burly guards.

    Outside the office, another security guard's torch beam found Gray's motionless body on the grass verge.

CHAPTER 35 - MCAS Airbase aftermath

May 26th 8:30 a.m.

Maximilian was outside Jensen's cell. "You can let him out now Sergeant Phillips!"

He smiled, "Inspector, what a remarkable story you gave the guards last night. Captain Gray is now being guarded by security personnel in a military hospital. The rest of the 25th Wing Unit on this base, are being interrogated at this moment. I expect that Gray and his men will face many years in a civilian cell."

"We found video tapes, and documents in a pile on his office floor which contained Osprey flight plans and cargoes to Hachijo-jima. They verified the account you gave my guards last night, so, you're free to leave this base."

"General, what happened after the gunfire?"

"Ahh, we captured five mercenaries, and killed seven. The five we captured are being interrogated now, however, several more got away. We lost thirteen good men, and considerable damage was done to my airbase. The power station will be out of action for months, so until its fixed, I guess everyone's going to have to pay a bit more for their electricity bills!"

"We have naval patrols surrounding the island, but as you are well aware, Okinawa is a tourist attraction. The mercenaries that escaped might already be back to wherever they came from, or they could still be on the island posing as tourists?"

"We have computer databases on our enemies, and we're trying to match the faces of the mercenaries we captured. The dead ones too! We have tightened up security on all exits from Okinawa. If they are still on the island, there's still a good chance that we can get them!"

8:50 a.m.

Jensen was then taken by Maximilian into another building containing a secure room. It contained several cabinets, a table, and four chairs, but purposely no windows.

Maximilian put on the lights and closed the door. "Do sit down Inspector. Would you like anything to drink?"

Jensen spotted a coffee percolator in the corner of the room, "A cup of coffee, thanks."

Maximilian, walked over to the percolator, then thought twice, and after a pause walked over to a filing cabinet and brought out a bottle of Napoléon Brandy and two glasses.

"Join me instead in a glass?"

Jensen nodded.

He then poured two glasses and passed one to Jensen.

"Thanks," said Jensen. "Did they get what they came for?"

"Unfortunately, yes! They found crates in the armoury holding bay which were destined for Hachijo-jima. They opened them, searched the contents, and then destroyed everything inside with hand grenades. They now know the name of the island, but they do not know where the unit is based!"

"We have not informed the unit in Hachijo-jima, or any other intelligence station, that some of the mercenaries got away, in fact, quite the reverse. We have broadcast to the intelligence units that all the mercenaries were either killed or captured."

"We did this to dampen any tension on the rogue members in the 25th Wing Unit in Hachijo-jima. As we will have to arrest all of them soon, we do not want any of them fleeing before we get there."

"But that means the unit will be facing the CCP hired mercenaries soon!"

"Quite so Inspector, along with my men too!"

Jensen thought carefully for twenty seconds, then put his brandy down on a shelf and looked at Maximilian. "If I was part of that unit, I wouldn't feel confident about staying on Hachijo-jima unless I received a confirmation from Captain Gray or one of his commands?"

"Yes, indeed Inspector, as several from of his unit will now face many years in prison, I'll sort that problem out."

"Jensen, I think it's worth your while to witness the end of this little enterprise!"

"Depending on the weather conditions, Hachijo-jima is about four hours away by Osprey. Will you come along with us?"

"Yes, it's been a long investigation, and I'd like to see the end of it!"

"Excellent Inspector, let's drink up, then you can pick up your luggage from your hotel and meet me here outside this building at around 10 o'clock."

CHAPTER 36 - **Station recapture**

May 26th 10:30 a.m.

The Seven Seas Adventurer scheduled a return to the island's harbour every three months to load up tungsten missiles.

The ships communications officer contacted the 25th Wing Unit on Hachijo-jima, and the harbour control. He informed them that the ship was on schedule for docking at the island in 19 hours. The communications officer would also report to the 25th Wing Unit on the island every three hours.

12:00 p.m.

The 25th Wing Unit at the base in Hachijo-jima island were busy loading up two tucks with crates containing 10 assembled missiles.

The Seven Seas Adventurer would easily be big enough to take onboard both lorries. Inside the ship, they would be able to park them in the spaces at each side of the shuttlecraft. The shuttlecraft was in preparation for a launch off the Macquarie Island in a two weeks' time. It's mission, to refuel and top-up the missiles in the stealth spacecrafts that were in orbit.

2:50 p.m.

Maximilian's Osprey hovered above the entrance to the Hachijojima Oriental Resort next to the 2 1 5 highway and sea. The rear door was opened, two ropes were attached to the airframe doorway and the remainder of the ropes dropped to the ground. 22 combat troops from his 24th Wing Unit then descended down the ropes to the ground. Maximilian and Jensen were the last to leave.

The ropes were then retracted and the Osprey circled the area waiting further orders. The troops dashed up the road leading to the underground basement carpark. On entering the basement, they took up strategic positions amongst the pillars supporting the hotel.

One of his men equipped with an AirTronic Shoulder-fired Rocket Launcher, pointed the weapon at two locked enforced solid steel doors. The doors led into the secret basement control room.

Maximilian walked up to the security camera scanning his troops from above the steel doors, and pressed an intercom button, that was positioned to the right of the door.

"As you are aware men, I'm Lieutenant General Maximilian. Surrender now, or I'll bring this hotel down on you all!"

Sixty seconds passed, then the locks on the doors were released and his troops walked into the secret communications base. The troops held their rifles outstretched anticipating trouble.

Inside they found four electronic engineers holding up their hands. Behind them were several large banks of servers, computers and radio equipment.

"Where's your Commanding officer, Lieutenant Pearson?" demanded Maximilian.

The senior communications officer spoke up, "He's taken several crates in a truck to our warehouse at Kaminato Port Sir."

"Who is going to collect the crates, and when?"

"The crew from a giant converted car transporter, Sir. It's due to dock in twelve hours."

"Converted to do what?" asked Maximilian.

"To launch satellites into space, Sir."

"100-foot satellites?" asked Jensen.

"Yes, Sir."

Both Maximilian and Jensen, were taken back with the reply, they both realised that the Kaminato port authorities would have inspected the ship at some point in the past. In not having reported the ship's activities, they must be complicit too, and affiliated with the SEAATA organisation.

Jensen asked, "How much communication have you had with that transporter ship today?"

"Every three hours, Sir."

Jensen turned to Maximilian, "The CCP probably has spy listening stations fixed on this island and most likely have been observing any transmissions. There's probably been enough time for them to triangulate this site using several transceiver stations!"

"Yes, you're right Jensen, we may be too late to save this base, and the ship."

Maximilian turned back to the communications officer. "OK, get a message to the American Fleet Admiral. See if he can spare a frigate or a destroyer to escort the ship into the harbour. If he can't spare a ship, then contact the Japanese Fleet Admiral!"

"Yes Sir."

"I don't want the captain of the transporter changing course. Maintain the three-hour contact and assume the position that all is fine. Otherwise, face the rest of your life in a prison cell!"

"Yes Sir."

Maximilian radioed the Osprey pilots, "OK, move that Osprey away from the hotel, it's a target here.

Park the Osprey close to the island's runway, then stay there to defend the Osprey at all costs."

Maximilian thought carefully, then said, "I want a man to guard the prisoners, and two volunteers to arrest Lieutenant Pearson at the port warehouse. Take one of these prisoners to identify the warehouse. Then take them both to the aircraft, and hand them over to the pilots, then return here. The rest of you, open up the armoury, everyone equip yourself with pistols and rifles and take up defensive positions around the hotel. We'll probably be expecting gunfire from mercenaries within the next 24 hours!"

CHAPTER 37 - **Hachijo-jima invasion**

May 27th 3:30 a.m.

The night air was warm and the sea relatively calm as the Seven Seas Adventurer powered towards Hachijo-jima. Captain Hu Zhang was pleased with the ship's progress.

He was only a few hours away from docking and looked forward to visiting the island again. He looked at the radar screen and was a little disturbed to see a blip heading towards his ship. He pointed out the blip to the officer on watch. The officer on watch reached for his binoculars. His binoculars had up to 120 magnifications, but it was not sufficient in the night to identify the ship heading in his direction.

Most of the crew were sleeping, and the night shift staff were relaxing, or walking around the deck. Some of them were drinking from bottles of spring water, fizzy drinks, or non-alcoholic beer. They were all looking forward to a few days break.

4:00 a.m.

A periscope from a Type-039C submarine, broke the surface a third of a mile off the ferry port on Hachijo-jima Island. Two hatches opened up on the hull, and four dinghy package containers were passed through them by the crew. The dinghies were extracted from their container covers and inflated on the deck. Petrol motors were passed through the hatches and attached to each dinghy.

Sixteen mercenaries climbed out of the hatches, and in each dinghy four men made themselves comfortable. The submarine crew then retained the dinghy package covers, re-entered the submarine, and closed the hatches.

Shortly after, the submarine quietly submerged below the surface leaving the dinghies floating in the bay. The mercenaries purposely ignored their power motors and took out the onboard paddles, heading for the harbour.

4:30 a.m.

Onboard the Seven Seas Adventurer, the officer on watch had been simultaneously observing the radar, and looking out to sea through his binoculars. He alerted Captain Hu Zhang.

"Sir, a large ship approaching, possibly Chinese Navy."

Captain Zhang took the binoculars off the officer and viewed the ship. He then picked up a phone and contacted the onboard Space Control Room.

"Do you see the ship on your radar?"

"Yes Sir, what do you want me to do?"

"As it's are heading directly towards us, assume it's hostile, put each spacecraft on alert and bring them over its head."

"Yes Sir!"

Seconds later, navigational rockets fired at the sides and rears of the spacecrafts. Their orbits changed and headed in the direction of their assigned rendezvous.

#

5:15 a.m.

The Hachijojima Oriental Resort lit up with explosions.

Maximilian and Jensen had anticipated the use of mercenaries. They knew, no country at this time would want to be held responsible for invading Japanese sovereign territory.

Jensen located two 6-foot single bed mattresses and then found a good position on the right-wing rooftop facing the 2 1 5 highway. He placed the mattresses one on top of the other, and then hauled them over against the perimeter stone baluster wall. Then lying flat on his stomach and on top of the mattresses he looked through the rifle's infrared sight, and searched for any mercenary foolish enough to fall into its view.

Minutes later Jensen identified a mercenary approaching the hotel. He aimed the rifle and shot at the man's legs, making him collapse instantly to the ground. Another mercenary, dragged the man away, while another threw a hand grenade into the basement at the rear of the hotel. The explosion blasted chunks off several concrete pillars, but the enforced solid steel doors leading to the secret control room held.

Maximilian's men had found good positions in the hotel and the grounds. They were able to pick off the mercenaries as they fell into their infrared sights.

The man guarding the prisoners, told them that it was time for them to leave. They left through a rear passageway into a tunnel under the hotel. The tunnel led to broken-down lifts and stairways. In its heyday the tunnel had been used for discreet movement of laundry.

On seeing a missile heading for the roof domes, Jensen quickly shielded himself between the mattresses.

The missile blast ripped into the larger dome, destroying the hidden antenna-transmitter dish inside. The shockwave further shattered the antenna into jagged pieces. The larger and smaller dome collapsed through the top floor and fell down into the centre of the hotel. The dome pieces crashed into the lobby and on top of the

Reception Desk. This brought down more parts from the top roof and the roof from the next lower-level with it. Jensen managed to grab and hold onto a small brick wall facia until the subsidence and rattling stopped.

    Jensen thought about the mercenaries taking on such a high risk for this mission. He was sure that they would be very well paid for their efforts, assuming they survived to collect the reward.

    A mercenary's missile found its target, and blasted open the steel doors that were securing the secret room. The next missile entered the room and exploded. A resulting fireball consumed the area within.

    The noise from explosions cchoed around the harbour, startling people and triggering car alarms. The police at the central station had been notified earlier of possible trouble. They now armed themselves, rushed to their cars and headed for the abandoned hotel.

    Two further missiles blasted into the control room and destroyed any remaining radio equipment, along with the missile crates. Fortunately, there was no-one left inside.

    A mercenary entered the remains of the control room. He saw the destroyed remains of a transmitter-receiver, the remains of swivel chairs, tables, cabinets, cupboards and in the far-right corner, workbenches with large contorted metal crates. Some of the crates had burst open in the earlier explosions revealing damaged parts of missile equipment. To satisfy himself he decided to finished the job with hand grenades.

The mercenary quickly left the basement to avoid the blasts. Maximilian found the man in his sight, fired and watched him drop to the ground.

Two mercenaries dragged the man away. Then the gunfire fell silent.

6:00 a.m.

Maximilian assessed the situation and shouted out, "MEN, they've all gone. There's nothing left here. They won't risk a landing at the airfield with our men there. It's too risky to land a helicopter in this rubble and visibility, so they'll escape by sea! Every man available, get to the harbour now and try to track them down from there!"

6:05 a.m.

On the Seven Seas Adventurer, three blips on the radar had been showing for some time. One blip was very prominent, it was about a half a mile away. That blip was the radar return from the approaching frigate.

A radio message was sent from the frigate to the great ship:

"CAPTAIN OF THE SEVEN SEAS ADVENTURER."

"THIS IS THE CHINESE NAVY, STOP YOUR ENGINES AND PREPARE TO BE BOARDED, OR YOUR SHIP WILL BE DESTROYED!"

Fear began to spread amongst the crew on the Bridge, as they realised that their fates would be shortly changed.

Captain Zhang realised that he could not outrun the situation and the game was almost up. He knew what was coming, so picked-up a microphone and spoke to the whole crew.

"Attention All! Attention All! There is a Chinese Navy frigate approaching us! I know you have all put your hearts into this project to protect your countries from the tyranny of dictatorship, I salute you! I now give the sad order to abandon ship. All are to make for the island, with exception for the essential crews. Essential crews are the staff manning this Bridge, engine staff, the Space Control Room, and the shuttle engineers and pilots. We cannot leave any technology in the hands of our enemies! We have vast resources and we'll continue our mission sometime soon. I'll see you all again then. Thank you again for your service, and out!"

6:15 a.m.

A message was sent from the Space Control Room to one of the spacecrafts which then relayed back the message to the approaching frigate on all naval bands, through an artificial voice:

"ABORT YOUR MISSION, OR YOUR SHIP WILL BE DESTROYED IN 20 MINUTES"

Then twenty seconds later, "19 40" was transmitted through the artificial voice.

The commander on the frigate contacted Beijing with the warning message, and waited for further orders.

The orders from Beijing were blunt and direct. The frigate was instructed to locate the signal in space and then feedback the co-ordinates to them.

Ten minutes later, six DF-17 hypersonic missiles were fired from artificial islands in the China Sea, and headed for space.

The artificial voice messages continued:

"ABORT YOUR MISSION, OR YOUR SHIP WILL BE DESTROYED IN 15 MINUTES"

Then twenty seconds later, "14 40" was transmitted by the artificial voice.

The instruments onboard the spacecrafts detected the missile launches and relayed the information back to the Space Control Room. The spacecrafts were hidden from radar, however every 20 seconds one sent the countdown message, which fixed their position for a split second before being lost again. The spacecraft was then instructed to stop sending the warning message, and both spacecrafts to apply code 'AI Route S', and continue towards their set rendezvous.

All non-essential crew had left the Seven Seas Adventurer and were now in lifeboats and life rafts, about fifteen miles off the island.

Fifteen minutes later, the Captain Zhang contacted the Space Control Room.

"How are we doing?"

"In position within minutes, Sir."

"Good, give the frigate until the last second of the countdown. If they fail to abort by then, then fire on the vessel!"

The 'AI Route S' instruction sent from the Space Control Room instructed the spacecrafts to make strategic manoeuvres to prevent any CCP artificial intelligence computer from working out their exact spaceflight trajectories.

The DF-17 missiles reached their set projected targets in space and exploded. One spacecraft was caught in the shockwave and blew apart. Its missiles and other onboard components, were sent into higher orbits on trajectories heading for other satellites and space junk.

#

6:20 a.m.

Jensen, Maximilian and his men reached the harbour. They could hear powered motors from dinghies out at sea, so commandeered five power boats and headed in pursuit of the mercenaries.

Jensen joined five of Maximilian's men on one of the boats. Fortunately, it was a twin-engine craft and had plenty of power. However, once free of the harbour, the waves buffered, tossed and spun the craft. Without safety constraints, the men slid across their bench seats and were soaked in sea spray.

#

6:30 a.m.

The bulbous front of the remaining spacecraft opened. A support platform extended two stealth missiles until they were clear of the spacecraft.

Sections of the missile support platform changed elevation from the horizontal position to the vertical. The missiles now pointed directly towards Earth.

"Fire one, Fire two," came a voice from the Space Control Room. Computer command instructions were sent to the spacecraft.

Seconds later nozzles at the rear of the missiles sprang to life and fired. The stealth missiles released themselves instantly from their support platforms and headed to their target and destruction.

As the missiles picked up speed, the thermal tiles wrapped around the tungsten armaments exceeded 2000 degrees Fahrenheit. 115 seconds later at 47,520 feet, the missiles passed from the Stratosphere into the Troposphere. Five seconds later, the missile travelling near 8.5 Mach, tore through the upper decks into the frigate's armoury.

No one within 50-feet of the impacts stood a chance. A wall of fire sprang out of the armoury, anyone in its path was instantly incinerated.

The remaining crew on the Seven Seas Adventurer and those in the lifeboats and life rafts saw the blasts, and flames, which climbed out of the frigate to hundreds of feet into the sky. Initially shocked at the devastating scene, they recovered their spirits and began to cheer.

The frigate looked to be dead in the water. It was taking on water, sinking, and being abandoned.

As they powered in their boats towards the horizon, the mercenaries and Maximilian's men suddenly became aware of the Seven Seas Adventurer and the burning frigate.

6:40 a.m.

Onboard the frigate, the missile control room had survived the impact. A dazed officer, recovered his composure and balance. He looked up and down his display panel, and then contacted the commander.

"We still have two active missiles, Sir!"

"Then fire on that ship when ready."

Captain Zhang could now see fourteen blips on the radar. The original blip was now dominant, a further two blips were following the dominant blip in the same direction. There was another strong blip near the coast and ten weaker blips coming from the same direction.

Two short range missiles were launched from the crippled frigate. Both found their targets.

The Bridge on the Seven Seas Adventurer blew away, killing Captain Zhang and all the crew around him.

A second missile tore into the lower decks at the rear of the ship. Shockwaves travelled out from the ship creating 15-foot waves, nearly toppling several lifeboats.

The waves reached the mercenary dinghies. One dinghy survived the waves, but the other three dinghies were toppled into the sea. The pursuit boats homed in on the dinghies, but Jensen and Maximilian's men were further startled to see a conning tower rising above the sea.

The Space Control Room onboard the Seven Seas Adventurer survived the blast. The crew faced a problem. They needed to get to the onboard shuttle and destroy it along with any sensitive equipment.

When they arrived at the shuttle, they were joined by the shuttle engineers, and two of the crew who piloted the shuttlecraft.

"What should we destroy first," said a technician.

A shuttle engineer cut-in, "Wait a minute, let me try this first!"

He then went over to a control room panel and pressed several buttons.

The stricken vessel jolted as bolts were released separating the shuttle craft from its booster rocket stage. Further jolts occurred as the bow doors slowly opened.

The commander on the crippled frigate contacted the missile bay again.

"Have you got any more missiles?"

"I've launched from all our active tubes, Sir, but I can reload them."

"Sink that bloody ship!"

"Yes, Sir!"

The Chinese submarine resurfaced nearby.

7:00 a.m.

A thunderous roar echoed from the belly of the Seven Seas Adventurer.

At the same time, a missile launched from the frigate.

A huge flash of metal shot out of the bow of the Seven Seas Adventurer, and skipped across the waves, just like a pebble being thrown and skipping across a pond.

The missile from the frigate hit the Seven Seas Adventurer in her upper decks, followed by several huge explosions.

The launched shuttlecraft did not sink, but on being given full thrust, bounced off the seventh wave, and rocketed into the sky.

As the shuttlecraft headed to the sky, the crew members from the Seven Seas Adventurer gave out a huge cheer from their lifeboats.

The Chinese submarine commander, observing the scene from his conning tower, in retaliation ordered two torpedoes to be launched at the Seven Seas Adventurer.

Everyone watched helplessly as two streaks of white pillowing water, left the submarine, and streaked across the bay and then blasted into the centre of the great ship. The great ship broke in half and quickly sank.

Two Destroyers approached the scene, one was American and the other Japanese.

The Chinese submarine commander had lined his top deck with gun crews. He was aware of the two Naval Destroyers closing in on him. There was just enough time to rescue four mercenaries in the one surviving dinghy and to bring in his gun crews. He then gave the order to dive.

    Maximilian's boat was first to reach the abandoned mercenaries struggling in their soaking outfits in the sea. The mercenaries had been used and spat out by their masters. His crew hauled in five of them and left the rest of them to be rescued by his men in the other four power boats.

CHAPTER 38 - Hachijo-jima aftermath

May 27th 11:30 a.m.

Jensen and Maximilian were walking through the rubble in the remains of the hotel basement control room. It was temporarily lit up by arc lights placed on tripods. In one corner, body-bags were filled with eight mercenaries, and three combat troops from his 24th Wing Unit.

Maximilian turned to Jensen. "Although the structure is still reasonably solid, this location is now known, so we will have to move to another island."

"General, what about the two spacecrafts in orbit?"

"One got destroyed by Chinese ballistic missiles. This sent bits of it along with bits of the exploded Chinese missiles on a collision course with other satellites. At least eight satellites were destroyed in the process. If the Russians and Chinese lost any satellites, they are keeping quiet about it! The remaining spacecraft is not in the same orbit. So, until our satellites find it again, there's not much to be done."

They then walked past several of Maximilian's men that were busily trying to salvage any remaining electronics. The senior communications officer that had been placed under arrest the day before, spoke up.

"Sir, I think there's a backup control room hidden somewhere on another island. Can I talk to you in private please?"

"Yes, later."

Jensen looked at the senior communications officer then looked back at Maximilian, "Please, keep me in touch, if you can?" He then thought of the death toll and turned to Maximilian.

"Has the CCP given any account of the incident?"

"Yes," said Maximilian, as you would expect, their version is quite different. The information they have released, states that while attempting to rescue a sinking car transporter, ammunition on their frigate Jiabao, exploded in an unexplained fire, causing the whole armoury to explode, leaving considerable damage to the ship's rudder and loss of control at the helm. The frigate was lost at sea. They have thanked the Japanese and US governments for helping to rescue their crew along with the crew of the transporter."

Jensen looked amused, "Propaganda Bullshit!"

"Yes, indeed," said Maximilian. "But, no World War III. However, when we've finished with the crew of that spacecraft launcher, we will need to thoroughly investigate this SEAATA organisation. We still have to decide on what information should be released to the general public?"

"Jensen, there's another Osprey on its way from Okinawa to pick-up the dead. The Osprey that we arrived in, is still parked at the airport as it cannot land here in this rubble. It departs at 1 p.m. for Yokota on the main Japanese Island. There's an air base there, shared between the US and the Japanese Air Self-Defense Force. It's easier for you to get to Tokyo from there than the Okinawa base. I'll arrange for you to get a lift in a helicopter back to Tokyo."

Jensen gave a firm handshake with Maximilian.

"Thank you, Sir, that's a big help. It's been a great pleasure working with you. I'll sign out of the hotel now and get to the runway!"

CHAPTER 39 - **London**

June 4th 9:00 a.m.

Jensen was delighted to be back in London. It was a bright sunny morning as he walked into the Ministry of Defence building. A meeting had been arranged at 11:30 a.m. with the Prime Minster Richard Harris, M I 5 Chief Rosemary Yates, M I 6 Chief Jon Barton, Defence Secretary Peter Mathews, Raymond French, and Sir Henry Gibson Foreign Secretary of State.

11:30 a.m.

Peter started the meeting. "As I see it Prime Minister, the investigations into the two spacecrafts belonging to SEAATA, are now under the control of the American and Japanese governments."

"We can only assume that the enthusiasm of some very rich and powerful people to protect their countries from tyrants had excessively got out of control."

"Do we now know who these people are?" said Richard.

Jon answered, "Sir, this will take some time possibly months? The Seven Seas Adventurer survivors, are being interrogated along with the officers at the Kaminato Port, in Hachijo-jima island."

"The Seven Seas Adventurer itself might have the answers! The US Navy has divers trying to re-float the two halves of the ship. There might be clues as to where the capital for the ship came from? For example, who paid for the refits to enable it to launch spacecrafts."

"The American and Japanese governments have to be careful with the sensitivity of the territory, as the ships sunk just outside the island's 12-mile Territorial Water Zone Limit."

"You mean, the CCP might have a claim on the wreck too?" asked Richard.

"Yes Sir," said Peter.

Richard cut-in, "What about the shuttlecraft? Does anyone know where it is now?"

Jon answered, "Yes Sir, it couldn't make orbit, and had to be talked down with the help of two Japanese American F-16 fighters. It made an emergency landing at the Ibaraki Airport, about 53 miles North East of Tokyo. The airport also serves as the Japanese Air Self-Defense Force under the name Hyakuri Air Base. The two pilots onboard are now being interrogated at the Japanese Defence Intelligence Headquarters, in the Shinjuku district of Tokyo."

Peter then turned to Jensen.

"Inspector Jensen will now fill us in on the bio-chips stolen from Gene Solar."

"Yes Sir, Professor Jannat Rashied, heading the Egyptian Forensic Department, updated me earlier this morning. The divers searching the wreck could not find any trace of the bio-chips in the secret control room onboard the Bluebell. She concluded that all of the bio-chips were destroyed in the fire, when the yacht was sinking."

"As you are all aware, Cheryl Brenton and her brother Richard, are now serving as CCP diplomats in Malta. However, as both positions were quickly arranged, they might be given other assignments very soon. In fact, Cheryl's former role as a researcher into bio-chip technology and her brother's role in satellite broadcasting are probably far more valuable to the CCP than their current postings!"

"It's thought that Alekos Alisavou and several of the engineers along with their wives, were kidnapped by Cheryl and Richard, and have since been taken to China."

Richard interjected, "Peter, Jon, as we are really dealing with spies, I want a surveillance team to watch over Cheryl and her brother in Malta. I want to know if they get assigned away from their current diplomatic duties. If that does happen and it's possible, I want an S A S team to bring either one, or both of them back to the UK, and make it unseen!"

"Yes Sir," said Peter.

Jensen continued, "Flight lieutenant Angela Carter, from the Cranfield Defence Academy has returned to Cyprus. She is working with the local police to investigate any further connections to Alekos and Harald Haugen."

Jensen summed up, "Harald and two other people, Svein Thorsen, and Anne Westrum are believed to be behind the financing of the spy satellite hacking operation. They are still at large. Roger Phillips and Lucy Matthews from M I 6, and Rebekah Petersen a Danish journalist investigator, are searching for them!"

"Thank you, Inspector," said Peter.

Richard looked troubled! "OK, what's the latest on Gene Solar Ltd?"

"Well Prime Minister," said Peter. "We can now use bio-chips to crack downloaded encryption codes from enemy spy satellites, but so too can the CCP. However, as they were specifically designed for the UK Defence Shield, the apparatus supporting them will now require further modifications to prevent any hacking from any foreign intelligence surveillance organisations."

Richard interrupted, "And how much will all this extra cost? Would it not be cheaper to close this program down? What about GPT AI, it's spreading across the world and growing rapidly. Can we not utilise this AI in some way instead?"

"I'll have my accountants to do some investigations, Sir!" said Peter, looking a little strained!

Peter continued, "The initial project stage for using Gene Sola Ltd. was to investigate the structure of the squid's brain. This was due to its high intelligence and rapid speed in changing its camouflage over seabed objects in different environments. This is what drew the creature to the attention of our scientists. They thought the brain structure and function could be adapted for monitoring our radars from space, and of course our radars on land and sea, covering the UK."

Peter then summed up the case for Gene Sola Ltd:

"The second stage is to create a replica synthetic brain to match the rapid responses of the cephalopod squid. This is to be based on its neural network along with our research into AI. This is similar to the software architecture now used for GPT AI."

Richard gave Peter a hard look. "I'll look forward to reading your reports Peter, and the accountant's report into the investigations."

CHAPTER 40 - **Resurgence of evil**

July 21ᵗʰ 9:00 a.m.

At his flat in Swansea, Jensen woke from a bad dream. He had realised that stress was affecting him and he had taken a week off work. After a quick breakfast he went for a walk along the bay. It was a lovely warm morning.

There were a couple of small sailing dinghies in the bay. He watched them sail for over an hour and longed for September when he could take a full holiday and hire a boat too.

11:00 a.m.

Jensen headed for his favourite cafeteria 'Fiona's', and ordered a coffee. If the weather was fine, Fiona liked to place several tables outside the cafeteria on her balcony. Fortunately, she had done that earlier in the morning. He found a vacant table, sat down on a chair and relaxed.

His coffee was delivered, and he thanked Fiona. He stared into the cup, brought it to his lips and took a good sip. That did the job. He then looked out at the bay, and stared at the horizon over the sea. His mobile phone rung, bringing his thoughts back to earth.

"David Jensen."

"Hello David, it's Rebekah."

"I've been informed of all your adventures! Too bad, I was looking forward to a trip to Malta, but there might be little to investigate there now?"

"Good, investigators have run into grief there! If you do go Rebekah, you'll need a good bodyguard!"

"David, for the moment, forget Malta! I've done some research through the dark web, and I've also been working with Interpol. There are two businessmen fitting certain profiles that will be looking over a 200-foot yacht in a couple of days."

"Now that's interesting Rebekah, where?"

"Bremen, enough information David for you to leave what you're doing for a few days?"

"I'll need to make a couple of phone calls first."

Rebekah added, "I'll be at the Radisson Blu hotel in Mitte."

"OK, I'll let you know whether I get permission to travel!"

12:00 a.m.

Jensen was in a meeting with the Police Chief at the Swansea Central Police Station. Chief Superintendent Alex Jones was sat behind a mahogany teak table, in a meeting room on the top floor.

Jones was in his early-sixties, he had a thinnish face, with dark brown eyes. His eyebrows were cut short and thin, which matched his short thinning hair, giving way to baldness on the top of his head. He was wearing standard uniform black trousers, and a white shirt with two front pockets. His jacket was hung around the back of his chair.

"Thanks for allowing me to arrange this meeting Chief."

"Rebekah Petersen phoned me an hour ago, she has a lead on Harald Haugen. She's been working with Interpol, and they believe that they have traced him to Bremen where he is about to buy a replacement yacht."

"Germany! Inspector, I'd prefer you leave this type of work to your former colleagues in Whitehall. But, OK, considering you're officially on holiday this week, you don't need my permission to go there."

Jones continued, "Whitehall called me earlier today too. Lieutenant general Maximilian has been in contact with them. He's located a backup control room for the remaining spacecraft on a nearby island called Aogashima. He was interested to know if you might be reassigned out there soon?"

"For the moment, Whitehall have said no, as both Roger Phillips and Lucy Matthews from M I 6, are in Malta at the moment, and will be reassigned to help him along with a CIA agent Brad Jackson."

"Inspector, I have a few additional comments!"

"Chief?"

"Alekos and some of his top men are presumed to be in China, God knows what will become of them? But then again, knowing what they got up to, I don't care a bit, unless of course they start working for the CCP! But, thanks to Cheryl and her brother, the CCP officials probably know your home address too!"

"Quelle est la qualité de votre français?" (How good is your French?)

"Assez pour s'en sortir!" (Enough to get by!)

"Why are you asking Chief?"

"Interpol has recently moved to a new central office in Paris, the National Central Bureau (NCB). It might be in your interest to disappear from this area for a couple of years. If you were to apply for a position with them, I'll write you an excellent reference?"

A smile appeared on Jensen's face as he thought of Rebekah. "Give me some time to think it over?"

"One last observation Inspector."

"Chief."

"Based on the documentation that's been sent to me from GCHQ, Harald Haugen is a very wealthy man. Even if we get some of his tax havens to cough up the money that he's stashed away, he'll still be a very rich man."

"Yes Chief, that worries me too!"

Jensen then paused for a thought, "So, why does he need to generate more wealth?"

"GCHQ made the same observation Inspector. Good luck with your investigation in Bremen."

"Thank you, Chief."

CHAPTER 41 - **Bremen**

July 23rd 9:00 a.m.

It was the start of a warm day in Bremen, with the temperature approaching 60-degrees Fahrenheit. Gerald Spieler and Carl Bergmann, both wearing dark greyish business suits, were in a taxi heading out from the city centre. They had been to Bremen several years earlier on similar business, but decided not to proceed with their business deal at that time.

Bremen is in Northern Germany and is the largest city next to the Weser River. It lies 37 miles from the North Sea. It is a major cultural and economic centre, and home to many art galleries, and museums containing historical sculptures and priceless paintings.

Bremen was known for its role in the maritime trade, as represented by the Hanseatic buildings in the Market Square. The Hanseatic League was a commercial and defensive confederation of merchant guilds and market towns in Northwestern and Central Europe that dominated maritime trade in the Baltic Sea from the 13th to the middle of the 17th century. Bremen had joined the Hanseatic League in 1260.

Today, Bremen is known by its luxury ship building companies, the most famous being Lürssen, which built luxury yachts. Gerald and Carl had already been to Lürssen two days earlier.

The two men had already been acquainted with the city for four days. They had visited several museums and had gone to the theatre in the evenings. However, they were not there to specifically sample the local culture.

Gerald had no time to wait the two to three years for a new yacht to be built for him. He wanted to buy a recently built yacht, but no more than two to three years old. Millionaires, having generated enormous sums of money from their successful businesses, would consider an offer on their yachts after two or three years, in order to buy bigger and to improve their status.

A yacht broker informed Gerald that a yacht called the Southern Star was under maintenance and a small refit at the Weissman yards, and the owner was open to offers.

He and Carl were there to look the yacht over. If they were happy with the yacht, there might be some months of negotiating ahead. Also, due to the nature of the duties he would assign his crew, once the yacht was delivered to its new location, the present crew would all have to be replaced. So, he and Carl needed to start on the task as soon as possible.

9:30 a.m.

The taxi pulled up at the Weissman luxury yacht's office, and Gerald and Carl were introduced to Sales Manager Christoph Mullner.

"Good morning, Mr. Spieler and Mr. Bergmann. I'm very pleased you could make it here on time. On such a fine and sunny day too! Gentlemen, would you like a little refreshment before the tour of the Southern Star?"

"Why yes, thank you," said Gerald. "Thank you," said Carl.

"Please, come into my office, and sit down on the sofa and relax for a while." Christoph then walked to the rear of his office and opened the glass doors of a wine cabinet.

"Gentlemen, champagne, brandy, or scotch whisky?"

Both men asked for brandy.

Christoph brought the glasses over and passed the drinks.

Christoph was in his mid-fifties, he was slim built, had slightly greying hair, which was cut to his collar.

He stood at about five feet seven inches tall, in his slick pigment green suit. He was preparing to turn on the charm for his customers.

After getting his Business Studies Degree at the University of Mannheim, he had learnt the hard way how to sell yachts. This started with sailing dinghies at a marina in Bremenhaven, which was located at the mouth of the river Weser.

He picked up two brochures detailing the yacht, handed them to the men and started the sales pitch. He addressed the men confidently and positively.

"Gent's the Southern Star is a beauty; the yacht was designed to have a light and breezy appeal. She is a solid and stable craft. To prove what I've just said, she's been around the world three times already."

"She's very safe at sea, well stabilised and her engines are almost silent. She's been to Australia and sailed from New Zealand to Honolulu in Hawaii. She's been to French Polynesia, Alaska, and to Japan, Taiwan, and Manila in the Philippines. She did not have to stop once for maintenance in any of those countries."

"Here are her statistics:"

- "Length: 62 metres, 203 feet 4.9 inches
- Year: 2019
- Builder: Weissman
- Beam: 11 metres, 36 feet, 1 inch
- Draft: 4 metres, 13 feet, 1.5 inches
- Cruise speed: 15 knots

- Maximum Speed: 18 knots

- Staterooms: 6

- Guests: 12

- Crew: 14"

"Gentlemen, take your time with the brandies, and when you've finished, I'll show you around the yacht, she's in No.3 dry dock at this moment."

Twenty minutes later, Christoph started the tour.

"Everything inside you see has been designed by Italian designer, Marabella Bellotti. She's designed the interior to make you feel relaxed, and cosy."

"You will see many sculptures and paintings that have been exclusively picked by the owner."

On the Main Deck, they walked past two glass panel doors that had been slid back, and entered the Main Saloon. As far as the eye could see, a thick cream carpet stretched to its full length. Inside the saloon were two four-seater cream-coloured sofas, and two matching chairs.

Several wooden varnished sculptors were fixed to the walls. Two table lamps displaying stylish white shades, stood on top of two cream-coloured tables. The far side of the Main Saloon housed a set of cream-coloured draws. Setback two feet from the top of the draws, was an enormous 200-inch TV screen.

Behind the TV screen was an elegant dining room. A glass chandelier hung above a large dark crystal glass table. 12 cream coloured leather upholstery seats had been laid around the table. A large silk screen depicting a Caribbean Island scene in various colours of silk thread, divided the dining room from the lobby behind it.

The lobby contained a glass lift and a spiral stairway that part wrapped around the lift. The lift and stairway would take a person from the sleeping quarters directly to the Bridge Deck. Past the lobby was a gaming room for children, which contained a 100-inch TV screen and game controllers to keep them happy. Beyond the gaming room, were two large VIP master bedrooms.

Christoph then showed them the two VIP master bedrooms. They consisted of glossy light brown wood panelling, and cream coloured leather panelling that reached the ceiling, serving as a contrasting colour to the room, and as headboards for the beds. Fluorescent lighting lit-up the ceilings. All the bedrooms were covered in a thick cream carpet, and contained two sets of draws, a personal desk, inbuilt wardrobes and ensuite marble bathrooms with toilets.

Below in the Lower Deck were two further guest double bedrooms, and two guest bedrooms containing two single beds in each, with built in wardrobes, desk, sets of draws and ensuite bathrooms with toilets.

Next, they were shown the Upper Deck Owner's Deck, containing his Private Office, with an 80-inch TV screen positioned on the wall in front of the desk, and a Master Stateroom along with a marble ensuite bathroom. The deck matched the colouring of the other guest quarters, but was considerably grander, and designed to allow as much natural light to penetrate as possible. It also contained a private balcony which led to a set of sofas. The deck looked out through large glass windows over the bow, which when at sea, would provide a spectacular panoramic view.

The deck above was the Sundeck, and it contained one of the two jacuzzies onboard with built-in whirlpools. The final deck above was the Observation Deck which was fitted out with sun loungers and seating areas.

After a short break and refreshments in the Observation Deck, their tour continued. They saw the Main Deck with the Galley, which when at sea would be staffed continually by two chefs. They were then taken to the Lower Deck, shown a large laundry room, crew mess quarters, and the crew bedrooms.

Finally, they were shown around the engine room, engine control room and garage which contained a motorised tender and jet ski toys for the owner's and his guest's pleasures. They were then taken back to the private office in the Owner's Deck.

11:00 a.m.

"Now," said Christoph. "As you have already paid us €5000 to register an interest, and been given this tour of the yacht, the owner has given me permission to show you the yachts security features."

He then went over to the wall cabinet, moved a spinning world globe and stand, and pressed a hidden button in the centre of a wooden carved flower. A hidden door on the right side of the cabinet then popped open.

A stairway lit-up and descended to the Lower Deck leading to another illuminated room. Gerald and Carl, followed Christoph down the stairway. The room was equipped with radio equipment, an 80-inch TV screen, mahogany table, four swivel chairs and several cabinets. There was also a door leading to a bathroom and toilet.

"Sit down gentlemen please," said Christoph. Two years ago, the owner took this yacht for a refit at Alblasserdam, in the Netherlands."

"You are now in the Citadel Room. If I activate the button next to the door, the upper secret door closes, along with this door. The doors and surrounding room have ballistic protection. Nobody can now open these doors from the outside, unless you release them yourself from here."

"It's a safe place to hide away, in the unlikely event of unwanted visitors taking control of the yacht. Citadels override any satellite communication from the bridge. Here you can communicate to your satellite providers, and a police force or private security force will be sent to you, from anywhere in the world."

Christoph added, "This room has also its own independent ventilation system. If you are in remote locations the cabinets contain sleeping bags, rations and sufficient water and alcohol to keep your spirits up for several weeks."

Gerald looked pleased, "This room is ideal!"

It also brought a smile to Carl's face.

"Yes," said Christoph. "As you are probably aware, a Citadel Room, is now frequently requested at the super-yacht design stage."

"Now," said Christoph. "There are several other security features. The Bridge is equipped with anti-drone protection for privacy. A 500-metre electronic 'exclusion zone' can be activated, which jams signals from any drone controller, effectively rendering the drone useless, along with its 'return to home' command."

"There's an acoustic deterrent, which will deter attempts to board the yacht in sea areas where pirates are known to operate."

"The yacht is also fitted with an underwater sonar system that will detect and track skin divers, or underwater vehicles from 900-metres away."

Christoph then led Gerald and Carl back to his Sales Office, and offered them another glass of brandy while they collected their thoughts.

"Gentlemen, what did you think of the yacht tour? The owner is asking for €25,000,000. So, are you likely to take this offer any further?"

Gerald looked at Carl, and received a nod and look of approval from him.

Gerald replied, "Mr. Mullner, that was an excellent tour of the Southern Star, I'm very pleased with your professional service. It leaves us quite a lot to think about!"

"So far, we've been to the Lürssen boatyard. I have several other boatyards to visit before I arrive at a final decision. When I've decided upon a captain and chief engineer, I'd be grateful if you would provide them with a tour of the yacht. I'll forward to you the same €5,000 fee prior to their visit. If they like the yacht, we can negotiate the price."

Christoph was pleased, sending a captain and chief engineer to inspect the yacht was a good sign of their intention to buy.

"Gentlemen, it's also possible to arrange a meeting with the present captain and chief engineer?"

"Thank you," said Gerald. "I'll consider your offer."

Christoph concluded the visit, "Thank you Mr. Spieler, Mr. Bergmann. I'm pleased that the tour went so well. The Southern Star is completing her maintenance. Just now, a larger seawater purifying system is being installed. She will probably be with us for another six weeks. Is there anything else I can do for you both?"

"Yes," said Carl, can you arrange a taxi please?"

"No problem."

Ten minutes later, a Mercedes taxi pulled up outside the office. The men finished their drinks, and left for the taxi.

Christoph raised his hand and smiled at Gerald and Carl in the taxi, as it was leaving. All had gone well. He considered that he had played an excellent part.

When he saw several armed Interpol policemen spring-out from nowhere, then stop and surround the car, Christoph cut his smile, to look shocked.

Jensen appeared at the rear passenger window next to Carl, and then opened the door. Jensen looked at Carl, "Hello Svein."

Jensen then looked across at Gerald, whose face had now turned grim. "Hi Harald, long time no see!"

At the same time Anne Westrum was being hunted down in the Seychelles.

Rebekah took several photographs of Harald and Svein Thorsen as they were led away to a police transit van. For over six weeks she'd been working with Interpol. She had been contacting yacht brokers for updates on clients around the world. She knew, this time that she had her man, and a great scoop!

Rebekah had banked on Harald not being able to stay in the shadows for too long. Organisations that he sold intelligence reports to, were ruthless. They would be concerned if Harald's intelligence started drying up.

Harald was caught through his own network. Unless he restarted his business, he knew that within a year, his intelligence contacts in several unsavory countries would assume the worse, and would think that he had been taken captive, and in turn would sell them out to western intelligence agencies as a plea-bargaining chip.

Harald had two choices, to start gathering illicit intelligence reports again, or to disappear for several years. Harald was a narcissist; therefore, the second choice was unacceptable. It did not fit in with his long-term grand plan.

After the police transit van departed. Rebekah and Jensen walked over to Christoph.

Jensen smiled at Christoph and spoke, "Superb job Christoph! Congratulations on a splendid performance!"

Both Jensen and Rebekah shaked his hand. Interpol had visited Christoph a couple of days earlier. The police had wired him for any unforeseen trouble. He'd done his job; no finger would be pointing at him from any criminal organisation.

7:00 p.m.

Jensen was in his bedroom with Rebekah at the Radisson Mitte hotel. They were dressing to go out on the city, and later in the evening to have a meal at the Canova, which was famous for its seafood menus.

"David, I hope it's the last we see of that bastard and his merry men?"

Jensen attempted to put Rebekah at ease, "Harald and his buddies will be in maximum security for the rest of their lives!

"Rebekah!"

"What David?"

"I'm considering working for Interpol in their Paris office. How do you feel about moving your base to Paris?"

Rebekah realised that Jensen suggestion for working in Paris was to be near to her. "No, the French and the British are always at odds with each other; David you will not be happy there!"

"You love the Gower. Cardiff and Bristol have international airports; David, I can work from anywhere in Europe, including the Gower. As the CCP might now know where you live, why don't you sell your current flat in Swansea and buy another, or maybe buy a cottage instead?"

Rebekah continued, "When we're not at work, we can visit one of your favourite Gower beaches."

Jensen raised a smile, "I know a great place Rebekah where we can have a fabulous cup of coffee, stare out at the sea and watch the sailing yachts pass by, and just relax while the hours slip away!"

Rebekah teased, "You know, you're far too lazy! Wouldn't you want something better to do with your spare time?"

Jensen walked over to Rebekah and embraced her in his arms. He looked deeply into her bright blue eyes, "You mean like this?"

She smiled just before their lips made contact.

Several minutes later, Jensen broke the embrace. "Grab your coat girl, we're about 'to paint the town red' now!"

The End

PATHWAYS INTO EVIL

Researching the novel

Research into locations and countries have been achieved from actual visits by myself, or through visiting Google Maps. Night sky star positioning on actual dates was achieved using Starry Night Professional software.

In this novel, all historical information including dates, have been sourced mostly from Wikipedia and YouTube videos.

The Wikipedia articles that are adapted for this novel are under the 'Creative Commons Attribution-Share Alike License 3.0.' These adapted articles are referenced under 'Acknowledgements'. The YouTube videos from which I have made observations on, and which in turn have contributed towards this novel, are referenced under 'Acknowledgements'.

Some historical sources were quite vague concerning actual events and dates, while other accounts directly contradicted each other. Therefore, it's best to take the open-minded approach, as any Police Inspector would do today:

'That somewhere in the account, there was an element of truth, if not the full truth!'

Alan D Baker 2023

Pronunciations

Several text alterations have been made throughout this novel to provide easier pronunciations for optical text readers:

1. 999 to 9 9 9.
2. Biochip to Bio-chip.
3. Superyacht to Super-yacht.
4. MI5 to M I 5.
5. MI6 to M I 6.
6. LED to L E D.
7. Flybridge to Fly-bridge.
8. Submachine to Sub-machine.
9. 215 to 2 1 5.
10. SAS to S A S.
11. Some money values are partly written in text.
12. Walkthrough to Walk-through (in Ack.).

Acknowledgements

1. Chapter 1. Night Ride. Resources: a. Port Talbot was once the author's home town. b. Star positioning throughout the novel by Starry Night Pro software. c. Google Maps.

2. Chapter 6. Hong Kong. Adapted from: a. Wikipedia - 'Hong Kong', 'Repulse Bay'. b. YouTube - 'The Dark Side of Hong Kong' Explained with Dom. Singapore comparison: YouTube - 'How Singapore solved Housing' by PolyMatter, 'The Dark Side of Singapore's Economic Miracle', Explained by Dom. c. Google Maps for the 'The Lily' building.

3. Chapter 7. Limassol. Adapted from: a. Wikipedia - 'Cyprus', 'History of Cyprus (1878-present)'. b. YouTube - 'The Brand New Super-Yacht Najiba docking in Monaco!' by eSysman Super-Yachts. c. Google Maps for Limassol.

4. Chapter 8. The Bluebell. Adapted from: a. Wikipedia - 'Low Earth orbit', 'Medium Earth orbit', Geostationary orbit'. b. Satellite Bands and Orbits: Multiple sources on the internet e.g., 'NASA '9.0 Communications', PC Magazine 'satellite frequency bands', RF Wireless World 'Satellite Frequency Bands of operation', The European Space Agency 'Satellite frequency bands'.

5. Chapter 9. Alexandria. Adapted from: a. Wikipedia - 'Liberia, 'Samuel Doe', 'Charles Taylor', 'Prince Johnson', 'Sierra Leone'. b. BBC News - 'Charles Taylor caught in Nigeria'. c. Dates also double-checked with Bing AI.

6. Chapter 10. On Reflection. Adapted from: a. Wikipedia - 'Cyprus', 'Kingdom of Cyprus', Isaac Komnenos (also spelt as Commenus) of Cyprus', 'Richard I of England', 'Mercadier'. b. YouTube - There are many YouTube videos on Alexandria's classrooms and Roman Bathhouse remains, e.g., 'EGYPT: The ruins of ancient ALEXANDRIA' by Vic Stefanu.

7. Chapter 12. Trondheim. Adapted from: a. Author's personal visits to city. b. Wikipedia - 'Trondheim'. 'Nidaros Cathedral', 'Kristiansten Fortress', 'Vidkun Quisling'. c. Bekaa valley in Lebanon drug running – There are many articles on the internet. Also see Indian news channel Gravitas 'Taliban smuggling heroin via India'. Recent BBC updates on Taliban activity in response to poppy cultivation.

8. Chapter 16. Assessment. Wikipedia - 'Out of Space Treaty'.

9. Chapter 17. Copenhagen. Copenhagen Tivoli Gardens, Author's personal visit.

10. Chapter 18. Trondheim visit. a. Author's personal

visits, including the Radisson Blu Royal Garden Hotel. b. Google Maps.

11. Chapter 19. Central Police Station Trondheim. a. Wikipedia - 'Cone Snail' venom, 'Dimethyl ether', CAMEO Chemicals 'DIMETHYL ETHER'. New Jersey Department of Health and Seni or Services Hazardous Substance Fact Sheet 'DIMETHYL ETHER'. b. Google Maps.

12. Chapter 20. HMP Bronzefield. Adapted from: Wikipedia - 'HM Prison Bronzefield'.

13. Chapter 21. Central Police Station Swansea. Resources: Google Maps.

14. Chapter 23. Cheltenham. Adapted from: a. Author's personal experience from living there. b. Background research on Malta. Wikipedia - 'Malta'. c. YouTube - Many videos are available, e.g., 'Things to KNOW before you VISIT MALTA' by 'Creative Travel Guide', 'Geography Now! MALTA' by Geography Now. 'A mazing Places to Visit in Malta | Best Places to Visit in Malta – Travel Video' by Joyous Travel. c. Google Maps.

15. Chapter 24 Malta. Adapted from: a. Wikipedia - 'Malta'. b. YouTube - 'Why did Britain Refuse to Annex Malta'. c. Google Maps.

16. Chapter 25 Blast-Off. Resources: a. Wikipedia - 'Macquarie Island'. b. Google Maps.

17. Chapter 26 Bab Sharq Police Department: Google Maps.

18. Chapter 27. Flight to Japan. Adapted from: a. Wikipedia - 'Japan', 'Black Ships', 'Matthew C. Perry'. b. YouTube - 'Sites of Japan's Meiji Industrial Revolution – UNESCO World Heritage Site', by 'World Heritage Journey', 'History of Japan' by Bill Wurtz, 'Commodore Matthew C. Perry – The Man Who Unlocked Japan' by elfreyshira. 'End of the Samurai – Black Ships – Extra History - #1' by Extra History. There are many other YouTube videos available on the history of Japan and the Black Ships. c. Wikipedia - 'Carbon fibers. d. YouTube - 'Carbon – Carbon Composites' by Professor J. Ramkumar Department of Mechanical Engineering IIT Kanpur, Indian Institute of Technology Kanpur.

19. Chapter 28. Tokyo. Adapted from: a. There are many articles on discipline for Japanese children on the internet. b. YouTube - There are many YouTube videos on children's discipline, e.g., '8 Japanese Parenting Rules All Kids Need'. c. Districts of Tokyo, there are many articles on the districts of Tokyo, e.g., Wikipedia - 'Japan'. d. There are many YouTube videos on the districts of Tokyo e.g., - 'Guide – Explore the Dynamic

Districts of the Olympic City'. By Travel Obscurer. e. Wikipedia - 'Tokyo Tower'

20. Chapter 29 Emperor Tiles. Adapted from: a. Reference to Commodore Mathew Perry and Black Ships, same as Chapter 27. b. Reference to Tokyo Tower, Wikipedia - 'Tokyo Tower', also ask Bing AI. c. YouTube - Many references are available on the internet. e.g., 'The Complete Tour of Tokyo Tower | Amazing Tokyo Views' by I will Always Travel for Food. 'Tokyo Tower Club 333 Christmas Eve 2014' by lightmanga.

21. Chapter 30 Taiwan and Taipei. Adapted from: a. Wikipedia - 'Taiwan'. b. YouTube - Many videos are available, e.g., 'Why didn't Mao Conquer Taiwan? (Short Animated Documentary)' by History Matters. 'The History of Taiwan on Animated Map' by History on The Map. Wikipedia - 'Taipei 101'. c. Bing AI - 'Taipei 101'. d. YouTube - There are many videos on Taipei 101, e.g., 'Taipei 101 Observation Deck – Is it Worth it??' by Kevin Eassa, 'Top of the world! 101, 101st floor Skyline 460 outdoor observation' by taiwanreporter. 'Taipei 101' by Viator Travel, 'The Wonders of Taipei 101: A Skyscraper Like No Other' by Interesting Engineer.

22. Chapter 31 Wolfram Wire Ltd. Adapted from: a. Wikipedia - 'Tungsten', 'Tungsten carbide', 'How Tungsten Wire is Made' Midwest Tungsten Service,

www.tungsten.com, 'How is tungsten rod made?' by Knowledgemax organisation www.knowledgemax.org. b. YouTube - 'Tungsten: Ore to Wire' by gmpullman. 'Tungsten – The MOST REFRACTORY Metal ON EARTH!' by Thoisoi. c. Wikipedia - 'Okinawa Island', 'Battle of Okinawa', 'Cornerstone of Peace'. 'Okinawa Prefectural Peace Memorial Museum', 'Operation Downfall', 'Henry L. Stimson'.

23. Chapter 32 Okinawa. Adapted from: a. Wikipedia - 'Okinawa Island', 'Kadena Air Base', 'Marine Corps Air Station Futenma', 'United State Marine Corps rank insignia'. b. YouTube - There are many videos available to give you a flavour of the island. Many videos are positive but some are negative. c. Google Maps showing the MCAS airbase at Okinawa (front and rear entrances).

24. Chapter 33 Hachijo-jima. Adapted from: Wikipedia - 'Hachijo-jima'. b. YouTube - There are many videos available, search on: 'Hachijo-jima', 'Hachijojima Oriental Resort', 'Hachijo Royal Resort'. c. Google Maps show Island and the abandoned Hachijojima Oriental Resort hotel. d. Bing AI 'Hachijo-jima'.

25. Chapter 34. Battle stations. Google Maps showing the MCAS airbase at Okinawa (front and rear entrances).

26. Chapter 39 London. Adapted from: Reference to Hyakuri Air Base in Japan. a. Wikipedia - 'Ibaraki Airport'. b. Google Maps 'Hyakuri Air Base'.

27. Chapter 41 Bremen. Adapted from: a. Wikipedia - 'Bremen', 'History of Bremen (city)', b. YouTube - 'Town Hall and Roland on the Marketplace of Bremen (UNESCO/NHK)' by UNESCO. Updated video "Town Hall and Roland Statue in Bremen – UNESCO World Heritage Site' by World Heritage Journey. c. Southern Star Super Yacht walk-through and sales speech adapted from many YouTube videos e.g., 'FORMOSA | 60M/197' BENETTI Yacht for Sale – Super-yacht Walk-through' by Fraser Yachts. 'Walk-through Benetti 208' MOCA – Benetti yachts' by FGI YACHT GROUP. 'ALFA 170/230' Benetti Yacht for sale – Super-yacht walk-through' by Fraser Yachts. 'MINE GAMES: 203 Benetti Super-yacht' by Denison Yachting. '$19 Million Super-yacht Tour: 2004 Oceanfast' by AQUAHOLIC.

Printed in Great Britain
by Amazon